Praise for the
DONN

"Loaded with subtle emotions, sizzling chemistry, and some provocative thoughts on the real choices [Grant's] characters are forced to make as they choose their loves for eternity."   —*RT Book Reviews* (4 stars)

"Vivid images, intense details, and enchanting characters grab the reader's attention and [don't] let go."
                           —*Night Owl Reviews* (Top Pick)

Praise for the Dark Warrior series

"The world of the Immortal Warriors is a thoroughly engaging one, blending powerful ancient gods, fiery desire, and touchingly human love, which readers will surely want to revisit."   —*RT Book Reviews*

"[Grant] blends ancient gods, love, desire, and evil-doers into a world you will want to revisit over and over again."
                                   —*Night Owl Review*

"Sizzling love scenes and engaging characters."
                                   —*Publishers Weekly*

"Ms. Grant mixes adventure, magic and sweet love to create the perfect romance[s]."   —*Single Title Reviews*

More . . .

Praise for the Dark Sword series

"Grant creates a vivid picture of Britain centuries after the Celts and Druids tried to expel the Romans, deftly merging magic and history. The result is a wonderfully dark, delightfully well-written [series]. Readers will eagerly await the next Dark Sword book."   —*RT Book Reviews*

"Another fantastic series that melds the paranormal with the historical life of the Scottish highlander in this arousing and exciting adventure."   —*Bitten By Books*

"These are some of the hottest brothers around in paranormal fiction."   —*Nocturne Romance Reads*

"Will keep readers spellbound."

—*Romance Reviews Today*

SMOLDERING HUNGER

DONNA GRANT

St. Martin's Paperbacks

This is a work of fiction. All of the characters, organizations, and events portrayed in this novel are either products of the author's imagination or are used fictitiously.

SMOLDERING HUNGER

Copyright © 2016 by Donna Grant.
Excerpt from *Smoke and Fire* copyright © 2016 by Donna Grant.

For information address St. Martin's Press, 175 Fifth Avenue, New York, NY 10010.

ISBN: 978-1-250-07195-8

Printed in the United States of America

St. Martin's Paperbacks edition / January 2016

St. Martin's Paperbacks are published by St. Martin's Press, 175 Fifth Avenue, New York, NY 10010.

10 9 8 7 6 5 4 3 2 1

To my brother, Aaron—
We spent our childhood always at odds,
but I couldn't ask for a better brother.
I love you!

ACKNOWLEDGMENTS

To my magnificent, marvelous editor, Monique Patterson, for, well, everything. I love our collaborations, your excitement, and even your edits. You are a gift, and I'm honored to work with you.

To my beautiful, incredible agent, Natanya Wheeler. You always find answers to my questions and work tirelessly on my books. Thank you for all you do!

To Alex, Erin, Amy, the truly amazing art department, marketing, and everyone at SMP who was involved in getting this book ready. Y'all are astounding. Thank you!

A special thanks to my friends and family for the endless support and love.

CHAPTER
ONE

Edinburgh
Mid-November

His hands were large and rough as he jerked up her skirt. Her fingers delved into his long blond hair, feeling the silkiness of the thick strands.

She couldn't draw enough breath into her lungs. The way he pressed her against the building and pinned her with his body was . . . exhilarating.

No man had ever shown such passion, such need for her before. It spurred her own desires until she burned.

For him.

His kisses stirred her soul, leaving her gasping and hungry for more. They pulled her from the wasteland of her life, viciously and ruthlessly. With just one kiss she was clinging to him, silently begging him to show her all that one brush of his lips promised.

The feel of his arousal pressed against her stomach made her dizzy with need. It swirled low in her belly and began to consume her with each beat of her heart.

She closed her eyes against the night, against the world

that was falling apart around them. And she did the one thing she swore she would never do again . . .

She opened her body.

His palm scraped against her thigh. She felt the calluses against her skin and the warmth of his hand against the chill of the night.

Each kiss was like a wrecking ball, smashing through the walls erected around her heart without any difficulty. He had wanted her and sensed her own attraction to him, and he had acted.

When was the last time a man had done that?

Never.

She didn't have to think or act. All she had to do was feel. And he was like a riot of sensations swarming her, consuming her. Yet it didn't frighten her.

No, it excited her, delighted her.

Invigorated her.

She gasped when he cupped her sex. It soon turned into a moan as his fingers delved into her slickness and teased her clit before sliding within her.

Her head fell back against the building while his mouth left a hot, wet trail down her neck to her breasts. His lips fastened around a nipple and sucked.

She bit her lip and briefly wondered when her coat had been opened and her shirt unbuttoned. Then she forgot how to think as he began to flick his tongue over the rigid peak.

He suddenly lifted his head, and the next thing she knew, his hands moved around to her bottom where he lifted her so that she could wrap her legs around him.

Her eyes opened and she looked into his dark eyes. The shadows hid his face, but she didn't need the light. His image was branded into her mind from their first meeting.

He was dangerous, serious, alarming, and a bit threatening. He was everything she should stay away from. Despite her best efforts, she was pulled to him like a bee to honey.

There were no words between them. There wasn't a need for any. The passion and yearning said it all.

It frightened her how much she ached to have him within her. She knew very little about him, but her body didn't care. And frankly, at that moment, neither did she.

She ran her hands over his wide shoulders and his arms that were solid muscle. She felt the sinew move beneath her palms as he lifted her just enough so when he lowered her, she felt the head of his cock at her entrance.

Her lips parted and her nails dug into his shirt as she waited with anticipation for him to fill her. He leisurely lowered her, letting his rod stretch her with agonizing slowness.

She wasn't able to draw in a breath until she had taken his full length. All the while, he held her gaze, daring her to look away.

In his eyes, she saw his desire, his blatant hunger. In that moment, that very second, he allowed her to see the real him. And it caused her heart to catch, because she liked what she saw. Too much.

He groaned loudly before he took her lips in a savage kiss that was both tender and relentless. Then he began to slide in and out of her.

She could do nothing but wrap her arms around his neck and hold on. With his thick cock filling her faster and faster and his shirt scraping along her bare nipples, the orgasm came quickly.

As if he knew she was about to peak, he began to thrust harder and deeper, taking her to places she hadn't known she could go.

His kisses swallowed her loud cries as her body shuddered around him. Then he began to fade, turning to smoke. She tried to touch his face, but all she met was air.

Then she was alone. Just like before.

Sophie opened her eyes, hating when reality intruded upon her dreams. She sat up while trying to ignore how her body still pulsed from the climax.

How could a dream make her find pleasure as eloquently and vividly as she had in Darius's arms? She put her hand on her stomach and closed her eyes while she waited for her breathing to return to normal and her body to calm once more.

She didn't move when the alarm went off. Only when she had herself back under control did she reach over and shut off the alarm.

Sophie opened her eyes and threw off the covers before she stood. It had been two weeks since she and Darius had sex against a building, just steps from the hospital where anyone could have seen her.

She hadn't much cared who might have stumbled across them that night. She'd been too caught up in his raw masculinity, the consuming desire that swept through her.

Now, however, she wondered at her sanity. She didn't do such foolish, rash, or reckless things.

But it had felt good!

Sophie would only admit that to herself, and even that tiny concession threatened to turn her world on its axis. The blame lay squarely with Darius.

No matter how hard she tried, she still found herself looking for him when she left the hospital—day or night. With each day that passed and he wasn't there, a little more sanity returned.

She was almost to the point where she was pretty confident that she could turn him away.

Right, her subconscious said with a laugh. *That's why you dream about him every night, climaxing each time you remember what he felt like inside you, sliding in and out. Stretching you.*

She sighed, her stomach clenching at the memory. If only that wasn't the truth. Sophie stood in front of her closet staring at her clothes, but that wasn't what she saw. She saw Darius and the way he looked at her.

His dark eyes the color of chocolate had ensnared her. His gaze had promised passion, pleasure, and a multitude of other things she hadn't dared to think about then. And especially now.

Recalling it two weeks later still made her breath catch. It was a look she'd seen others get, but it was never directed at her.

It evoked memories, dreams, and desires long buried. Those were dangerous, because they were a part of her life where she hadn't been in control, where she had followed her heart.

"Never again," she whispered.

It was a vow she spoke so many years ago and repeated often. It was her mantra, her motto. It was the only way she had gotten through those first horrible months. Those words built the concrete walls around her.

She had to stop dreaming of that night and how Darius made her feel. Sophie held onto those amazing feelings because she hadn't thought anything would come of it.

Now, fourteen days later, she recognized how wrong she had been. Wasn't she? She'd expected to live her life alone, and she was comfortable with that. Or she had been.

Until Darius walked out of the shadows and into her life one night.

There was a way to end the dreams and any thoughts she had of Darius. And that was to think of that inauspicious day, seven years before.

Sophie had pushed that memory deep, but never too deep. It was always there, a reminder of her gullibility, her stupidity. But she pulled the thought forward and let all the hurt, the anger, the betrayal, the confusion, and the sorrow take her again.

For just a few seconds, she gave herself to the memory. It was a reminder of why she vowed to live alone, why she pushed away anyone that tried to get close to her. Then she forcefully shoved the abhorrent memory back into a dark corner of her mind.

"Never again," she repeated.

She was strong now. She was her own woman. She knew the truth of the world. It was dark, lonely, and merciless. She'd learned that the hard way, but she wouldn't be caught in that position again.

Sophie grabbed a shirt and pants from her closet and headed to the bathroom. Her thoughts were centered on her patients waiting at the hospital. No longer did Darius occupy any part of her mind.

Just the way it should be.

CHAPTER
TWO

On the other side of Edinburgh . . .

The warehouse was quiet and empty except for the four Dark Fae dead at Darius's feet. He stared down at them, wondering where all the other Dark were. Those four were all he'd killed since he began hunting the morning before. It was a full twenty-four hours later and all he had to show for it was four Dark.

He blew out a breath. Someone or something else was killing the Dark. Not that he minded the help, but he wished he knew who it was.

Blowing out a deep breath, Darius tried not to notice the stillness of the warehouse. Just a few weeks before it was a place where he and Thorn had come while they'd fought the Dark Fae who attempted to take over the city—and failed.

Now Thorn was back at Dreagan with his mate, Lexi, and Darius was in Edinburgh alone.

Alone. It was such an insignificant word. Or it had been for centuries. He'd sought out the solitude, had slept away centuries in his cave without hesitation.

And now? Now he hated the quiet.

He detested being alone.

It wasn't that he missed the other Dragon Kings. He could communicate with them via their mental link at any time. It was something much deeper, much stronger that twisted his gut.

He'd told the other Kings he wanted to end the war with the Dark Fae so he could return to his mountain and the dragon sleep. It had been the truth. For a bit. Now, he found himself searching for something he didn't understand or know.

No matter how many times he walked the streets of the city, no matter how many times he killed the evil Dark Fae who sought to slaughter the innocent humans, Darius was never satisfied.

It was as if he were missing something. That only made him hunt longer and harder. He'd tracked the last remaining Dark Fae who hadn't been smart enough to leave the city, running the bastards to ground.

Since the Dark fed off the souls of the humans, Darius took great pleasure in killing them. But not even that helped to ease the tension within him.

But it did help him remember that he was a lethal warrior. He did what he did not just for himself, but for his brethren at Dreagan who hid amongst the humans distilling world-famous whisky. And he did it for the humans.

The realm might've been the dragons' first and foremost, but the humans were part of that world as well. The Dragon Kings fought for themselves and the mortals who once tried to kill them.

Darius removed his shirt and folded it before neatly stacking it on the table on the other side of the warehouse. After removing his boots and setting them tidily together, he unfastened his jeans and stepped out of them. Folding them, he set the jeans beside his shirt and turned to face the dead Fae.

With just a thought, he shifted, his body transforming from that of a human into a dragon. He shook his great head and blinked his eyes as he fastened them onto the Dark.

The greed and extravagance of the Dark Fae had caused the city to erupt in chaos. Edinburgh hadn't been the only place bombarded with the Dark, however. Every major city in Scotland and England had been attacked.

It caused the Dragon Kings to take drastic action against the Fae. In doing so, the Kings played right into the Darks' hands.

The Dark Fae filmed the Kings on Dreagan flying, fighting, and shifting. That video was then released onto the Internet, and a fury storm of questions fell upon Dreagan.

Their leader, Constantine, King of Kings, ordered that no Dragon King could shift out of human form. Darius was doing what his brethren hadn't been able to do in weeks.

He wasted no time in breathing fire upon the Dark. There was nothing on any realm as hot as dragon fire, and it scorched the bodies into ash almost instantly.

Darius immediately returned to human form and dressed. He wouldn't stay in his true appearance when the others couldn't. It wasn't fair. And it only made him hate the Dark Fae even more.

Once, long ago, there was a war on Earth between the Fae and the Kings. The Fae Wars had lasted for decades with hundreds dying.

The Kings eventually won. It was supposed to have been a war that would never be repeated. It would've remained that way if the Kings hadn't had to hide their true selves. There was only one race to blame for that: the humans.

Darius dressed and left the warehouse. It was just after five in the morning. There was still time to do some hunting. Perhaps he'd get lucky and see who was killing the Dark.

He hadn't gone more than five blocks when he found himself turning to the left. Darius walked another two before he realized he was on his way to the Royal Victoria Hospital.

His feet halted instantly.

Every time Sophie entered his thoughts, he hastily squished it. She was a distraction he didn't need—and couldn't afford. Yet, when he walked the streets, every time he saw a flash of red hair, he hoped it was her.

There was only one time in the two weeks since he'd made love to her on the street, shrouded by shadows with a hunger for her riding him hard, that he had allowed himself to see her.

A day after their encounter he'd remained hidden atop a roof watching as she left the hospital. She hadn't even looked in the direction where they'd had sex against the building.

Did she remember how her nails bit into his flesh? Did she recall how her body shuddered with the force of her climax? Did she forget how he had to swallow her screams of pleasure with a kiss?

He had no trouble recollecting all of that and more. So much more. For days after he had the taste of her on his tongue. Even now he recalled the feel of her soft, warm skin beneath his hands. He knew the weight of her breasts and how sensitive her nipples were.

If he allowed himself, he could get drunk off her kisses alone.

It was for that reason alone that he hadn't returned to

the hospital or gone anywhere near Sophie's home. She was much too alluring and entirely too much of a temptation to put himself in close proximity to her.

So why was he now heading toward the very place he'd shied away from? His thoughts had been on the Dark and eradicating them forever from this realm. He hadn't even been thinking of Sophie.

Darius turned on his heel and retraced his steps. He had to get far from Sophie. Nothing good could come of him seeing her again.

For hours he walked without a trace of the Dark to been seen. It agitated him, but he knew there were still a few of the bastards in the city.

The sun climbed in the sky and then began its descent, all the while he marched through the city from one end to the other. A few times he thought he was being watched, but he could never discover who it was.

Darius made his way to Edinburgh Castle. He was sitting staring out over the city when he felt a push against his mind. He instantly recognized Con's voice in his head.

He opened the link to Con. *"Aye?"*

"How are things?" Con asked.

"If you're asking if I've discovered who else is killing the Dark, I've no'." Darius had hoped to have better news. The Kings needed some good news soon.

Con blew out a breath. *"It has to be Fae. They're the only ones who can remain veiled."*

"If it's Fae, then why no' show themselves? It doesna make sense."

"I never said it made sense, I just said it had to be them."

Darius could hear the weariness in Con's voice. He hadn't been to Dreagan since before the video leaked. Darius could well imagine that tensions were running high with everyone doing their best to appear as human as possible to MI5, who had descended upon their business and home.

"*And you?*" Darius asked. "*How are you?*"

There was a long pause before Con said, "*We're fine.*"

"*I didna ask about Dreagan. I know the bloody whisky is going to be fine. I asked how you were, you stubborn bugger.*"

"*How the fuck do you think I am?*"

Darius smiled when he heard the anger in Con's voice. Constantine was known for being as cold as ice in any situation. Few had seen him angry and lived to speak of it. "*I almost feel sorry for the Dark for what we're going to do to them.*"

"*They need to be wiped from this realm.*"

"*All Fae need to go. Even Rhi. They've caused nothing but problems.*" Darius expected Con to agree regarding the Light Fae who had helped them in many situations, but the silence stretched on.

"*Rhi has too many friends among the Kings.*"

"*And you want Usaeil as an ally.*"

"*The Light Fae queen has nothing to do with this,*" Con said tightly.

His tone made Darius frown. Was that a tinge of irritation in Con's tone? Over the Fae queen? Interesting. There were rumors among the Kings that Con was disappearing a lot of late. Many suspected he and Usaeil were now lovers.

That wasn't going to end well in any scenario.

Darius changed the subject. "*How is the tracking going on the Dark?*"

"*No' as well as before. Henry is making it his mission to track the Fae.*"

Henry. The only human who wasn't a mate of the Kings. He'd been allowed to know their secret and enter their private domain. Henry was no mere human, however. He was one of the best spies Britain had to offer.

"Are the nasty buggers back in Ireland like they're supposed to be?"

"Most. There's still some stragglers. Too many for my comfort."

"If they're in Edinburgh, I'll find them."

Con's sigh was loud enough to make it through the mental link. *"We have to find Ulrik, Darius, and make him answer for this video. I'll no' have any of you take to your caves to hide from the mortals again. We survived it once. I'll no' ask it a second time."*

"We understand what's at stake. Ulrik knows we're looking for him. We've been searching for weeks. Perhaps it's time we ask Broc."

"Nay," Con said with finality. *"The Warriors and Druids already brought attention to themselves during the battle with the Dark in Edinburgh. This is our fight. We can find Ulrik ourselves."*

"He'll no' stray far from Scotland, I'll wager."

"Just be on the lookout. And remember, Darius, he can no' be trusted."

Con severed the link before the last syllable was uttered. Darius looked over the lights of the city and thought of Con's words.

Ever since Darius woke and ventured from his cave a few months earlier, he'd known his time would be spent in battle. Con visited every King who slept and updated them on the world. Darius was well aware of Ulrik's growing threats before he walked from his mountain.

Now he, like the other Kings, was hunting one of their own. Ulrik was a menace to all the Dragon Kings. Ulrik might've brought Lily back from the dead for Rhys, but soon after he attempted to kill Darcy.

Ulrik's actions were chaotic and seemingly indiscriminate. Every time they thought they knew what he would do, Ulrik changed his motives. He surprised them with his decisions at every turn.

It was a brilliant tactic to keep them guessing and on edge, not knowing what he would do next. No doubt it was driving Con mad with fury.

Darius grudgingly acknowledged Ulrik's cleverness. Then again, it was no surprise. Ulrik was one of the strongest of the Dragon Kings. He could've been King of Kings, and probably would've been had Con not wanted the position.

The two of them had been close brothers. They were inseparable. Until Con took over as King of Kings. Ulrik never challenged him, even though it was Ulrik's right to do so. Instead, Ulrik stood behind Con as their leader.

Would things be different if Ulrik had challenged Con and won? Ulrik might've still been betrayed by his female human lover, but he wouldn't have exiled himself. No doubt he'd still have started the war with the humans, but Ulrik would have wiped the realm of them.

There's one thing for certain, if Ulrik was King of Kings, none of the Dragon Kings' problems would be there now. They wouldn't be hiding from the humans. Nor would they be in a war with the Fae. The Fae wouldn't be on the realm if it weren't for the mortals.

Perhaps Ulrik had been right all along. It was better to end the humans' existence from the beginning.

But that's not what happened. Con was ruler, and Con had put an end to Ulrik's war with the mortals. In order to keep the peace, their dragons were sent away and every Dragon King had hidden in their mountain on Dreagan for several centuries until the humans forgot about them.

The Kings hid once. They wouldn't hide again. It was already too much for them to curb when they could fly.

Before the disaster with the video, they were only able to take to the skies at night or in a thunderstorm, and they remained on Dreagan when they did.

Now, they were all effectively grounded since every mortal eye in the world was looking for a glimpse of a dragon.

Part of Darius wanted to show the humans exactly who had been living beside them for thousands of years. He wanted all the Kings to take to the skies and demonstrate their power once and for all.

The realm had been theirs from the beginning. They willingly shared it with the mortals, but now the Kings were shells of the great dragons they once were.

And it saddened Darius to see how they had fallen so.

He took a deep breath and pushed to his feet. He lowered his gaze to the streets around Edinburgh Castle. A frown puckered his brow when he thought he spotted a white-haired Fae on the street below, but in the next instant, he was nothing.

Darius stared at the spot for a long time. The Fae could veil themselves. However, none but the most powerful of them could remain hidden for more than a few seconds.

He scanned the streets and surrounding buildings, but saw nothing. Was he so desperate to kill that he was beginning to see Dark where there were none?

And a white-haired Fae? There was no such thing as far as he knew. The Light Fae had hair as black as the night and eyes as silver as moonlight reflecting off a loch.

The Dark Fae had silver streaked throughout their black locks. The more silver, the more evil they'd done. And their eyes were red as blood.

It was true a Fae could cast glamour that allowed them to change their appearance, but why would one intentionally bring attention on themselves like the white-haired one?

Darius rubbed his eyes with his thumb and forefinger. He was tense, his thoughts troubled, and the need to take to the skies and soar along the currents was strong.

How he longed to shift and spread his wings, to roar long and loud into the night and announce to one and all that he was there. How he yearned to feel the flap of his wings as he flew and felt the sun and moon upon his scales, to dip and dive, to turn and glide.

He rubbed his chest, wondering at the ache that had settled there. His gaze lifted to the moon half-hidden by the thick clouds. There was a hunger inside him, but it wasn't just to be in dragon form.

It was for a red-haired beauty who enchanted him with her fiery kisses and willing body.

Before he knew it, he was walking away from the castle. Darius was so lost in thought that he almost didn't see Ulrik before he turned the corner.

Darius quickly altered his steps and followed Ulrik. The exiled Dragon King walked alone. His steps were slow and unhurried as he looked around the city as if seeing what damage the Dark had done.

Ulrik wore thick-soled black boots that made nary a sound, dark denim, and a dark red sweater. His black hair was pulled back in a queue at the base of his neck.

A cold gust of wind howled through the street causing the mortals to hunker within their coats. Ulrik lifted his face to the gust.

Darius almost opened the mental link and called to Con, but he hesitated. It would be better to know where Ulrik was going and if he met with anyone first. If Darius notified Con, the King of Kings would want Ulrik taken immediately.

It was well known that Ulrik was working with the Dark Fae. If the Kings could know their plans before it happened, then they would no longer be on the defensive.

The Kings could be one step ahead of the bastards and win the war before it spilled over into the human world any more than it already had.

Darius smiled and his thoughts faded when Ulrik finally stopped walking and Darius found himself standing in front of the Royal Victoria Hospital.

CHAPTER
THREE

Sophie's back ached as she leaned against the nurses' counter and finished writing notes in the file of her latest patient. Her temples throbbed with a headache that wouldn't diminish, but at least her stomach had stopped growling.

She closed the file and handed it to the waiting nurse before grabbing the next chart. She quickly scanned it, noting the many fractures and broken bones the woman had received over the last five years.

"Another one, aye?" asked Claire as she walked past.

Sophie leaned an elbow against the counter and rested her forehead into her hand. "Yes."

"Do the arses really believe we don't know they're hitting the women?" Claire asked with a snort. "All you have to do is look at where the injuries have taken place."

Sophie hated these cases. She glanced up at her friend Claire, one of the best nurses at the hospital. "She's been admitted because he's injured her windpipe."

"You can't save them all, Soph," Claire said in her soft, kind Scots voice.

Unfortunately, Sophie learned that very early on when

she was still in medical school in London and her room-mate was beaten to death by her boyfriend.

She took a deep breath and straightened, chart in hand. "I know."

"There's a cute D.I. outside her room though." Claire shot her a wink. "It's been too long since your last date. It's time to go have some fun, doc."

Sophie smiled and laughed because it was expected. And strangely enough there was a funny feeling in her stomach, almost like she knew something was coming.

Seven years was a long time to be alone.

She paused. Had it really been that long? She tallied the months, shocked to realize so much time had passed. Her career had flourished during that time.

In truth, that was the only way she survived at first. She immersed herself in work, letting it consume every hour of her day—awake or sleeping. If she couldn't rectify her own life, she could save others. She'd done it so well and for so long that it became second nature, a habit she hadn't even comprehended she had.

The thing was, nothing changed. She worked late-night shifts at the hospital, saw to those patients who couldn't get to her, and was always ready to work if someone else wanted time off.

It was all going smoothly, just as she planned. No bumps, no waves, nothing to mess with her calm, uneventful life.

Then Darius arrived.

From the first moment she saw him, she felt as if her blinders had been removed. He'd calmly handed her the address to tend to a friend of Darcy's, and in the next breath, told her he wasn't a good man.

That should've sent her straight home without a second thought of him. Instead, she'd taken the address. Not because she never turned away someone in need—because she didn't—but because he asked her for help.

Why couldn't she stop thinking of Darius? Why couldn't she get him out of her head? It shouldn't matter that his touch made her ache or that he brought her such pleasure. He hadn't come to see her since that night. Fourteen days. Three hundred and thirty-six hours.

And today. She glanced at her watch. That made it three hundred forty-eight hours, seventeen minutes, and ten seconds.

Oh shit. What was happening to her?

"Sophie?"

She blinked and looked down to find Claire watching her with a worried look in her brown eyes. Sophie shot her a smile, but Claire cocked her blond head to the side and put a hand on her hip, telling Sophie she wasn't buying the act for a second.

"Just lost in thought," Sophie said with a shrug.

Claire raised her brows as she regarded Sophie. "By that look, I'd say it was a man."

A man? Darius was so much more. His presence seemed to make the earth still, waiting for his order. He commanded without a word, dominated with a look from his dark brown gaze.

Man? No man she'd ever met could be so strong and imposing.

And sexy.

Her mouth went dry thinking of the hard line of his jaw and his lips that were soft and insistent. His eyes could cut coldly, but they could also blaze with a fire so hot that it could melt the sun.

She knew what desire looked like reflected in his chocolate-colored depths. His eyes softened, turned downright sensual as he held her gaze, challenging her to try and look away.

All the while his gorgeous body with rippling muscles brought her higher and higher, giving her ecstasy the likes of which she'd never known.

And never known she could have.

If she hadn't been sore the next morning when she woke, she might have thought it all a dream.

"I don't know who he is, but you need to see him again," Claire said, breaking into Sophie's thoughts again. Her smile was wide, a knowing look in her eyes.

Sophie swallowed and smoothed a hand over her hair to make sure the thick length was still in place. "I don't know what you're talking about."

"Uh-huh," Claire said with a wink. "Two weeks ago you walked in here with a flush to your skin and a smile on your lips. You wore the look of a woman who had been ridden well. Ever since, you occasionally get that look in your eyes. I'm telling you as your friend, Soph, go see him again. Because if I could find a man who could make me look like that after sex, I'd chain him to my bed."

This time Sophie's laugh wasn't forced. She knew all too well Claire's issues with men. She was a petite, pretty woman who had a bright smile and infectious laugh, and yet every guy she was interested in preferred someone else. Worse, it was all the wrong sorts of men who were attracted to Claire.

If Sophie thought her years without a date was a long time, Claire wasn't behind her by far. It was why the two of them had become such good friends.

Sophie leaned down and whispered in Claire's ear, "The sex was out of this world, but he's also out of the picture."

She walked away, leaving Claire with her mouth gaping and questions in her eyes. Sophie inwardly laughed, because it was a rare thing when she got to shock Claire. Normally, it was Claire who astonished her on a daily basis.

Sophie turned the corner and found a man leaning against the wall staring at her. He was drop-dead gorgeous in his dark red sweater and jeans.

He wore a small smile about his wide lips as his golden eyes stared at her. His long black hair was pulled back, showing off the hard planes of his face.

It unnerved her how he watched her, as if she were something to be studied under a microscope. Sophie pulled her gaze away from him, and stopped dead in her tracks when she spotted Darius.

Her heart thumped in her chest and her stomach fell to her feet. She couldn't decide if she was excited to see him or surprised. Especially after just thinking of him.

The strands of his long, dark blond hair were wind-blown. Just disheveled enough to make him even sexier. His hair, in addition to the five o'clock shadow of a beard, made her blood race and her hands itch to touch him, to run her hands up his chest and over his thick shoulders once more.

He watched her with his deep brown eyes without a hint of any emotion. While she was reeling from seeing him after so long and her body instantly beginning to throb with need, he felt . . . nothing.

Sophie knew what kind of disaster lay with Darius. She'd sworn to never go down that path again. As tempting as he was—and good Lord was he *tempting*—she fortified the walls around her heart.

She walked into her patient's room without a backward look to Darius. If only it was as easy to erase him from her thoughts as it was to look away.

Yet, she couldn't. In the middle of examining a young boy's broken arm some time later, her hands shook as she thought about how Darius's warm breath had fanned her skin right before he'd kissed the spot on her neck where it met her shoulder.

Less than an hour later, her thoughts suddenly turned away from the chart she was reading to remembering how Darius's large hands had held her so gently and firmly as he rocked his hips into her with such force that she felt his balls slap against her legs.

Her eyes glazed over so that she had to read the chart four times before the words soaked in.

When Claire dragged her to get something to eat, Sophie thought about Darius's lips. How he kissed as if it were his last kiss, as if his very life depended upon it. From slow and sensual, to fast and fierce, he kissed her every way imaginable in a short amount of time.

And she remembered every one of them.

It had been so long since she'd last been kissed that he was seared upon her brain—every sound, every touch, every smell. It was as much a part of the memory as his kiss.

Sophie had forgotten how good a kiss could be. She hadn't recalled how a kiss could sweep her off her feet. Or how it could make her body sizzle and yearn to be touched. She had forgotten the desire, the heart-pounding hunger to quench the growing need a kiss could stimulate.

Why couldn't Darius be a bad kisser? It would've been so much easier had he been as bad as . . .

Sophie halted her thoughts right then. She almost said his name. Quickly, she changed her thoughts. If she were comparing the two of them, then things had progressed to a point that was worrisome.

Mind-blowing sex or not, Darius needed to be erased from her life from that moment on.

She didn't know why he'd shown up at the hospital after two weeks, but she wasn't going to find out. Whatever mad thoughts prompted her to throw caution to the wind and let him take her in the shadows were gone.

Sophie was in control of herself once more. The serene,

rational Sophie who never had fun or did anything reckless or wild.

Darius could stand naked in the hospital, and she wouldn't feel anything.

Like hell you wouldn't. You'd definitely *feel something.*

She blew out a breath. Her subconscious was right. She felt something now, but she wouldn't act on it. She couldn't.

"Never again," she murmured.

Claire eyed her suspiciously before she went back to her story of the men on an online dating site she'd signed up for. All the ones who wanted to talk to her were old, extremely unattractive, or just creepy. The few Claire had shown interest in hadn't bothered to even acknowledge her existence.

If anyone needed to be "ridden well" as she put it, it was Claire.

If only Sophie knew someone she could introduce to Claire. Sophie hated when people interfered in her love life, but Claire was different. Claire had been through hell and back with a man who strung her along for four years promising marriage, and then left her for another man.

Claire still believed in love and romance and everything that went with it. She deserved a man who opened doors for her, who called first, who brought her flowers for no reason, and who always had her well-being in mind. She merited a man who couldn't keep his hands off her, a man who only had eyes for her, and a man who pleasured her until she was limp.

It was ironic that Sophie once craved those very things, but fate had a way of forcing someone to realize how tragic and difficult life could be.

But Claire wasn't her. Claire had a chance, and if Sophie could help, she would.

Instantly, an image of Darius rose in her mind. Claire

might be her closest friend, but she wasn't about to share Darius. Darius was a secret Sophie would carry to her grave.

"One loser after another," Claire said as she scrolled through her "matches" from the dating site. "It's ridiculous who they think I'd want to go out with. Eww," she exclaimed at one individual.

Sophie swallowed her bite of sandwich and grimaced when Claire showed her the picture of what Sophie would've swore was a drunken mug shot.

"That does it," Claire said with a shake of her head. "I'm deleting my profile. I might as well invest in a better vibrator, because it looks like that's going to be my bed partner from now on."

Sophie opened her mouth to say something, but she clenched her legs together as she recalled Darius. No vibrator or dildo in the world could compare to the real thing after him.

CHAPTER
FOUR

Darius knew walking into the hospital was a bad idea. As soon as he entered, his gaze searched for red hair instead of keeping his focus solely on Ulrik.

Ulrik's path through the hallways had been casual, almost as if he were taking a stroll through a park. He didn't look inside the rooms or talk to anyone.

Darius remained far enough behind him not to be noticed, but Ulrik was a Dragon King. He knew Darius was there. The way Ulrik acted was almost as if he *wanted* Darius to follow him.

And when Ulrik finally halted and leaned against a wall while eating a bag of pistachios, Darius knew why. He prayed he was wrong for once. Then Sophie came into view and it was like a punch in his gut.

Darius actually took a step back. His gaze was locked on her and his lungs seized. How had he stayed away from her? He hadn't forgotten how stunningly gorgeous she was, from her pale skin that looked like cream to her vibrant red hair that had felt like cool silk in his hand.

He drank her in, as if he was starved for the very sight

of her. From her oval face to her almond-shaped eyes to her incredible lips, she was hypnotic, spellbinding.

Magnetic.

Darius licked his lips, recalling the captivating taste of her. Even weeks later he could still recall how it felt to have her tight sheath clamped around his cock as she peaked and feel her nails cut into his neck from her grip.

Dr. Sophie Martin might appear as calm and cool as a porcelain doll to the world. But he'd seen her fire. He'd felt it. And flamed it higher.

She'd been wild and uninhibited in his arms. The mask she wore had been stripped away without his even trying. He wasn't even sure she was aware of all she had shown him while in the throes of such passion.

Nor did Darius want to think about what he might have given away. He'd wanted her, but he had been wholly unprepared for his strong, visceral reaction to her.

It was why he'd kept away from her. Well, that among other reasons. Yet, now that she stood just down the corridor from him, he realized what an utter fool he'd been.

Darius forgot all about Ulrik, forgot why he had followed him into the hospital. Darius was about to go to Sophie and pull her into his arms for a kiss.

He watched as she looked at Ulrik. Then her gaze slid away and landed on him. Darius waited to see a look of delight or even a hint of a smile, but she turned away as if he were a stranger.

As if they hadn't shared an earth-shattering moment weeks earlier while Edinburgh burned.

Darius was so shocked by the cold reception that he could only watch as she disappeared into a patient's room.

When he blinked, Ulrik was walking away. Darius had no choice but to follow. He glanced inside the room

Sophie entered and saw her standing beside the bed of a woman who had obviously been beaten.

Darius could hear Sophie speaking softly to the woman, telling her that she would heal, but if she didn't take action against her husband that she might not be so fortunate next time.

He fought against his instinct to remain near Sophie. It was no accident that Ulrik entered the hospital or walked to Sophie's floor. Ulrik did nothing without a reason.

There was a slim chance that it was purely coincidence that Ulrik had gone to Sophie's floor, but Darius knew that thought was rubbish. But how did Ulrik know of Sophie?

Unless he'd seen Darius with her that night in the streets. Darius had been so wrapped up in the woman in his arms that he hadn't paid attention to anything else. It had shocked him how easily she'd managed to make the world fall away.

Darius took one more look at Sophie standing straight as an arrow with her long, thick red hair piled once more behind her head. He wanted to yank her hair down and shove her against the wall to take her once more.

He hadn't imagined the passion that blazed within her, and he wanted to prove it to her.

"Another time," he murmured to himself.

Even as he wondered why after swearing to stay away from her.

Darius lost Ulrik in the throng of people entering and exiting the hospital. By the time he found Ulrik a few moments later, Ulrik was flirting with a pretty brunette.

Still reeling from Sophie's reaction to him, Darius walked to a bench and sat, waiting on Ulrik. He was able to keep an eye on Ulrik as well as get a clear view of the hospital entrance.

Darius wasn't surprised when Ulrik ended his conversation with the nurse and came to sit beside him.

Neither said a word as Ulrik cracked another pistachio and popped the green nut into his mouth.

"I figured you'd remain behind and talk to her."

Darius clenched his teeth. Shite. Just as he'd feared, Ulrik was there for Sophie. He and Thorn had taken great pains to make sure Sophie was never seen helping them heal Lexi. That meant Ulrik discovered Sophie from Darius's carelessness.

Fuck. He'd really buggered things this time.

"What do you want with her?" Darius asked.

Ulrik tossed aside more empty shells and shrugged. "She's attractive. If you like redheads. I've always found them to be extremely enthusiastic in bed."

Darius didn't respond. There was nothing he could say that would help Sophie's case, especially when he wanted to tell Ulrik to kiss off.

Ulrik cut him a look, a sly smile upon his lips. "I didna think you'd be so careless as to get tangled with another female, Darius. Not after your . . . past."

Darius took a deep breath and slowly released it, attempting to keep his anger under control. He'd woken from his long sleep as angry as when he sought out his cave. Consequently, it didn't take much to set him off.

It took an incredible amount of effort for him to keep his mouth shut and his hands to himself when all he wanted to do was shift into dragon form and go for Ulrik's jugular.

Instead, he took a page out of Constantine's book. He pushed all the rage and all his emotions aside until there was nothing. Only then was Darius able to respond. "I'm no' anything with the doctor."

"Always the same response given. I was hoping you might be more creative."

"How do you know I have no' already contacted Con?"

Ulrik turned his head and shot Darius a smile. "Because

of the doctor. You want to know what I'm about before you inform Con I'm here."

That had been Ulrik's gift before he went rogue and was exiled from Dreagan. He had always been able to figure people out, no matter what they hid.

"Con knows you're here."

Ulrik laughed and reached into the bag for another handful of pistachios. "If he did, he'd be here. Oh, wait. He can no' get here fast enough since he has to *drive*."

Darius wanted to wipe the smirk from Ulrik's face. The crowd of people around them kept him where he was. The smugness in Ulrik's voice as he mentioned how none of the Dragon Kings could shift and take to the skies threatened to break Darius's calm, but he managed to hold onto it.

"My battle with Con is coming soon," Ulrik said. "Pitting us against each other here willna do anyone any good. No' at the moment, at any rate."

"You've done what you wanted. You've clipped our wings," Darius said. "For now."

Ulrik finished chewing and swallowed before he said in a tight voice, "I wasna able to shift into my true form for thousands of millennia. Doona talk to me about having your wings clipped."

For the briefest second, Darius saw the fury in Ulrik's gold eyes before it was tempered. He'd gone a mere few weeks unable to take to the skies, but Darius had been able to shift. Ulrik hadn't been able to do either for too many centuries to count. As awful as Darius imagined that was, it didn't excuse Ulrik from the atrocities he'd committed in the past few years.

"If you hate Con so much, why no' just go after him?" Darius asked.

Ulrik stood and wadded up the empty bag. "Because fucking with all of you is too much fun."

Darius knew it was more than that. Ulrik was too cunning to waste time causing trouble. Each assault, each strike was calculated. "So you'll destroy our entire race because you were exiled?"

"I wasna merely exiled, or have you forgotten so easily?" Ulrik's half smile hardened, his gold eyes becoming icy. "All of you killed her. That was my right for her betrayal. And instead of wiping the mortals from our realm, you and the others chose to protect them. The verra ones who were going to try and kill me. The ones who were responsible for our dragons being sent away. You want to know if I'll destroy all of you? I'll do it with a smile on my face."

"If you're the only Dragon King left, you willna be able to fight the Dark Fae who will want to take over this realm."

Not a shred of emotion crossed Ulrik's face. Darius hoped to read something in his old friend's visage to help determine what Ulrik planned, but once more Ulrik was proving to be a master at hiding his plans.

Darius stood, putting them eye to eye. "You want to fight Con? Then fight him. We all know what's coming is between the two of you."

"Do you now?" Ulrik chuckled softly.

"Aye."

Darius kept his gaze on Ulrik even though he wanted to look around the hospital. Ulrik had proven in the past that he was more than capable—and willing—to kill any woman who could be a mate to a King.

Darius wasn't going to allow Sophie to become mixed up in this. He'd do whatever was needed to keep her out of harm's way—which meant away from Ulrik.

She was only involved because they had brought her in. Darius made it worse by seeking her out to make love to her. If he walked away now, there was a chance Ulrik would turn his attention from her.

"I want all of you to understand how it feels to be trapped in human form without any way out. Unless you have a warehouse big enough for you to shift and burn Dark bodies."

So Darius had been followed. How had he not known of it? He was normally very attuned to that sort of thing. It grated on his nerves that Ulrik one-upped him again.

"So your focus is on me now?" Darius asked. "You saved Lily for Rhys, only to kill Darcy to hurt Warrick?"

Darius left out the part about how they saved Darcy who was living happily with Warrick at Dreagan.

Ulrik tossed the bag into a nearby trash bin. "Perhaps I'm here to save Sophie."

Darius didn't believe that for a moment. Ulrik had proven that he wasn't to be trusted an inch. Yes, he had helped save Lily, but he'd also harmed the Kings in more ways.

"You doona believe me." Ulrik dusted off his hands. "I could tell you all my secrets right now, and you wouldna believe them."

"You've proven yourself a liar who is only after his own agenda."

"And you were no' after your own agenda two weeks ago when you took the pretty doctor against the building?" Ulrik asked nonchalantly. "You seemed rather intent on your agenda."

Darius fisted his hands to keep from striking Ulrik's smug face. So they'd been watched. By Ulrik.

Ulrik had seen her passion, her desire. He'd heard her cries of pleasure. The bastard. Darius wanted to make him pay for witnessing what he alone should've seen. Never mind the fact that he had taken her on the street.

Ulrik laughed softly. "That blank stare you're giving me

reminds me of Con. Unfortunately, your clenched hands tell a different story. You care for the doctor."

"She was a female. It had been a long while since I had such a release. That was all."

"Is it?" Ulrik asked with a smirk. "With that kind of passion? Doona bother with such lies, Darius."

Darius closed the distance between them so that he was almost nose to nose with Ulrik. "Too many innocents have paid the price for our war. I doona want her—or anyone in that hospital—harmed because you believe I hold some feelings for the mortal."

Ulrik stared at him a long time.

"If you wanted to hurt me, you've already done that by making sure I can no' fly. You've done what you wanted. Leave," Darius demanded.

"My plans are just getting underway. Besides, I've no interest in leaving Edinburgh just yet. Go ahead and tell Con. We can have our battle right here."

Darius knew Con would never condone such a thing. Con took his vow to protect the humans too seriously to battle Ulrik to the death in front of them.

He moved in front of Ulrik to halt his turning away. "I'm no' going to tell you again to stay away from the doctor."

"Ahh," Ulrik said with a sneer. "Is one of you finally going to step up and challenge me?"

Damn. Darius couldn't. Con had already called that option.

"I didna think so." Ulrik gave a bark of laughter. "What a pity. I thought the old Darius might've returned. But you're still the same broken dragon."

He glared into Ulrik's gold eyes. "If you're looking for a fight, I'm right here. Though it willna be a fair fight with you only having some of your magic."

Ulrik's smile was cold. "You think you know so much.

You know nothing. None of you do. When it all comes down, you'll realize just how many pieces of the puzzle all of you were missing."

"Trying to change the subject?"

Ulrik held his gaze, his smile hardening. "No' at all."

A shout of pain pulled Darius's gaze from Ulrik over his shoulder to a woman who was on the ground writhing in pain.

"Keep pushing me, Darius. I've no problem hurting any of these . . . beings," Ulrik said.

Darius thought of Sophie and the hundreds of people in the hospital. He recalled his oath to protect the humans, and though it went against everything he was, he didn't slam his fist into Ulrik's face as he wanted.

Or rip him apart. That's what Darius really wanted to do.

The warrior of old, the lethal dragon that struck without remorse or hesitation reared its head. Darius thought he'd lost that warrior spirit long ago. He'd felt a stirring of it a few weeks ago—then more and more each day.

Then, today, he knew it was back. *He* was back. The dragon he'd been before tragedy struck.

Now he had a target—and someone to protect. Ulrik wasn't going to know what hit him by the time Darius was through with him.

The woman's screams became louder as people gathered around her and hospital workers rushed out to help her. This wasn't the time to remind Ulrik of his place in the world. That would come soon enough.

Darius thought of Sophie working in the building behind him, saving lives. He pictured her olive eyes, her smile. And he managed to remain where he was, in complete control of his fury.

"One day soon you'll know the secrets Con has been

so desperate to keep from all of you," Ulrik said as he walked away, his smile too smug for Darius.

The woman's screams stopped and she was helped to her feet a moment later.

Darius wanted to talk to Sophie, but he followed Ulrik instead. Right up until Ulrik vanished into thin air a minute later.

CHAPTER
FIVE

Balladyn stared at the ruins of Pompeii, remembering how he tracked Rhi there. He'd searched all over the realm for her. Every time he got close, she slipped away. He felt her, just as she had felt him.

He still wasn't sure why she stopped running from him. But he was glad when she did.

From the time she was a young hellion of a Light Fae, she'd run rampant over everyone and everything. It wasn't just Fae who were drawn to her. It was everyone and everything—plants, animals, wind, water, and even the sun.

She was a force to be reckoned with, and she wasn't even aware of it.

Though all Fae were naturally beautiful, Rhi had an inner glow that no other Fae possessed—not even Usaeil, the Light Queen.

It was his friendship with Rhi's brother, Rolmir, that had afforded Balladyn the privilege to know her. For centuries he'd loved her from afar, waiting until she was old enough to want a husband.

Instead of following in the footsteps of most female Light, Rhi followed him and Rolmir. She trained with them, fought with them, and earned herself a position as the only female in the Queen's Guard.

It was one of the highest honors a Light Fae could ever achieve. It was truly a day of celebration. For Balladyn, it was doubly so because it he was able to spend more time with Rhi.

However, while he was eating meals with her, training beside her, and dreaming of her at night, Rhi was falling in love with a Dragon King.

Balladyn still remembered the sensation of a dagger slicing him open when she told him all about the Dragon King she'd met. It was all Balladyn could do not to tell her how he felt.

Caution stopped him, urging him to give her time. Because surely whatever was going on with the King would never last.

As if fate conspired against him, the affair went on much longer than he ever thought possible, and then just when he was ready to give up, the King abruptly ended the affair.

The next thing Balladyn knew, he was holding Rhi as she cried unending tears, her anguish tearing him apart. Balladyn went from hating the Dragon King, to wanting to cut him into tiny pieces for breaking Rhi's heart.

For days he remained by Rhi's side comforting her as best he could, even when all she did was cry. It was enough that she'd turned to him. It meant she knew he'd always be there for her.

Then Usaeil summoned him. Never in his wildest dreams did he imagine Rhi would venture into the darkest side of the Fae realm where no Light Fae dared to go.

But Balladyn had been ready to follow her. Only he saw Rhi's Dragon King go in after her first. To this day, Rhi had no idea who brought her out of that death trap.

Balladyn dropped his chin to his chest as those memories assaulted him. He'd sworn to stay beside her always. So he was prepared to wait for her to get past her broken heart—except the Fae army was called to war. As a Queen's Guard, they led the charge.

He touched his left shoulder where he'd been hit with an arrow from a Dark. The tip came so close to piercing his heart he was still surprised he hadn't died. In some ways, it would've been better had it killed him instead of him ending up in a Dark Fae dungeon where he was consequently turned.

All the love he once held for Rhi was then twisted to hate. He made it his mission to capture and turn her. When she ventured into Taraeth's domain, Balladyn had scarcely believed his fortune.

For just a second, he'd believed she was there for him, to try and bring him back to the Light. Then he learned of the Dragon King, Kellan, who was being held. Despite all that Rhi's lover had done to her, she was still helping the Dragon Kings.

It infuriated him, exasperated him. And he'd been determined to do something about it.

Balladyn got his justice. He caught Rhi. And how he tortured her. The Dark King, Taraeth, had been ecstatic, believing he would have two former Queen's Guards with him.

Except Balladyn pushed Rhi too hard too quickly. She destroyed his fortress, and in the process showed him the sheer amount of power within her.

Being near her once more also revealed something else—he still loved her.

Deeply.

Balladyn proceeded to chase her all around the world. Not to turn her Dark, but to be near her. His heart had leapt when he'd found her at Pompeii and she placed her hand in his.

He hadn't known what to do after that. Rhi was no longer running, but she still wasn't his. Balladyn knew then he would have to tread slowly with her. Their first kiss had rocked him to the pit of his black soul.

The more he was with Rhi, even for mere seconds, the more he felt himself changing. She consumed his thoughts day and night, asleep or awake.

He'd waited thousands of years for her. He didn't want to wait any longer.

Then she'd come to him, asking for help. She had touched him, kissed him. Whether she wanted to admit it or not, she felt something between them. There was no denying it, not the way she returned his kiss.

In order for them to be together, Balladyn had to figure out how they could both escape Usaeil and Taraeth or take them both down. He'd watched Rhi in action recently as she, along with Con and Thorn, attacked Mikkel's manor to save a human.

All was going well until Rhi had been struck with Dark magic. Reliving that moment still made him feel powerless and so damn angry.

Balladyn rubbed his chest where his heart should be and teleported to the desert. It was the place they'd shared their first kiss, the place they returned to time and again.

He sat in the hot sand, letting the tiny grains burn his hands as he buried them. The sun baked him, but he didn't feel any of it. He kept seeing Rhi thrown back by the blast of magic at the manor and then lie unmoving.

Balladyn had attempted to go to her, but Ulrik stopped him. It was Constantine who took Rhi to Dreagan. All Balladyn could hope for was that the King of Kings used his power to heal her.

It was not knowing how Rhi fared that was slowly killing Balladyn. He hadn't heard from or seen Rhi in weeks. Each day that went by without word from her was its own special kind of torture.

He called to her repeatedly. She either didn't answer because she couldn't, or she didn't want to. With Rhi, it could be either option.

Rhi was loyal to a fault. She had a good heart that he soured during his torture of her. She was amazing with a sword, and someone you knew you could trust explicitly.

She wasn't without her faults. She loved to meddle, and had a penchant for shopping daily. Her fingernail polish collection was unrivaled, as was her affinity for having her nails painted.

The fact that she couldn't lie without feeling extreme pain was a boon for anyone close to her. Rhi always told the truth, no matter how painful it might be. There were no lies or deception with her. Just honesty and laughter.

That laughter had been missing from her eyes ever since she'd broken free from the Chains of Mordare while in his dungeon. He'd done that to her. He'd nearly snuffed out her light.

How could he have done that if he loved her?

He loved the Rhi that ran laughing through a field of flowers with her black hair loose and her arms out.

He loved the Rhi whose silver eyes shone with mischief whenever she played a prank.

He loved the Rhi who would bounce up and down with excitement anytime she had a surprise for someone.

He loved the Rhi who would close her eyes and lift her face to the sun as if seeking its warmth.

All that had drawn him to Rhi. And he'd crushed it. It was the darkness within her that allowed him to find her. It was that which called to him.

He'd hated her for what he had become, and yet he was

responsible for turning her in the same direction. That is, if she lived.

Balladyn dropped his head in his hands, a tight band gripping his chest. Life without her would be . . . impossible. He couldn't be here without her. She was his everything, his reason for breathing.

"Please, Rhi. Come to me," Balladyn whispered. "I need you. I love you."

He looked up, hoping she would suddenly appear, looking at him as if he were pathetic.

Instead, only the sound of the wind over the sand met his ears.

Dreagan Distillery

Rhys stood in the doorway gazing at the bed where Rhi lay unmoving as she had for the past two weeks. He visited every day, and each time he fully expected her to be sitting up demanding Con bring her a tray of food.

"Still no change?" Con asked as he came to stand beside him.

Rhys glanced at the King of Kings and shook his head. Con's black gaze was trained on Rhi. "None."

"I doona understand," Con said as he walked to the bed and put his hand on Rhi's forehead. "I healed her. All of her injuries. She should've woken by now."

"I know." Rhys shoved away from the door and moved to the chair near the bed. He sat heavily and sighed. "Something's wrong."

Con straightened with a nod. "I agree."

"But what? The Dark magic?"

Con shrugged his shoulders, his white dress shirt stretching over his arms at the movement. He slid his hands into his pants pockets. "She's been through a lot lately. We doona know what all happened to her at Balladyn's hands."

"She's no' Dark," Rhys said through clenched teeth.

"I never said she was."

"You implied she might be."

Con glanced away. "All I'm saying is that we doona have all the facts. We know she was tortured. I saw her, Rhys. I didna recognize her when I walked into that dungeon. Whatever Balladyn did, he did well."

"It was weeks after Ulrik carried her out of Balladyn's fortress before we saw her," Rhys admitted.

"And she's no' been the same. Her light is . . . diminished. No' gone, but she's different."

Rhys shook his head sadly. "Even I can admit you're right in that assessment. I fear the Dark magic is somehow going to eviscerate whatever is left of her light."

"Rhi is too strong for that."

Rhys eyed Con. "How she'd love to hear you say that."

"It's because she's asleep that I'm able," Con replied with a slight smile. That smile died as he shifted his gaze back to her. "But it's worrying that she's no' woken. I doona know what else to do. Usaeil wants her at the castle."

"Nay," Rhys stated as he rose. "Rhi isna leaving Dreagan."

Con's forehead puckered for a moment. "She's a Light Fae. She should be with her own kind, no' here with us Dragon Kings."

"This is exactly where she needs to be. With friends. She left the Queen's Guard. Rhi wouldna want to return there."

Con gave a nod of his head. "I'll only be able to keep Usaeil away for so long."

"You're King of Kings. You can keep her away indefinitely." Rhys suspected something was going on between Con and Usaeil, and the more he spoke with Con about the queen, the more he thought he was right.

"I can, but I doona want to."

"Since when do you bow to the Fae?"

A muscle jumped in Con's jaw. "Never."

"But you are to Usaeil. There is talk you two are having an affair. Is there truth to that?"

"Since when do you listen to rumors?"

"Since it involves Usaeil. Answer the question," Rhys pressed.

Con held his gaze for long moments. "I didna ask you who you took to your bed. I'd like the same courtesy whether it's a Fae or a human. It's my business."

Rhys watched Con walk from the room knowing he had his answer. Now all Rhys could pray for was that Rhi never discovered the truth.

CHAPTER
SIX

It wasn't the first time Sophie had a day that seemed to never end, but this one took the crown. And then some. It was one craptastic event after another.

After seeing Darius, it was as if fate wanted to remind her of him constantly. She turned the corner at the hospital and saw a portion of a man's face with people surrounding him. Her heart raced, thinking it was Darius.

Until the crowd moved and she got a full look at him.

The disappointment when it wasn't Darius only made her angry. So what if he had come to the hospital? He hadn't spoken to her.

It wasn't like you gave him a chance. You didn't even smile.

Smile? She wasn't thinking of smiling when she'd looked at him. She'd thought of hot kisses, ragged breaths, and skin sliding against skin.

She walked to her locker and opened it. Smile. As if. There was no smiling when her body was heated in such a way.

You could've at least let him know you were happy to see him. I wouldn't have talked to you either.

Sophie hung her white doctor's jacket in her locker. She then grabbed her purse. It was fine. Better than fine, actually. She didn't want to talk or see Darius. Hadn't she told herself that earlier?

"Never again," she repeated.

You don't have to talk when a sex god like him is doing you. In fact, you don't even have to look at him.

With her hand on the locker, prepared to close it, Sophie hesitated. But she did want to look at him. He was sinfully gorgeous. There was also an air of peril around him.

You always wanted to know what it was like to be attracted to a bad boy.

Darius wasn't a "bad boy." He was something darker, something more wicked. He hadn't been lying when he said he wasn't a good man, and yet she trusted him.

Odd since she didn't trust men in general.

It was his eyes.

Yes, his eyes. Those deep orbs the color of rich, dark chocolate. He hadn't tried to be glib or charming. He simply was.

Was that what drew her? Was it because he told her the truth, uncaring what she thought of him? She hadn't known men were capable of such things.

He hadn't flirted with her or tried to be charismatic. In fact, he'd said very little the first time and nothing at all the second.

Instead, his large hand had cupped the back of her head and held it while he kissed her mindless. Her senses had been assaulted with his taste, his heat, his desire, and his smell. Even now she had only to think of sandalwood and chills raced over her skin.

Sophie blinked and found herself staring at her reflection through the small mirror in her locker. Her eyes were dilated, her lips parted, and her chest heaved.

Her sex ached to feel Darius's length slide inside her once more, to have him thrust hard and fast. Her breasts swelled and moisture soaked her panties.

My God. What was wrong with her?

He rode you good.

Sophie slammed her locker shut and turned on her heel. It was past midnight, and she wanted a few hours of sleep before she was back at the hospital for her next shift.

On her way out, she stopped by to check on the woman whose husband had beaten her. The woman refused to press charges or to realize that if she didn't take some kind of action, she could end up dead.

Sophie paused by the door when she heard voices within. She peered around the corner to see a man with her. He was crying, swearing he would never do it again.

How many times had he said those same words? By the woman's medical records and all her broken bones, it had been many, many times.

Sophie had done her part. She'd given the woman the same advice they gave every victim of domestic violence. The ball was in the woman's court. Sophie could only pray that she took a stand and got her life back.

As she walked out of the hospital, Sophie felt the wind hit her face with a blast of cold air. A light snow had fallen two days ago, and more was on the way. Even after seven years, she still wasn't accustomed to the harsh Scotland winters.

Still flushed from thinking of Darius, she didn't bother to button her coat. Her heels clicked on the cobblestones as she made her way to the street.

Unable to help herself, she glanced to the spot where she and Darius had given in to their passion. The shadows hid the location, but she didn't need lights to know where it was.

For a short time, Sophie had forgotten her past and the

betrayals that shaped her into who she was. For a brief space she had just been Sophie—a woman who craved Darius's touch like she needed air.

And it had felt so good to give in to that.

She looked at the ground and swallowed. Damn Darius for showing up again. And damn her own mind for not being able to forget about him.

When she raised her head, her eyes clashed with chocolate ones. Sophie halted inches from running into Darius. She gripped her purse in one hand and her black medical bag in the other while she wondered what to do.

"Walk around me," Darius said.

She frowned, anger cutting through her. Hadn't he been the one to come to the hospital, her place of work? Wasn't he the one in front of her now?

"Keep walking, Sophie. I'll find you later and explain," he said in a low voice.

She rolled her eyes and walked past him, making sure she ran her shoulder into him hard enough to throw him off balance.

Why had she romanticized their dalliance? Why had she once more found herself making a man into something he wasn't?

Darius had told her he wasn't a good man. Yet she went and made him out that way. All those nights dreaming of him, of their passion and desire, created a man in her head that couldn't possibly exist.

After this run-in, she was sure Darius would be well and truly out of her mind for good. She didn't have the time or inclination for men like him.

But still, the idea that her life might've been changing was a heady one. As had the thought that Darius could be the kind of man she didn't think existed.

She opted to walk home instead of taking her usual cab. The air was brisk, and with the snow coming, it might be her last chance for a while. The stroll felt good despite her feet hurting from two back-to-back shifts.

Sophie was exhausted by the time she entered her flat. She tossed down her keys, purse, and bag at the entryway table. Then she hung up her coat and kicked off her shoes on the way to the bathroom.

She was unbuttoning her shirt when she paused to turn on the water for the bathtub. After her clothes were in the hamper, she walked naked to the tub and poured a large portion of bubble bath in before lighting the candles set all around the claw-foot tub.

While the water filled, she turned on some music and shut off the lights. Her newest favorite was the soundtrack to *Outlander*. She climbed into the tub with the haunting melody playing in the background.

Sophie sighed as she leaned back and let the water and bubbles surround her. When the water was high enough, she turned it off with her foot.

Her eyes were closed as she relaxed. Slowly the tension and stress began to ease from her muscles. Her head lolled to the side. Her fatigue was so great she could fall asleep right there if she wasn't careful. The only thing that would've made everything perfect was wine.

And Darius.

With the music playing, Sophie couldn't help but think of him. She'd come across a few Highlanders while in Edinburgh, but none compared to Darius. She didn't even have to ask if he was a Highlander.

It was in the way he held himself, the way he spoke. It was a look that couldn't be faked or copied. Whatever made a man a Highlander was in his blood, in his very soul.

Movies and romance books loved to have Highlanders as heroes. Truth be told, Sophie had always found herself drawn to such men. Highlanders valued loyalty, honesty, and family. The alphas who would give their very lives for those they loved.

At one time she'd dreamed of finding such a man for herself. She hadn't actually thought it would be a Highlander, however. She'd been content to find her man closer to home.

But all that changed so quickly. Her world was shattered in a dizzying display as the layers were pulled back and the lies were revealed.

Sophie didn't ever think she would forget that feeling of drowning when she realized everything had been a lie and she'd been made into the biggest fool of them all with her fiancé's affair.

That's what she got for thinking men were like those portrayed in films and books. Those were characters written by those who crafted them.

They weren't real people.

No matter how much she wished they were.

Darius was the closest she'd ever come to finding those heroes she used to read about. Then he proved he was as flawed as she was. Which was a good thing. She needed that so she didn't find herself wanting him more than she already did.

She didn't need anyone. Hadn't needed anyone in years. She lived her life the way she wanted without having to answer to anyone or take their bullshit.

It was just the way she wanted it.

Liar.

Sophie silenced her subconscious with a vicious kick. So what if Darius made her realize just how lonely she was? Or that he made her think—for just a heartbeat—how it might be not to be alone anymore.

She knew exactly what she wanted, and though a quick tumble with Darius did wonders for her mentally and physically, she knew better than to think of more.

She shifted in the tub and saw the candles flicker through her eyelids. Sophie opened her eyes, her mouth falling open when she saw Darius leaning against her sink watching her.

Had her thoughts conjured him?

"What . . . ? How . . . ? There's no . . ." she began, only to find her brain shut off.

His gaze blazed with unreserved longing while his hands gripped the sink tightly. Despite his lounging, his body was strung as tight as a bow.

How long had he been in her bathroom? How had she not heard him? And what did he want?

Regardless of the questions running through her head, none made it past her lips. Sophie fought against the tide of desire that swept over her like a surge. It didn't help that Darius looked at her as if he were about to toss her over his shoulder and take her to bed to make love to her.

Sophie's sex throbbed just thinking about it. There was no way she'd be able to carry on a conversation if she didn't get her body under control. And there had to be a conversation followed by Darius quickly leaving.

There would be no sex.

Umm. Did you say something?

Shit. She was in trouble. The kind that would have her waking up in the morning groaning from—

Soreness?

—bad decisions. And Darius was definitely a bad decision.

His gaze dropped from her face to the water. A harsh breath left him. Her eyes traveled down his chest to his waist and lower where she watched the outline of his cock lengthen and harden right before her eyes.

Her nipples tightened in response. When Darius murmured something beneath his breath in a gravelly tone, she jerked her gaze back to his face.

That's when she realized her nipples had broken the water's surface, and the bubbles now drifted around her breasts. Sophie sank farther beneath the water.

Darius closed his eyes briefly and drew in a ragged breath. When he looked back at her, he was once more in control.

Too bad she wasn't.

For long minutes, they simply stared at each other. Sophie mentally undressed him, thinking how she'd run her hands over his body and feel his heat and hardness.

"What are you doing here?" she finally managed to ask.

As if her words were a punch, he turned his head away for a moment and said, "You're in danger. If you ever see me, pretend you doona care. Make sure that anyone who is around thinks you'd rather see anyone else but me."

"I can do that."

Had he winced? She was sure he'd winced. Now that was a shock. Since when did her words ever hurt anyone?

"I only came to tell you that," he said.

Sophie was suddenly wretched that he might be leaving. After all her erotic dreams—and daydreams—of him, he couldn't just leave. But what did she say? "Thank you."

He released the sink and pushed away from it. Darius walked to the tub and leaned down. "Be safe, doc."

His lips briefly touched hers. A moan left him the same time her hand snaked out of the water to wrap around his neck.

CHAPTER
SEVEN

Darius was on fire, smoldering from the inside out with an inferno of need that threatened to devour him if he didn't have one more taste of her.

In truth, he'd been burning for Sophie's touch before he ever followed Ulrik to the hospital and saw her again. But it was discovering her in the tub that did him in.

He'd known as soon as he walked in that he was a goner. Yet he hadn't left. His feet refused to move, and his body . . . well, his body demanded he climb into the tub with her and remind her just how loudly he could make her scream.

When she opened her eyes, Darius had been transfixed. The way tendrils of her flame-colored hair clung to the sides of her face and neck was one of the sexiest things he'd ever seen—or ever would see. Then there was the flicker of the candlelight moving seductively over her skin.

The knockout punch came when Sophie shifted ever so slightly in the bath. Her breasts rose from the water, parting the thick bubbles. Darius's mouth had watered at the sight of her puckered pink nipples. Every bit of blood rushed to his cock as he fought to remain where he stood.

What possessed him to walk to her to say farewell? And to tempt himself with another taste of her lips, no matter how light? He must be daft to put himself in such a position.

All it took was one sample, one small press of their mouths to push him over the edge. All the yearning, all the hunger he felt for her that he told himself wasn't real, came rushing back like a tsunami.

It consumed him, devoured him. Leaving was no longer an option. He had to have her again.

Darius moaned when her lips moved beneath his. He braced his hands on either side of the tub, even as her arm wrapped around his neck.

Water slid down his neck and along his back. Bubbles that clung to her fingers tickled his ear. Water lapped loudly against the side of the tub when she brought her other arm up to his neck.

Darius was supposed to have been in and out of the flat. All he wanted to know was that she was safe. And he needed one last look at her.

He wasn't supposed to be kissing her, and he sure as hell wasn't supposed to be thinking of sliding his aching rod between her legs.

The sound of bubbles squishing was nearly as loud as their harsh breathing as he dipped one arm in the water and pressed her against his chest.

With the music still playing in the background, Darius kissed her with all the pent-up need and longing he'd been discounting for days.

He stood straight, bringing her with him. Water trickled down her body into the sloshing tub. Darius stopped kissing her long enough to see thick handfuls of bubbles sliding down her back, shapely ass, and legs, returning to the water.

"Don't stop," she whispered with her olive eyes heavy-lidded.

As if he could. Darius bent and scooped her into his arms. He pivoted and carried her dripping wet to the bedroom. Just as he was about to lay her on the bed, she pulled his head down for a kiss.

Darius was powerless to pull away. Her kisses had a way of making his brain stop functioning properly. With just a coax of her lips, he was putty in her hands.

He put his knee on the bed and leaned forward, catching them with his free hand. Darius couldn't contain a growl of pleasure when he found himself nestled between her legs.

If only his clothes weren't in the way of feeling her sleek, damp skin against his.

As if Sophie was thinking the same thing, she yanked his shirt up to his shoulders. Darius jerked off the offending garment.

His breath locked in his lungs when he felt her breasts against his chest. How could he have even dared to think their first time together would be the best? Especially when he hadn't seen or felt all of her?

With her hand traveling over his shoulders and down his back, Darius gazed into her eyes that were a beautiful mixture of green and silver.

He hissed in a breath when she wrapped one long, lean leg around his waist, bringing him closer to her sex. Through his jeans he felt the heat of her core.

Her hand paused at his backside, pressing just enough as she ground against him. Darius gritted his teeth as he rocked into her. His cock jumped, aching for more.

Two weeks was too long to think about Sophie and not take advantage of the time given to them. Darius rose to his elbow and began to grab for the waist of his pants. In a heartbeat, Sophie's hands were there.

A second later, he was helping her push them down his

hips while he kicked off his boots. It took entirely too long to take off his clothes and once more be against her.

But when they were flesh to flesh, both held quiet and still in the moment.

Until the passion took over once more.

They began to frantically kiss each other. His hands were in her hair, tugging the length free from the pins. Then he was touching her arms, her hips, and her legs before he cupped her breast and found a pert nipple waiting for his attention.

When he bent and took the peak into his mouth, her back arched and her nails dug into his back. Darius watched the pleasure move over her face, which only spurred his desire higher.

He was so intent on learning the weight of her breasts in his palms as well as how sensitive her nipples were to his fingers, lips, and mouth that he didn't know what her hands were about as they roamed over him until she wrapped her fingers around his cock.

Sophie sizzled through every particle of her body. She was so close to orgasm that if she rocked against Darius once more, she would shatter. It was the yearning to feel his length inside her that kept her still.

Was it because she'd gone so long without having sex before Darius? She kept herself busy enough that she didn't think about easing her body too often.

Or was it Darius who brought out the shameless abandon? And did it really matter?

It felt good. *He* felt good.

Sophie ran her hand up and down his thick length as his tongue teased her nipple mercilessly. Each flick, each soft suck drove her closer and closer to the edge.

It was only fair that he be there with her. Sophie loved

the feel of his arousal. It was like warm velvet gliding over steel. She hadn't realized he was so large. No wonder he'd stretched her so that first time.

A bead of pre-cum formed, and she rubbed it around the head of his shaft. After, she cupped his ball sac and rolled them around in her palm before she softly scraped her nails over them.

Darius hissed, his cock jumping in response. She smiled, and in return, he lightly bit her nipple. Sophie cried out from the pleasure as it tightened low in her gut.

She could do nothing when he raised her arms above her head and held her there with one strong hand. With a slow, wicked smile, Darius kept eye contact with her as he lowered his head and nipped her breast. Then he drew her nipple deep into his mouth and suckled while his tongue lapped at the turgid peak.

While his mouth did wonderful, decadent things to her breasts, his free hand skimmed along her stomach to her hips. He shifted his body to the side so he could then slide his fingers into her small triangle of red curls at her sex.

Sophie's legs fell open on their own. Her breathing was harsh, her body trembling as she anxiously awaited his finger to touch her and ease some of her need.

But he didn't touch her. Instead he stroked the inside of both thighs, coming just close enough to her sex that she could feel the warmth of his hand—but never touching. All the while he had her nipples so hard they hurt.

Sophie tried to move her hips to get in contact with his hand, but Darius kept out of reach. Her sex throbbed she was so close to climaxing.

He lifted his head and cupped her sex. She stilled instantly at the contact. Then he ran a finger along her sex to her swollen clit and back to her entrance again.

"Is this what you need?" he asked.

Sophie couldn't form words so she nodded.

One finger slid inside her. Her eyes closed from the bliss.

"So damn wet," he murmured. "I need to taste you."

He was nestled between her legs before she knew it. "No," she cried as he licked her.

"Nay?" he asked, pausing long enough to say the word before he found her clit.

Sophie gripped the comforter and fought to speak past the rising passion. "I want to taste you too."

That got him to lift his head and look at her. She waited, her chest heaving as her sex clenched for more.

"You're dripping wet," he said as he looked down at her. "You're verra close to release."

Yes, but why did that matter? She wanted to know more of him to add to her memories. Feeling his body atop hers was amazing, just as it was to learn the thickness of his arms and the width of his shoulders. Not to mention his stomach that was lined with hard muscle.

"Are you sure?" he asked with a gleam in his eyes as he circled her clit with his thumb.

Darius watched her eyes roll back in her head. Her legs were spread and her sex open to him. She was magnificent. The little triangle of red curls was trimmed neatly and the rest shaved to show her sex gleaming with her arousal.

He spread her woman's lips and found her clit. Bending, he lapped at the bud with his tongue while her breathing grew more ragged as soft cries fell from her lips.

She tasted as wild and fiery as her passion. Her sex greedily clenched against his finger when he slid a digit inside her.

Just as he suspected, he only had to move his fingers two pumps before a hoarse cry filled the room as she peaked. But Darius wasn't nearly done with her.

With the walls of her sex still clenching around his

finger, he withdrew his hand and rose above her. He positioned the head of his cock at her entrance, and slowly penetrated her.

His own eyes closed when he felt her orgasm squeeze him. She was so hot and wet that he couldn't be inside her and not move.

With his hips thrusting softly at first, he set up a rhythm that she soon joined in. He braced his hands on either side of her face and steadily drove within her tight sheath.

She urged him on with her hands and legs. Her seductive gaze held his, and the wonder and pleasure he saw in her depths surprised him.

With his own orgasm rapidly approaching, Darius thrust harder and deeper. He saw the flush on her chest and her eyes glazed over a moment before her body stiffened.

He watched in amazement, as once more she climaxed. It was such a beautiful sight that he couldn't get enough. The slight curve of her lips, the way her breasts heaved, the carnality that shone in her eyes.

It all sent him careening over the edge.

Darius pumped inside her with hard, fast strokes before he buried himself deep and let the orgasm take him. The pleasure was intense, potent.

As he stared into Sophie's olive eyes, all he wanted to do was kiss her again. He lowered his head and took her lips while their bodies still shuddered from the ecstasy.

When he withdrew from her, Darius didn't get dressed and leave. He rolled to his back with his fingers entwined with Sophie's.

For every moment that he remained, it grew harder and harder to leave. Yet, if he wanted her far from the war that the Dragon Kings were involved in, he needed to do just that.

Darius turned his head toward her, ready to spout a lie that would allow him to leave. Only he found her asleep.

He turned toward her and ran the back of his fingers along her cheek and jaw. "Farewell, doc."

CHAPTER
EIGHT

Rhi was floating in darkness with pinpricks of light coming from thousands of miles away. She looked at them, curious. Were they stars? No. She knew what stars looked like. These were something entirely different.

She wasn't afraid. For the first time in a very long time she felt . . . nothing. No happiness, no sorrow, no anger, no regret. It was as if everything had been wiped away. Like the slate was clean, allowing her to start over.

What a load of crap that was. No one started over. The baggage always remained. She learned that the hard way. It was what one did with said baggage that made the difference.

Rhi knew she was at Dreagan. And she knew because of *him*.

He was in the room with her again. It wasn't the first time her lover had come to see her. She wished she could see his face. She wished she could speak so she could shout at him and demand to know why he was coming to her now.

Was it because she was injured? Did he care *now*? Had he ever really cared?

That was the question that haunted her. If the love he once claimed to have for her had been real, then he wouldn't have been able to let her go so easily. Nor would he have sent Darius to tell her.

She couldn't look at Darius without hearing those words that had torn her world to shreds in a matter of seconds. One minute she was on top of the world.

The next, she was drowning in misery and confusion, trying to find her footing with the hand fate had dealt her.

She didn't hate Darius exactly. Though he could've refused to give her the news. Her lover should've had the balls to tell her himself. Was he afraid she'd go nuclear on him as she'd done at Balladyn's fortress?

Rhi paused. She most likely would have, now that she thought about it. But that didn't make his pansy-ass any easier to swallow.

She hated that he was in the room with her, standing beside the bed.

And she loved that he was there.

Her heart ached at his nearness. How she wanted to grab his hand and bring it to her face to feel him touching her once more.

She was pathetic, pitiful.

How many centuries needed to pass without him coming to her before she could let him go? She kept asking herself that same question, and each time it get easier to answer.

She'd been saying for a while now that she needed to let him go. Ulrik had told her that, as had Balladyn. Both held grudges against the Dragon Kings, and in some ways those resentments were justified.

"Wake up."

His voice was like a punch in her gut. She felt tears gather, and hated him for it. She loathed herself for having such a reaction to him.

"You've made your point, Rhi. It's time to wake up."

She wasn't ready. If she woke she'd have to face Balladyn. Worse, she would need to confront Usaeil, and she wasn't ready. Then there was the issue of the darkness inside her.

It was growing. She couldn't deny that any longer. How long before it stamped out her light? How long before she became Dark?

The prospect didn't frighten her as it used to. Perhaps she'd been destined for this path from the very beginning. Maybe that's why Balladyn was Dark, so he could help her when she turned.

Balladyn. If he could, would he be there with her? She knew the answer to that. It was an unequivocal yes. If she were anywhere but Dreagan, Balladyn would be beside her.

That warmed her heart. After all the rejection from her lover, Balladyn—as always—never failed her. Sure he'd tortured her to turn her Dark, but she'd gotten away. That kind of attention was preferable to being disregarded and ignored.

A great love. That was what she and her King had claimed they shared. If it was so great, where had he been? Why had he ended it? Why . . .

She halted the questions. Did it really matter anymore? She'd gone thousands of years without answers, and it wasn't like she would get them. Ever.

Her body couldn't move. It wasn't the blast of Dark magic that kept her sleeping. She did that. She was at a crossroads, and she still wasn't sure what to do.

If she remained on her path, loving a man who didn't return her affection and letting the darkness continue to grow, she'd become that which she hunted—Dark Fae.

If she took the other path, she didn't know what lay ahead. It could be with Balladyn or someone else.

"How is she?" said a voice with a British accent.

Henry. She sighed. Sweet Henry.

He was a good kisser, and she loved the way he looked at her. But he was human. She already crossed a line by kissing him and giving him hope that something would develop between them. That was something she needed to set straight soon.

"There's no' been a change."

Rhys. He was back again? Somehow Rhi wasn't surprised.

Henry let out a loud sigh. "I'm worried."

"As we all are," Rhys stated.

"I was looking for Con earlier. Someone said he was in here."

Rhys grunted. "Aye. He was."

"His power is to heal. Can't he bloody well do something?" Henry asked angrily.

"He already has," Rhys stated. "She's healed."

"Then why does she not wake?"

She hated the worry and fear she heard in both men's voices, but she wasn't ready to face things yet. Rhi sunk deeper into her sleep so she wouldn't hear any more.

Right before she drifted off, she felt her watcher's eyes again. He hadn't left her side. She was more than curious as to who it was that could remain veiled so long.

It was one of the first things she would discover when she woke. Later. Much later . . .

Sophie knew before she ever opened her eyes that Darius was gone. She reached over and felt the spot where he had been. The bed was cold, informing her he'd left some time ago.

She opened her eyes and rolled to her back. Normally she had a hard time having an orgasm with a man, but Darius made it so easy.

The first time with Darius she attributed it to the fact that it had been a long time since she'd been with a man, but last night? Darius hadn't just given her the climax of her life. He'd given her two in a very short space of time.

Sophie bit her lip when she moved and the sheet rubbed against her nipples that were still highly sensitized from his teasing.

She carefully lifted the covers and climbed from the bed. Shutting off her alarm a minute before it was supposed to go off, she made her way to the bathroom.

There she halted and stared at the bathtub full of water. The candles had been blown out. Darius must have done that.

Sophie quickly unstoppered the tub to let the water drain and grabbed her towel. She turned on the shower and waited for the water to heat up before she stepped in.

But under the hot stream of water, she could only stand there thinking about being in Darius's arms. For two weeks she'd dreamed of him taking her against the building because it had been so erotic and amazing. Last night far exceeded the first. It could well last her an entire year's worth of dreams.

It wasn't until she was drying off that she remembered what Darius had said. She was in danger, and if she saw him she had to act as if she couldn't stand him.

That was easy yesterday, but after another night in his arms? She wasn't so sure. There was no doubt Darius was infuriating. He told her cryptic things like that, snuck into her flat, and then made love to her as if he would die if he didn't have her.

Sophie couldn't remember the last time a man made her feel that way. When he looked at her, he saw only her. Not his mobile phone, not his computer, not his friends or work. Just her.

And that felt . . . amazing.

She blinked and realized she was standing in front of her sink holding the towel as she thought of Darius. Dimly, she recognized the *Outlander* soundtrack still played on repeat.

And her glorious mood was soured as she feared she might never see Darius again.

Ulrik crossed another name off the list and stared at the few who remained. It was taking longer than he wanted, but he was slowly learning who Mikkel's spy at Dreagan was. He closed the file and tucked it in a false bottom of his desk drawer with others.

One of his mobile phones rang. He answered with a curt, "Aye?"

"He's no' been here, boss," said the deep voice on the other end of the line.

Ulrik sat back and grinned. "Are you positive?"

"We are. I kept watch on the front of the building while Jonas watched the back. Darius didna pay the doc a visit."

"Did you watch the roof?"

"Aye, boss. Just as you ordered."

Ulrik sat there a moment. After what Darius had gone through, he'd be the last of the Dragon Kings who would get embroiled with a mortal. Ulrik needed to be sure he was telling the truth, however. It looked like Darius had been.

Except he recalled how infuriated Darius became when he realized Ulrik had watched them make love.

"Follow the doctor to work. Discreetly," Ulrik cautioned. "I doona want her seeing you."

"Will do."

Ulrik replaced the mobile with the others on the corner of his desk. His interest in Dr. Sophie Martin went deeper than finding Darius with her. She'd helped Thorn and Lexi.

Sophie worked outside the hospital, often going to visit those who couldn't get to the hospital or who couldn't afford it. It was by chance that one of Ulrik's spies had seen her going into a building with Thorn. The same building where Darcy's flat was located.

That building was now decimated by the Dark, so there was no hope of Ulrik finding anything among the rubble. Depending on how much she knew, Sophie could be an asset. He rubbed his jaw.

With the right amount of coercion and persuasion, Ulrik could turn her and use her as a spy. With the Kings' penchant for showing up in Edinburgh and any mortal around them becoming injured, it was only natural that they'd call Sophie.

They trusted her, which meant they wouldn't hide things from her. It would be another blow to the Kings. Though he was pleased by the video leaking the Dragon Kings to the world, that was only a small fraction of his plan.

Once Mikkel made himself known, Ulrik had no choice but to alter his plots somewhat. Now he didn't just have to worry about fighting—and beating—Con, but he had to kill his own uncle as well.

It was either that or Mikkel killed him, and Ulrik hadn't suffered through all the millennia as a mortal not to have his revenge.

As for his uncle, he continued to let Mikkel think he was doing his bidding. So far Mikkel accepted everything while keeping a close eye on Ulrik. But Ulrik wasn't worried. There was much Mikkel knew, but even more that his uncle didn't.

While the scales dipped in his favor, Ulrik was all right. However, he hadn't gotten to where he was by letting fate decide his path. He made his own way, forging alliances and unions that would ensure his outcome.

Mikkel would try to kill him by a sneak attack. It was

one reason Ulrik never slept. Nor did he trust anyone. Which led him back to ties. Sophie Martin would be a nice addition to his allies.

His decision made, Ulrik rose and went to change. He had a trip into Edinburgh to make.

CHAPTER
NINE

Sophie was thankful for the craziness of work to take her mind off Darius. She'd gotten there at six in the morning, and the next time she looked up, it was four in the afternoon.

She leaned against the nurses' counter and jotted something in a file. It wasn't until Claire took it from her that Sophie looked at her friend and smiled.

"You saw him last night," Claire said in a whispery voice, her eyes wide.

Sophie tried to deny it, then she gave up and shrugged.

Claire looked to the ceiling. "Thank you, God. Now, if you don't mind, send one my way. Bob is getting tired."

"Who's Bob? You've not told me about a Bob," Sophie said, a little hurt.

"I have too," Claire said and gave her a little shove in the arm. "Bob is Battery Operated Boyfriend. B.O.B."

Sophie laughed, because only Claire would come up with such a name for her vibrator.

Then Claire batted her eyes and did her best Southern accent to mimic her favorite character, Kaylee, from the movie *Serenity* as she said, "Goin' on a year now I ain't had nothin' twixt my nethers weren't run on batteries."

Sophie had to grab her sides she was laughing so hard. Leave it to Claire to make her smile.

"What?" Claire said with an innocent expression, keeping her Southern drawl. "Was somethin' I said funny?"

Sophie held up a hand when Claire started to continue with more lines from the movie. "No more, please."

"It's all that coffee," Claire said as she eyed the cup Sophie set down a moment ago. "Water, Soph, water."

"Yes, but water doesn't have the caffeine I need to keep going."

"With Mr. Do-It-Right in your bed, I don't think you're going to need much caffeine."

It was a reminder that Darius had come into her life out of the shadows, and he'd disappeared back into them. Sophie tried to keep the smile in place, but Claire knew her too well.

"What is it, honey?" she asked.

Sophie waved her away. "Nothing. It was just sex, nothing more. And he's gone now. He won't be coming back."

"What a wanker. At least he wasn't perfect."

Only Claire would immediately come to her side and find something wrong with Mr. Do-It-Right, as she'd called him. Sophie smiled wryly. "He was kinda perfect."

"Everyone has flaws. Did he snore?"

"I've no idea."

"I bet he snored," Claire said with a firm nod. "Was his thingy bent? It curved to the side, didn't it?"

Sophie shook her head.

"Was he . . ." Claire trailed off and wiggled her little finger.

"Mr. Do-It-Right?" Sophie asked with a flat look. "He certainly wasn't small."

Claire rolled her eyes. "Hey, some small guys can do it right. It just feels better when the man is well hung. So maybe he couldn't kiss. That's it. He was a bad kisser."

Sophie shook her head again.

Clair threw out her hands and let them slap her thighs as they fell. "I give up. Looks like he was perfect except that he left. That definitely makes him a wanker."

"It's better that he's gone."

"It's absolutely not better if you think that. If you're glad, then that means he struck a chord in you, Soph. And I'm sorry, but after seven years, you need several chords struck. Repeatedly. And often."

Sophie checked her watch and winked at Claire. "Thanks for the pep talk. Gotta run."

"We're not done here," Claire called as Sophie walked away.

Sophie merely lifted her hand and waved, not bothering to look behind her. It was a conversation she and Claire had been having for years. She met Claire six months after moving to Edinburgh, and they had bonded during one incredibly long shift.

During a girl's night out a year later, Sophie had drank too much and ended up telling Claire the entire awful story. Claire was the only person in Edinburgh who knew the sordid details.

No matter what Claire said, Sophie was happy with her life. She had everything she wanted. Her career was on track, she loved her job, and she had a close friend. It was all she needed.

Except, with Darius, she'd begun to long for so much more. That dream of a husband and a happy life began to sprout again.

It was a dangerous thing, hope.

Especially to someone like her and all she'd endured. The humiliation, the shame.

Sophie turned the corner and ran into a man. She bounced back, but his hands grabbed her by her arms to steady her. "I apologize," she said and looked up into gold eyes.

He smiled, though it didn't quite reach his unique eyes. "It's my fault. I wasna looking where I was going."

She recognized him from the day before. "It's fine. These halls are very busy."

"I've a confession," he said as she started to walk around him.

Intrigued, she asked, "Oh?"

"I put myself in your path. I've been trying to get your attention all day."

Sophie looked at the hand-sewn suit he wore and shook her head. He practically oozed money and old-world class. "A man like you can have any woman he wants."

"What do you mean, a man like me?"

"Handsome, rich, and charming."

"But you doona find those redeeming qualities?" he asked, watching her intently, with a half-smile in place.

Sophie shrugged. "Handsome is always a boon. Money comes and goes easily, so that shouldn't make a difference."

"But it makes life easier."

"That's true," she conceded. "As for the charm, I've learned that men use it to get what they want, but it's rarely genuine."

The fake smile dropped as he looked at her differently, as if he were seeing her for the first time. "You're no' wrong, lass. However, men are no' the only ones to use something to get what they want."

"Ah, but I'm not one of those women who use their bodies to get something. I've a brain."

"Which is why I'm interested." He held out his hand, "I'm Ulrik Dunn."

Sophie hesitated for a moment before she accepted his hand and shook it. "Sophie Martin."

"Doctor," he corrected with a grin.

She found herself returning his smile. "Just what are you after, Mr. Dunn?"

"Ulrik, please," he said as he released her hand. "I've learned a lot about you, Dr. Martin. I know that you often help those less fortunate with your house calls."

Sophie immediately retrieved her hand and took a step back. "It's not against any regulations."

Ulrik held up his hands and bowed his head. "I was in no way saying it was. I'm merely pointing out that it's your side work, as it were, that has drawn me."

"Why?" Sophie was suddenly leery of him.

"You think of others. It's a trait I admire."

She held the chart against her chest and wrapped her arms around it. There was something about Ulrik that didn't quite meet up. His words were right, but his eyes lacked . . . humanity.

Darius's words of caution the night before came back to her. "So you've been following me?"

"Word of your deeds reached me. I checked you out, of course."

"Of course," Sophie replied tightly. She met his gold eyes and said, "Mr. Dunn, I enjoy what I do. My hours are filled here at the hospital and helping others. I don't have any spare time for whatever it is you want from me. I'd also appreciate if you quit following me."

"You're going to leave without even hearing my proposal?"

She paused as she was about to walk around him. "I am."

"You doona trust me," he replied with a hint of surprise in his deep voice.

"As a general rule, I don't trust anyone." She wasn't sure

why she told him that, since it wasn't true anymore. At least not when it came to Darius.

Whether she wanted to or not, she found she trusted Darius.

Ulrik put his hands in his pants pockets and gave a slight nod of his head. There was something in his golden gaze. It had been there for a second, so fleeting it was gone before she could realize what it was. But there was no doubt it was a bit of sadness and a heavy dose of anger.

He'd been hurt deeply.

Sophie didn't want to feel a connection to him. Ulrik wasn't a man to be trusted—ever. He was too controlled, and entirely too handsome. Men like him were a volcano waiting to erupt.

And when they did, they took out everyone around them.

Unlike Darius who was more like water. Soft at times, and yet unyielding and dangerous. Why then did she want to trust him?

She tried to keep walking, but something held her back. Sophie turned her head to Ulrik. He tilted his slightly, a question in his eyes.

"What is it?" he asked.

By his confused look, he had no idea of what he'd revealed. Most people wouldn't have seen it, but Sophie knew all too well how deep the wounds of a betrayal were. Those who had those same wounds could see them in others, no matter how well hidden they might be.

"I'm going for coffee. You're free to walk with me," she told him.

His cocky grin was back in place. "While doing my best in that short time to convince you of my proposal?"

"Yep."

Sophie started walking, and just as she expected, Ulrik was beside her. He held the door for her, as a perfect gentleman would. Yet there was a precarious current around him.

It was different than what she felt with Darius. Darius was electrifying, a temptation. Being near him was heart-pounding and hazardous to her health, but exhilarating all the same.

With Ulrik, she got the feeling that being near him almost certainly meant death. It put her on edge, making her tense and uneasy.

With coffee in hand, they sat at an empty table. Sophie set the chart in her lap and filled her coffee with loads of cream.

"Why did you invite me?" Ulrik asked.

Sophie focused on fixing her coffee. "I'm not sure. You make me uncomfortable, and you know I don't trust you."

"Exactly. You should be far away from me, and yet here you sit."

She lifted one shoulder in a shrug as she sipped her coffee. "I told you I'd listen to what you have to say. Once I decline it, you can leave."

"I'm more interested in why you agreed to hear me."

Sitting back and placing her coffee on the table, Sophie regarded him. He'd changed tactics. No longer was he the suave businessman who was trying to sell some proposal and wanting her involvement.

The man before her now was focused on one thing—the reason she didn't walk away.

Sophie could lie and make up something, but it would do neither of them any good. Ulrik was the kind of man who could spot a falsehood a hundred miles away.

"As silly as this sounds, it's because I saw your pain," she admitted.

All emotion was wiped from his face in a millisecond. "Excuse me?"

"Someone betrayed you." She slowly turned her cup

with her fingers. "I'm guessing by your reaction that few people are able to pick up on that."

"You could say that." His words were clipped, cold.

Sophie released a slow breath. "I can usually spot someone who's been betrayed deeply. You hid yours very well. I almost didn't see it."

"But you did." He tapped the rim of his coffee cup with his index finger. "You notice what you yourself hide."

"It's not something I share, but yes. I, too, was betrayed."

His golden eyes held hers, refusing to allow her to look away as he gazed deep inside her. Sophie shifted uncomfortably in her seat. Finally, she was able to lower her gaze. She found herself staring at the tie knotted at his neck.

"Let me take you to dinner."

Sophie lifted her gaze to him to find him running a hand through his long black hair. Her first thought was of Darius. "Thank you, but I must decline."

After a few minutes in silence, Ulrik pushed his chair back and stood. "That is your right, Sophie."

With a nod, Ulrik walked away, leaving Sophie more confused about his arrival than before.

CHAPTER
TEN

Darius was feeling restless and agitated. He needed to find a Dark Fae to take his frustration out on, but he'd scoured the city three times and couldn't find a single one of the buggers.

He was there to rid Edinburgh of the Dark. It was something that helped to keep his mind off Sophie and the need tearing through him.

But without Dark to fight, all he could think about was her.

Darius paused beside a hotel and leaned back against the building. Somehow he managed to skirt the hospital without going inside and searching for Sophie.

With no more Dark in the city, he should notify Con and return to Dreagan. Or at the very least see if any of the other Kings needed help in their cities.

Yet Darius did nothing. He knew the right thing to do was continue the mission and defeat Ulrik and the Dark. With Ulrik in the city and showing up at the hospital, this was where Darius needed to be.

Sophie was beautiful and fiery—and mortal. Not only that, but Ulrik already begun to focus on her. Darius didn't wish to carry the weight of her death for eternity. He already carried too much.

His mission was complete. The Dark were gone.

And suddenly there was Ulrik.

Darius should tell Con about his run-in with Ulrik. He wasn't sure why he hadn't yet. With all the searching Con did for Ulrik, Con was going to be furious.

Darius saw something out of the corner of his eyes that had him jerking his head to the left. There, for a half of a heartbeat was a man with long white hair. That was the second time he had caught a glimpse of the man before he disappeared.

His hair wasn't silver, so Darius didn't think he was Dark. And though he'd seen plenty of Dark with more silver than black in their hair, never had he seen—or heard of—a Dark with solid white hair.

But if not a Dark, then who could the man be to disappear as rapidly as a Fae?

"Well, this is a first," said a deep voice filled with humor behind him.

Darius sighed and turned around to find Constantine, King of Kings and CEO of Dreagan Industries, behind him. Shite. So much for Darius updating Con via their mental link.

Con wore a dark gray suit with a crisp white shirt and a steel gray tie with silver pinstripes running vertically down the tie.

Con was grinning, his wavy blond hair trimmed short and neat while his black eyes saw everything and everyone. The half-smile faded. A small frown puckered his brow. "What is it?"

"Have you ever heard of a Dark with white hair?"

"Nay," Con said with a shake of his head. "No' even one with all silver hair."

Darius looked over his shoulder where he'd seen the

white-haired man. "That's what I thought. It's twice now I've seen him."

"And his eyes?"

"I doona know," Darius said as he turned back around. "I'm only able to catch a glimpse. It's the hair. Both times I caught him out of the corner of my eye, and by the time I turn, he's gone."

Con put his left hand in his pants pocket. "Twice, aye?"

"Aye. His hair is long, Con, and white as snow. It's no' something I can miss."

"If you've seen it, others have as well."

Darius grunted. "As if a mortal would pay him any mind. They color their hair all sorts of weird shades now. White means nothing."

Con nodded as he stood silent for a moment. "And our situation here?"

"All but taken care of. I've no' even found a Dark using glamour. It's like they're gone. Yesterday I was still killing a few, but now there's nothing."

"It's the same in the other cities. I think it's time you returned to Dreagan with the rest of us."

It meant leaving Sophie behind with Ulrik. Which wasn't going to happen.

"I saw Ulrik yesterday."

Con's black gaze narrowed. "Why did you no' tell me sooner?"

"Because it'd do no good." Darius shrugged and glanced in the direction of the hospital.

"Tell me what happened. All of it," Con said in a low voice tinged with anger.

Darius glanced at the ground. "I found him entering the Royal Victoria Hospital and followed."

"The hospital? Why?"

"Do you remember when Lexi became ill? Thorn called

Warrick, and Darcy was able to tell him of a doctor who would come to Lexi."

"Since Thorn couldna take her to the hospital," Con finished.

Darius gave a bow of his head. "Exactly. The doctor's name was Sophie Martin. She came to Thorn as he was staying in Darcy's flat with Lexi. Dr. Martin was able to heal Lexi."

"And you believe Ulrik is interested in this Sophie Martin because she helped Lexi? There's more. What are you no' telling me?"

Darius stared at Con for a long moment before he said, "It's been a verra long time since I satisfied my body."

Con turned away, mumbling something beneath his breath as he ran a hand down his face. He pivoted back to Darius, his black eyes icy as the Arctic. "You fucked her."

"We shared our bodies, aye." It infuriated Darius that Con put so base a word to what they had done, even if it was the truth.

"Does she know what you are?"

"She knows nothing." Darius raised a brow and glared at Con as anger simmered. "Do you want to know where I took her? How about the position or how many times she came? Since apparently that's all tied to Ulrik."

"I didna ask those questions."

"You didna have to." Darius now understood how Thorn had felt under Con's scrutiny of his and Lexi's relationship. "Sophie was a mere tumble. She eased my body."

Con's entire demeanor changed. He relaxed, looking almost bored. "You bed her once, and Ulrik comes to the hospital. Did he speak with her?"

"Nay. I followed him outside. That's when he spoke."

"He . . . what?" Con demanded heatedly, rage making his black eyes dance with emotion.

Darius had seen Constantine furious twice in all their millennia together, but there was no denying the indignation that Con allowed him to see.

"The conversation wasna long. He was after Sophie because he thought I was interested in her."

Con's nostrils flared. "Why?"

"He saw us together."

"Fucking?" Con asked with a curl of his lip.

"Aye."

"Did you no' know someone was looking in your window?"

Darius didn't need to explain anything to Con, but if he didn't answer, it was just like Con to go to the hospital and find Sophie. Darius would rather answer the questions than pull Sophie further into their war.

"I took her outside the hospital against a building."

Con's eyes widened a fraction. "Have you lost your damned mind? When was this?"

"The night Edinburgh was burning."

Con closed his eyes and stood as still as stone for several minutes. When he lifted his eyelids, there was censure there, and it irked Darius.

As if Con hadn't done anything foolish and rash before. Then again, Con was perfect. He'd never done anything out of line or wrong, Darius thought mockingly with a snort.

"While you *fucked* Sophie," Con said, emphasizing the word *fuck*, "Ulrik was watching you. He obviously saw something that made him believe you've an interest in her."

"As I told him. He's wrong."

"How many times have you fucked her?"

Darius was barely holding onto his own rage. He kept silent, his gaze holding Con's.

Con smirked as he gave a dry chuckle. "How many times have you slept with her?"

"Twice."

"When was the second time?"

Damn. Con just had to ask, didn't he? Darius knew his answer would look bad. "Ulrik made it clear he'd target anyone the Kings show an interest in. I followed Sophie home last night to make sure Ulrik wasna there."

"And?" Con urged expectantly when he paused.

"And," Darius said angrily, "I told her if she ever sees me to pretend that she hates me."

Con raised a blond brow in question. "I suppose you want me to believe that you walked from her flat then?"

"I did. After we had sex."

"What if Ulrik was watching?"

"He wasna," Darius assured him.

Con nodded and blew out a breath. "All right. Let's say he wasna at her flat. How do you know he wasna following you?"

"I'm no' a fool, Con. I know how to make sure no one is trailing me."

"And the Dark who are allies to Ulrik. You doona think one of them would track you?"

Darius folded his arms across his chest. "None of them can remain veiled for longer than a minute or so. I wasna followed."

"You believe Ulrik is going to take your word regarding Sophie?"

That had nagged at Darius all day. "I'm going to make sure of it. She helped Lexi, and I had sex with her. That's all she is."

"Why did you no' let me know you were there with Ulrik? I could've captured him."

Darius glanced to the side. "Ulrik pointed out that since we Kings can no' fly anymore, that even if I alerted you to his whereabouts, he'd be gone before you could drive here."

"He is ahead of the game. For now." Con's chest expanded as he drew in a deep breath. "That willna always be the case."

Darius knew that Ulrik had to be taken out. His need for revenge against Con was disrupting everyone's lives. The one place the Kings had always been safe was Dreagan.

Ulrik had shone a spotlight on their home, making it more of a prison than a refuge. Ulrik's alliance with MI5 and the Dark Fae were just a portion of it. If Ulrik had proven anything, it was his ability to work the humans into helping him.

The worst—and harshest—of things Ulrik had done was curse Rhys so he couldna shift. Then there were Ulrik's attempts to kill Darcy and Lexi.

Any female—mortal or Fae—that a Dragon King showed attention was going to be on Ulrik's radar. Which meant those females were as good as dead if the Kings weren't around.

"How serious was Ulrik in wanting to talk to Sophie?" Con asked.

Darius shrugged, thinking back over the conversation. "I suspect he wanted to see how attached I was."

"Do you think he'd return to Sophie today?"

Darius dropped his arms to his sides. "It's a possibility."

"Then you should get to her. Now."

"I told her I was staying away."

Con tilted his head to the side. "I was in agreement with that statement a few minutes ago. No longer. I need to know if Ulrik speaks to her, and I need to know what he says. Sophie could help give us an edge."

"You said that about Darcy as well," Darius pointed out.

"You can be near Sophie, or I'll send someone else to the doctor. Your choice, Darius."

As if there was a choice. Darius turned on his heel and walked toward the hospital.

CHAPTER
ELEVEN

Sophie was still thinking about her peculiar visit with Ulrik as she pulled the takeout carton from the bag. She used to eat right out of the container, until she realized she'd gone two months without washing a single dish.

From then on, she always put her takeout on a plate. It was a nice pretend game she played, allowing herself to believe she actually cooked the meal.

In reality, cooking for one was nearly impossible unless she wanted to eat the same thing for three to four meals, and she couldn't handle that. Besides, she never liked cooking.

Eating, however, was an entirely different story. She loved food. She enjoyed visiting all sorts of restaurants and sampling what a chef could create. It had been months since she had been to a restaurant.

Work had been busy with her picking up all the extra shifts from doctors who wanted out of Edinburgh until all the deaths stopped. Even sleep had been a luxury she could ill afford. She caught naps at the hospital when she was able. Sometimes it was even easier to stay there instead of returning to her flat.

Maybe it was time to take a night and go have a nice dinner. It wasn't like she enjoyed eating by herself, but she learned to do it years ago. The trick was not looking as if you were about to break into a million pieces because you were lonely.

Sophie didn't mind eating alone. She didn't have to worry about keeping a conversation going, or worse, pretending to find a guy interesting.

She put the sushi on her plate and filled a glass of white wine. After she sat at the table, she pulled out her mobile phone and checked the calendar. She had the next two days off. It wasn't by her choice. The hospital administrator had insisted. Apparently she'd worked for three weeks without a day off.

Someone had to do it. Why not her? She had no family or anyone waiting at home. Not even a cat. She was the most likely candidate to cover those shifts to allow the others with spouses and children to get home to them.

"I can sleep in," she said aloud and took her first bite of the roll.

Sleeping in. What was that exactly? Her inner clock would have her awake at five with or without a day off. She was banned from even going to the hospital for the next two days. What was she going to do?

What *did* people do on their days off?

There were a few patients she could check on that she saw outside the hospital, but that would only take a few hours. What in the world was she going to do with the rest?

Sophie glanced at the telly. She couldn't remember the last time she turned it on. There were movies. She could go see a movie. That would eat up a couple of hours. And then what?

She ate the rest of her sushi roll and was sipping on the

wine when she rolled her shoulders. A nice soak in the tub would help to work out the kinks.

As soon as she walked into the bathroom and saw the tub, images from the night before filled her mind. Darius. The man set her aflame with a single look. It wasn't fair that he had that kind of control over her.

"It's not control," she told herself. "I've just not relieved my body in a while. That's all it was."

Horse shit.

It was complete horse shit. Darius did it for her in so many ways she couldn't begin to count. His hair, his eyes, that amazing jaw and cheeks. That mouth!

And his hands.

She sighed just thinking about his large hands skimming over her flesh.

"No," she said and firmly put him out of her mind.

Darius was gone from her life. He'd appeared as suddenly as he vanished. If she hadn't touched him herself, she would almost think him a ghost.

Sophie lit the candles around the tub and turned on the water. She sat on the edge of the tub until she got the water just right, then she put in the bubble bath and clicked the remote that turned on some classical music.

The hauntingly beautiful strings began to play. Sophie danced around the bathroom as she undressed. She couldn't help but smile as she realized that for a brief moment in time, she'd had her own Highlander.

Now she knew that men like that really did exist. They were rare—and usually already claimed by someone—but they were out there.

If she actually thought she could be in a relationship again, she would begin searching for a Highlander. A man who prided himself on loyalty, honor, and love.

Not true. She'd search for Darius.

She might actually view men a little differently if she'd met Darius years earlier. Then again, Sophie knew she wouldn't have. A year after she came to Edinburgh she was still too bitter.

Hell, seven years later and the bitterness had faded. Some.

Sophie stepped into the water and sank back against the tub. She closed her eyes, listening to the music. Halfway through the soundtrack she opened her eyes thinking Darius might be there. But he wasn't.

She finished her wine and remained in the water until the bubbles began to fade and the water turned tepid. Sophie toweled off and wrapped her robe around her, clicking off the music as she walked out of the bathroom.

After sorting through her mail for the past week and tossing out junk, she took the magazines onto the couch with her and looked through them. That wasted another thirty minutes.

Finally, Sophie gave up and untied her robe as she walked to her bedroom. She tossed the robe onto a chair and slid between the sheets.

For a long time, she stared at the ceiling thinking of Darius. Of his hands on her body, his mouth, and how wonderfully he kissed.

She finally closed her eyes and let it all replay in her head. Even as sleep claimed her, she wondered where Darius was and if he was thinking of her.

It was the chill that woke her. She looked to the window to see her curtain billowing into the room from the wind. And standing in the shadows was a man.

Sophie knew him instantly.

Darius.

She didn't know why he'd returned, and she didn't care. Her body heated instantly, aching to feel him inside her.

He turned to shut the window, and that's when she

realized he was naked. She shifted to her knees, breathless with excitement and desire.

Darius pivoted to face her and slowly walked toward the bed. She licked her lips when the mattress dipped as he placed his knee on it.

She stared into his dark eyes and touched his face. With a growl, he slid his hand along the back of her head and jerked her to him.

He claimed her mouth with passion and fury, a driving need they could only quench with each other. She groaned in response when her nipples scraped against his chest.

Before he could touch her, Sophie pushed him back onto the bed and kneeled beside him. He looked up at her, a slight smile of anticipation lifting his lips.

He was a man who was always in control, a man who liked to please his bed partner. But this time, she was going to be the one in control. This time she was the one who was going to be in charge.

She leaned forward and ran her hands from his chiseled jaw down his thick chest to his impeccable abs. Sophie glanced at his arousal and grinned.

He had driven her insane last night with his mouth, hands, and body. It was only fair she do the same to him. And oh, the things she wanted to do to him.

Sophie trailed her fingers past his navel to his rod. She wrapped her fingers around him and felt his cock jump in her palm. That wicked grin was gone, replaced with a hunger that made her stomach catch.

She pumped her hand up and down his length a few times while she leaned forward to lick and kiss his chest. His hands came up, not to stop her, but to take the pin out of her hair so that the length fell around her shoulders and draped on either side of her face.

"Damn," he whispered.

Sophie looked up at him. The way he whispered that

word, as if he were enthralled with her made her want to cry. If he didn't stop doing things like that, she was going to be in real trouble where he was concerned.

To shift the focus, Sophie moved and brought her mouth to his arousal. He ground out her name, his hands clutching at the comforter.

Sophie took him deep in her mouth. His fingers delved into her hair, almost as if he were afraid she might stop. She had no intention of stopping anytime soon.

His breathing was hoarse in the silence. She could feel his gaze on her, and it made her want to pleasure him even more.

She sucked in a surprised breath when his hands grabbed her and turned her so that she lay on his chest with her legs on either side of his face.

Sophie let out a sigh when his tongue found her clit and began to tease it. She had never done 69 before, and she wondered, why not? To give pleasure the same time as receiving it? It was perfect.

But the more pleasure he brought her, the harder it was to concentrate on her task. To get back at him, she sucked him hard, squeezing his ball sac gently.

When she tasted the pre-cum, Sophie smiled. He was almost there. She didn't plan on stopping until he came in her mouth. There was one thing she forgot while making such arrangements—Darius made his own rules.

One moment he was beneath her, and the next she was on her hands and knees and he was filling her from behind. Sophie moaned as he filled her with one thrust. Her body sighed, missing the feel of him.

He held her hips and began to move. She could feel his balls slapping against the back of her thighs as he increased his tempo.

With his teasing of her clit, she was so close to climaxing. Then he leaned over her and cupped her breasts, tweaking her nipples as he did.

She rocked back against him. His cheek rubbed against hers, his whiskers scraping her face. She closed her eyes. There was no use fighting against a force like Darius. He knew just where to touch her to give her the most bliss.

Her chest heaved and her breasts swelled at his touch. She didn't think the passion could get any better until his hand lowered to her sex and found her clit.

He fondled the swollen bud until she was crying out from the intense pleasure. She could hear him telling her to give him more, to give him everything.

Sophie could feel his thick arousal drive into her time and again, touching her womb he was going so deep. The more he filled her while teasing her clit, the higher she went.

Until the orgasm swarmed her. It ripped through her with the force of a tsunami. She screamed, even as the pleasure consumed her. And still he pounded into her, still he circled that tiny bud.

Just as the first orgasm began to subside, another arose, this one even more intense than the first. All Sophie could do was lock her arms and give herself over to the ecstasy.

Her head hung between her arms when the last vestiges of the orgasms began to fade. Darius's grip was tight on her hips as he pounded her.

His breathing hitched right before she felt his warm seed shoot inside her. Sophie couldn't believe she hadn't thought about a pregnancy or using protection any of the times she was with him.

Was Darius able to make her forget everything but him so easily? She was a doctor. She knew better than most what could happen with unprotected sex.

He pulled out of her and held her against him as he

rolled to his side. Sophie opened her mouth to speak when his hand caressed down her hair to her back over and over again.

She let herself relax once more. Darius had that affect on her.

She really should be worried, because she was beginning to want Darius around.

Never again.

But . . . maybe with Darius.

CHAPTER
TWELVE

Darius held Sophie against him as he stared at the opposite wall. There was no longer any denying the fact that he craved her like he craved to fly.

It was a feeling he never expected to feel again. And he shouldn't be feeling anything even close to this. And yet . . . there was no refusing to acknowledge it.

He wound a long lock of her red hair around his finger and listened to her breathing begin to even. Damn Con for insisting he remain close to Sophie.

Then again, Darius had intended to do it anyway. It was just easier to blame Con than to admit what was confusing the total shite out of him.

Sex with Sophie was incredible. Her touch, her scent, her body—everything about her was as if everything he'd ever wanted had been brought to life.

It shouldn't be happening. It couldn't be happening. He'd already found—and lost—his mate.

"What are you thinking about so hard?" Sophie asked in a husky voice.

His cock stirred at the sexy sound of her British accent. "Too much."

"Obviously." She shifted her head so that she was looking up at him, a worried frown puckering her brow. "Do you want to talk about it?"

"No' particularly."

But he was going to have to. How much did he tell her before she began to ask questions? Sophie was intelligent. She would figure things out if Darius wasn't careful.

Under no circumstances would he be responsible for her discovering his secret and putting her in Ulrik's line of sight. He would get what he needed from her and leave quickly. It was as much for her sake as it was for his.

Her hand lay over his heart while her body was pressed against his. The feel of her warm skin was heady. Lying with her in such a way was dangerous.

"I didn't expect to see you again," she said into the silence.

Darius drew in a deep breath and slowly let it out. "I tried to leave."

"I'm . . . glad you stayed."

He kissed the top of her head. "Me too."

The truth of it hit him hard. It wasn't about Ulrik. He would've stayed regardless, but Ulrik's interest only spurred him to admit what he'd been fighting to ignore— his ever-growing need to have Sophie.

"Am I still supposed to act like I don't like you?"

"Aye."

She was silent for a heartbeat. "Why?"

"A dangerous man I've been dealing with."

"Dangerous?" she repeated nervously. "And this has to do with . . . ?"

Darius said the only thing that made sense, and because he didn't want to lie. "Business."

She chuckled softly at his words while she rolled onto her back. Sophie scooted just enough away so that they weren't touching. It didn't go unnoticed by Darius that she had done it on purpose, as if she needed to break contact in order to catch her bearings.

"Right," Sophie said. "Business. I knew the moment I met you and Thorn that you were not the typical men in the city. Do you work for the government?"

"Something like that." It was as good of a cover as any, and it would allow him to keep most of what he did a secret.

But for how long? A day? Two? If he continued to hang around Sophie he'd have to tell her everything because she'd eventually see something.

That in itself frightened him. A part of him worried that she wouldn't be able to handle the truth of who he was. Then there was the matter of his past.

He was going to have to face that sooner rather than later. Darius would rather do it much later, but memories were assaulting him constantly.

She tucked her hair behind an ear and turned her head to him. "You look like that type to work for the government."

Now that intrigued him. He rolled toward her and propped himself up on an elbow. Darius made sure not to touch her as he did. "Type? There's a type?"

"Of course."

"And what exactly is that?"

She cut him a look, her olive eyes holding warmth and teasing. "The type that keeps to the shadows. The type who needs doctors to come to him instead of going to the hospital. The type who disappears without a word, only to suddenly reappear seemingly out of nowhere. The type who has an air of mystery and a large dose of 'don't fuck with me' attitude."

Darius grinned, he couldn't help it. Did she really see him that way?

Her face softened as if in wonder. "He does smile."

"I smile." Didn't he?

"Not like that." She reached out and touched his bottom lip. "It transformed your face. You should smile more."

"I could say the same of you."

Her hand dropped while her eyes lowered even as she turned to face him. "I don't have to ask to know that something bad happened in your past."

"Because I doona smile?"

Her smile was sad when her gaze met his. "It's your eyes. Your view of the world is colored."

"As is yours."

There was a long pause before she nodded. "Yes."

Darius was suddenly curious, but he stopped himself from asking. If he wasn't willing to share his secrets, why would she? It wasn't fair of him to ask about her past or what had turned her so hard.

"You're not going to ask?"

He shook his head. "You doona wish to talk about your past any more than I want to talk of mine. Tell me why you became a doctor."

"Um . . . let's see," she said with a grin. "Even as a little girl I'd play doctor with my dolls. I mended their broken bones, stitched them when needed, and even operated."

"I gather your dolls were gladiators or the like."

She laughed. The sound was magical. It utterly captivated him. All he wanted was to hear more of it.

"Not gladiators, though they did fight often. It's amazing how rough a doll can get with another," she said, still laughing.

"I can only imagine."

"From there I carried a box of Band-Aids, gauze, and antiseptic at all times. On the playground, if one of the kids got hurt, I tended them. My bag of medicines began to grow the older I became. As I walked the streets of London, I often stopped and tended anyone who needed it."

"And they let you?"

She shrugged her shoulder. "Surprisingly, they did. I didn't think anything of it at the time, but looking back now they must have thought I'd gone daft."

"You're a natural healer."

"I think each of us is born with a special gift. For some like me, we realize it fairly early and grasp it. Others find it later. I feel sorry for the ones who've either rejected their gift or not found it yet."

Darius lifted a lock of her hair from the bed and rubbed it between his fingers. "You're verra lucky."

"I know. I love healing others, and it kills me when they don't take my advice. What about you? Have you always known you'd do whatever it is you do?"

"Aye," he answered without hesitation.

"Then I think we're both lucky." Her gaze shifted to his neck.

Darius knew exactly what she was looking at. The head of his dragon tattoo that peeked over his right shoulder. Her interest made him want to fidget.

"Is that a tattoo?" she asked.

The first time he took her, he'd been clothed. The second time they'd been too frantic to notice anything like that. This third time was in the dark where she couldn't see. It must be the streetlight behind him that shed just enough light to make out the tat.

"Aye."

Her curiosity piqued, she sat up. "May I see it?"

Darius pushed into a sitting position as she turned on the lamp on her bedside table. When she faced him, he felt the urge to pull her into his arms and kiss her. Instead, he remained still as she crawled closer.

The first contact of her hands on the dragon head made his breath catch. Her touch was soft and light, inquisitive. He didn't want it to stop.

* * *

Sophie was awed by the elaborate detail of the dragon head. It peered over his shoulder as if seeing who Darius was talking to. The ink was neither black nor red, but a mixture that shouldn't even be possible.

She moved on her knees around to see his back and could only stare in mute silence at the beauty of the artwork. The dragon took up Darius's entire back.

The dragon was perched, as if climbing Darius's back to his shoulder. The detail was so impressive that she could even see the dragon's claws digging into Darius's back. The dragon had his wings half open while its tail curled at its tip, stopping just above his ass.

She ran her fingers over the tattoo, unable to keep her hands off it. It wasn't as if she knew Darius particularly well—or at all really—but she hadn't expected him to have a tattoo. Yet, she wasn't surprised by the revelation either.

"Why a dragon?" she asked.

He shrugged, causing his muscles to move and the dragon to look as if it were alive. "I like them."

"It's gorgeous."

Darius turned his head to look at her over his shoulder. "You like it?"

"Yes," she said with a smile. "I've seen a lot of tattoos as a doctor, and I can honestly say that is one of the most beautiful I've ever seen."

Sophie laughed when his arms snaked out and dragged her around to his front. His chocolate eyes held hers for a long moment.

"What do you know of dragons?"

She scrunched up her face. "I've never been one to love anything in a fantasy element, so I don't know a lot about them. I know they're in most cultures in some form— sometimes as good, sometimes as evil."

"And they're the largest mythological creature in the world."

"True," she admitted with a nod. "Is that why you chose it?"

His smile caused her heart to miss a beat. "You were born to heal people. It was chosen for you."

"So the dragon was decided for you?" she asked.

"It was."

"I didn't take you for a man who was rooted in fantasy elements."

He nuzzled her neck. "I never said I was."

"But you've a dragon on your back," she said as her eyes slid closed and her arms wrapped around his neck. His lips were doing wonderful things to her neck and throat.

"Enough talking," he murmured.

Sophie forgot what they were discussing when he tweaked her nipple with his fingers. She ran her hands through his thick hair as he kissed down her throat to her neck and down to her breasts.

A sigh escaped as she dropped her head back and gave her body once more to his skillful mouth.

Dark Palace, Ireland

Taraeth drummed his fingers on the arm of his throne. He'd been waiting for Balladyn for over an hour. It wasn't like his right hand to not come when summoned.

Then again, Balladyn had been acting strange of late. Ever since he kidnapped Rhi and tortured her. That wasn't true. Balladyn showed his true worth as a Dark Fae when he tortured her.

It wasn't until Rhi somehow broke out of Balladyn's dungeon and escaped that he changed. Balladyn was determined to get her back. He promised Taraeth she would be Dark, but as the weeks passed, Taraeth was beginning to wonder if Balladyn would even be able to find Rhi.

Taraeth rubbed the stump of his left arm. None of his considerable magic was able to stop him from feeling as if his arm were still attached. That's how powerful a Fae blade was. The strength of the steel was unmatched, but it was the Fires of Erwar where it was crafted that gave the weapons the power to destroy a Fae as no other weapon could.

Except dragon fire.

Taraeth refused to think of that. The Dragon Kings were the Dark's greatest enemy. The Kings not only had magic that was unmatched, but their fire burned hotter than anything.

Just as Taraeth lost patience and was about to send men to find Balladyn, the throne room doors opened. Balladyn walked in with his head down. He didn't stop until he kneeled before Taraeth.

"My king," Balladyn said.

Taraeth leaned forward and braced his right arm on his leg. "You better have a damn good reason for keeping me waiting."

CHAPTER
THIRTEEN

Balladyn clenched his teeth together. He'd given his full loyalty to Taraeth. He'd proven himself time and again, and the first time he was late, Taraeth dared to threaten him.

It was with great effort that Balladyn didn't reach for his sword and sever his king's head from his body. Balladyn instead rose to his feet and met Taraeth's gaze.

"You wanted me to watch Mikkel."

"I said we needed to watch him. I never put you on that duty," Taraeth said, his red eyes filled with contempt.

Balladyn rested his hand on the hilt of his sword and smiled. "I'm your right hand. I know what you want before you give me the order."

"You've always been too cocky for your own good. Even as a Light Fae you thought you could get away with anything."

"Because I did," Balladyn answered. "It's why you wounded me and turned me Dark."

Taraeth turned his head away and replied grudgingly, "True. Are you going to tell me what you found?"

"I wasn't able to get close enough to Mikkel."

The king's head swiveled back to him, anger radiating from his red eyes. Taraeth stood, his long black and silver hair flowing loose down his back. "You kept me waiting for nothing?" he asked in a furious tone.

"I never said that." Balladyn shifted his feet. "What I did see was Con and another Dragon King attacking one of Mikkel's manors."

"Why?" Taraeth asked with his brow puckered.

Balladyn shrugged. "I don't have an answer, but I can assure you that Con still has no idea he's been fighting both Mikkel *and* Ulrik."

"Was Ulrik there?"

"As if Mikkel allows him too far out of his sight."

Taraeth nodded as he returned to his throne. "Mikkel doesn't trust his nephew, and he's wise not to."

"Ulrik doesn't trust him either."

"Another wise choice."

"Who's going to win?"

Taraeth smiled wickedly. "That will depend on who I choose to help."

"Ulrik knows you're aiding Mikkel, but has Mikkel figured out you're helping Ulrik as well?"

Taraeth gave him a droll look. "Mikkel is too caught up in his plans to realize that. Yet. He will soon enough. It's why I'm playing things very safe for the moment. I'll not always be able to do that. Knowing what those two are up to at all times helps to keep me ahead."

"Who's watching Ulrik?"

"A female Dark I sent to him the last time he was here. She'll discover all that I need without Ulrik comprehending what she's about."

"Be careful with him, sire. Ulrik's need for vengeance far surpasses what Mikkel is about."

Taraeth sat back in the throne and sighed. "That I know.

Ulrik is calculating and cunning. If I guess right, he'll take out Mikkel before I ever have to make a decision."

In Balladyn's mind there was no decision. He would get behind Ulrik because he was the stronger of the two. "Is there really a choice?"

"There's always a choice. Ulrik might be ahead a little, but Mikkel brings other things to the table that Ulrik doesn't. Either choice is a good one, but which one is the best for the Dark?"

What Taraeth really meant was which one was better for him. Balladyn was no fool. Taraeth had been on the Dark throne far longer than most Dark Fae who claimed it, and if Balladyn had anything to do with it, Taraeth wouldn't be there much longer.

Balladyn just had to bide his time a little longer. He could take Taraeth now, but why get in the middle of a war between Ulrik and Mikkel if he didn't have to?

He'd already made his choice, though it hadn't been easy. Balladyn would help Ulrik if only because Ulrik would become King of Kings and then wipe out all the other Kings. That would free Rhi to love again.

Mikkel claimed to want to kill all the Kings as well, but if he did, he would have no one to rule. Mikkel wanted others to bow before him. His younger brother, then Ulrik, had been King of the Silvers.

Whatever magic or being decided who would be King never chose Mikkel until he was the last Silver on the realm after Ulrik had his magic bound. For those few minutes, Mikkel had been a Dragon King.

It was a taste, and he yearned to have it all. Though Mikkel wasn't a complete fool. He knew he could never defeat Constantine. That's where Ulrik came in. Ulrik wanted to kill Con anyway for his betrayal.

But if Ulrik did manage to slay Con, that made Ulrik King of Kings, which would never do for Mikkel. There would be another betrayal to Ulrik if he wasn't careful. Then again, Ulrik sniffed those things out well enough. Who in Mikkel's circle would dare to take on Ulrik?

There were plenty of Dark Fae that Mikkel paid to be by his side, and Taraeth allowed it to happen. Ulrik didn't pay any of them. He indebted the Dark to him so they either willingly helped or he forced them.

It showed the Dark who was the stronger dragon—Ulrik.

Some might say it was Mikkel because he used money instead of brawn. But Ulrik used his intelligence and shrewdness and muscle when need be.

Balladyn blinked and focused, realizing that Taraeth had been talking.

"That's where I am," Taraeth said. "Mikkel edges out Ulrik by a hair, but in the end we want this realm. We have prime feeding by the billions waiting for us. The mortals are a weak race. They were made to be dominated. The Dragon Kings were fools not to enslave them from the beginning."

Balladyn thought of Rhi and how many times she had helped out the humans. She wouldn't want them enslaved by anyone, but most especially the Dark.

"What's your opinion?"

Balladyn hesitated for a moment, then said, "I still think Ulrik would be the better bet. As for the mortals? They've been ours for thousands of years. It's time we have free rein over them."

Taraeth smiled and leaned to his right where his good arm was braced against the arm of the throne. "I thought you hated all Dragon Kings."

"I do, but as you said, this is for us. We need the strongest one who will give us what we need."

Taraeth nodded, approval shining in his red eyes. "Next time, don't keep me waiting. I won't be so lenient in the future. What of the Light Fae? Have you found her?"

"I'm still trailing her. She's been at Dreagan for a few weeks. She was with Con battling Mikkel. She was wounded with Dark magic."

"Is she strong enough to mend?"

"Con took her with him. He'll heal her."

"Good. I want her before me within a month, Balladyn. Now go."

Balladyn turned on his heel and walked out of the throne room. There was no way he was bringing Rhi before Taraeth. He'd lock her up in his dungeon, and Balladyn might never get to see her again.

That meant Balladyn would have to move up his plans to be king of the Dark. He had a month to plan how he was going to kill Taraeth.

Con stared out of the window of The Balmoral Hotel. Ulrik was out there somewhere. Darius spoke with Ulrik and hadn't bothered to alert him.

Was he losing his men? Were they turning against him as they once had?

The thought made his stomach sour.

Ulrik had been responsible the first time, and it infuriated Con that he was guilty yet again. Con wouldn't lose his men. Not again.

If he had to take out Ulrik in the middle of Edinburgh, he'd do it. Anything to be rid of such a troublemaker that had ruined their lives.

He took a drink of whisky, letting the liquor slide down his throat. Dreagan. The best whisky on the planet. Despite the distinction of the company, every move one of them made was being watched and recorded.

MI5 had six people following Con, and it wasn't the faction of the group of spies loyal to Ulrik. Not even Henry could convince them to lay off, and Henry had tried.

To think that Con trusted a mortal as much as he did

Henry. It still boggled his mind, but there it was. Henry had proven himself on many occasions, and his connections to MI5 had helped them out in the past. No more, however.

Even now Henry was being called back to London. When he refused to go, he was notified that he, too, would be watched.

Con pretended to ignore the imbecile across the street taking pictures of him. Con went centuries without being photographed, and now MI5 would have record of him.

That would never do. One way or another, Con was going to destroy every picture, every recording, and every documentation of him that any government agency had—regardless of what government it was.

At least the room hadn't been bugged. It took Con a good hour to thoroughly check his room and the ones on either side of his that he'd also rented for the night.

"Why the long face, lover?"

Con closed his eyes at the sound of Usaeil's voice. He slid the curtains closed and turned to face the Light Fae queen. "You know I'm being followed. You can no' be here."

She smiled from her position on the bed. Usaeil was on her side wearing absolutely nothing. Her long black hair fell behind her in a curtain of onyx. She patted the bed and winked at him. "You've kept me waiting for days."

"I told you I needed some time. You know what's going on," he said and softly set down his glass of whisky. "You being here is risky. MI5 is searching for anyone connected to me."

"You think I'm worried?"

Con raised a brow. "You should be. The entire world knows you as an American actress. Can you imagine if you're connected to me?"

"I could think of worse things. Besides, I believe it's time others knew."

Others, meaning the Dragon Kings. "You know how your people reacted when Rhi was caught dallying with a Dragon King. Do you think they'll accept you repeating her mistake?"

"I'm their queen," Usaeil stated in a regal voice. "They'll do what I command. And I don't want to talk of Rhi."

Con kept his distance from the bed, even when Usaeil ran her hand over her breasts to tempt him. It was time Con figured out how much Usaeil knew about Rhi. "Has she done something again?"

"You mean besides walk away from me and her duty?" All desire vanished from Usaeil as she sat up and glared at him with her silver eyes. "I've not seen or heard from Rhi, and I've sent plenty of Fae out looking for her."

"Why? Are you going to punish her for leaving the Queen's Guard?"

Usaeil scooted to the end of the bed and crossed one bare leg over the other. "Why are you so concerned?"

"Because the Fae love her. If you go against her so publicly, it could be bad for you."

The queen rolled her eyes and fell back on the bed with her arms spread. "You worry too much. I'm queen, and have been for millennia. There's not a single Light Fae able to take my place, and every one of them knows it."

"If they discover we're lovers and you go after Rhi for leaving the Queen's Guard, you might verra well lose your people."

"Never going to happen." She turned her head to him. "Now are you coming to bed, or must I come to you?"

When he didn't immediately move, Usaeil swiped her hand in the air, removing his clothes. She smiled when she lowered her eyes and saw his erection.

"Just as I thought," she purred.

CHAPTER
FOURTEEN

Sophie woke to the most exquisite pleasure. Darius's fingers were between her legs, stroking her. She opened her eyes to find him watching her.

His dark eyes burned with desire that made chills race over her skin. Could he really want her that much? It seemed impossible, and yet the thought of it made her own passion blaze hotter.

She lifted her face to his and pressed her lips against his mouth. He moaned as he kissed her with such abandon that it left her breathless.

As his fingers filled her, his thumb circled her clit in agonizing slowness. Almost as if he knew she was ready to peak, but was drawing things out.

She gripped his arm, silently begging him to give her more. It didn't budge him.

Sophie gasped at the pleasure and tore her mouth from his as it overwhelmed her. Her lungs couldn't draw enough breath, but none of that mattered as the desire coiled tighter and tighter within her.

"I need you inside me," she begged him.

He smiled. "Oh, I will be."

She tried to stop him, but it felt too good. He held her gaze, refusing to release her as his experienced hands brought her to the brink of climax, holding her there for a few seconds, and then gently pushing her over the side.

Sophie opened her mouth to scream, but it was locked in her throat from the sheer force of the orgasm. It rocked through her, seizing her body as it washed over her as powerfully as a waterfall, as fiercely as the sun.

When she was able to draw breath into her lungs again, he was kissing her. It was slow, sexy. Sensual.

And it totally rocked her world.

The Silver Dragon, Perth

Ulrik sliced off a sliver of the apple with his knife and brought it to his mouth. He chewed it as he glanced at the open folder on his desk.

He walked around the shop, but he wasn't looking at the antiquities he'd purchased throughout the years. No, he was thinking of Sophie Martin.

Dr. Sophie Martin.

He'd wanted to know her story from the moment he learned she helped Thorn. It took only one call to discover all the details.

Ulrik expected to find something he could use to black-mail her into doing what he wanted—as it was with any-one he dug into. But Sophie was different.

She was a loner, mistrustful, and wary of any man. And knowing what her fiancé had done to her, he understood it.

Her past also explained why she left London, though there was no reason as to why she chose Edinburgh other than one of her old professors from Oxford practiced med-icine in Edinburgh. At the Royal Victoria Hospital.

Sophie had no family in Scotland. She had no family anywhere.

Knowing all of this before he met her, Ulrik went to his first meeting with Sophie intending to be just the right amount of charming without making her suspicious. He was going to play on her sympathies of helping the less fortunate. Yet she'd turned it back on him and brought his past into the conversation.

For a woman who didn't date and rarely paid attention to the opposite sex, Ulrik had expected a certain reaction from her.

He hadn't gotten it.

It meant he was going to have to change tactics.

Ulrik cut off another slice of the apple and paused to study the file. There was a connection between the beautiful doctor and Darius. Ulrik just needed to find it.

With the other Kings, they hadn't been able to stay away from the mortals. But so far, Darius was also doing the opposite of what Ulrik expected.

Ulrik thought back to seeing Darius and Sophie having sex. It had been so wild and rough that it was born of a clawing hunger between them that wouldn't be denied. They had to have each other, to experience pleasure.

The way Darius had kissed her though . . . Ulrik was going to have to keep a closer eye on Sophie. If he knew anything about Darius it was that he took his responsibilities seriously. Even if Sophie were nothing more than a quick shag, Darius wouldn't leave Edinburgh without ensuring that Ulrik left Sophie alone.

Ulrik smiled and wondered what Darius would think if he knew Ulrik had coffee with the lovely Sophie. It made Ulrik chuckle just thinking about it.

It was so easy to rile the other Kings. Just threaten a mortal, and they lost their minds. How pathetic did they have to be?

He continued his walk around the shop, his mind returning to Sophie once more. Ulrik wanted her working for him. She could be a great asset. Even more so if he could get her to spy for him. Darius trusted her. The trick was convincing Sophie it was the right thing to do.

She kept to herself. There was only one friend he could threaten, but he suspected that move would only alienate her altogether. No, he couldn't threaten the short blonde.

If Ulrik was going to get to Darius through Sophie, then he would have to change tactics. He'd try once more to pull Sophie onto his side. If that didn't work, then he had something that was sure to do the trick.

Most humans were easy to decipher, but Sophie was different. She didn't date, didn't hang with friends, or have any kind of social life. All that mattered to her was healing people.

Ulrik sliced off another piece of apple and ate it. Even though his men hadn't seen Darius at Sophie's flat, that meant nothing. The Kings were nothing if not predictable. Now that Ulrik had shown up at the hospital, Darius would keep an eye on Sophie.

How long would it be before Darius had to tell Sophie about the Dragon Kings, the Fae, and even about Ulrik?

If Sophie was nothing more than a single shag, Ulrik might be doing all of this for nothing. But he had a feeling that wasn't the case. Darius was too predictable. So was Con.

Darius would tell Con about their chat, and Con would demand that Darius remain around to see what Sophie learned and what move Ulrik made next. Which meant Darius wouldn't be able to keep his hands off Sophie.

Ulrik laughed as he threw the knife, embedding it in the center of the picture of Con. "My move."

Darius couldn't believe how quickly the night passed. He hadn't brought up Ulrik with Sophie. How could he when he couldn't keep his hands off her? Being near her was impossible without touching her.

He lost count of the many times they had made love. Each time he saw the pleasure cross her face, he wanted to see it again and again and again.

While he pretended to sleep, Sophie quietly made coffee in the kitchen. He cracked open an eye and watched her through the doorway wearing nothing more than an ivory robe and her long red hair falling down her back.

It made him smile every time he thought of her sleeping naked. She surprised him with things like that. With the way she wore her hair always up and every strand in place, he figured she would wear flannel to bed.

Darius rolled over and watched her as she sifted through her mail. It was so mundane, and yet it fascinated him. Then again, everything about Sophie captivated him.

He rose from the bed and put his jeans on, not bothering to button them as he walked from the bedroom. Her head lifted and she smiled.

There was a part of Darius that realized that simple action was dangerous for him. But still he walked to her, still he allowed himself to become entangled in something that could easily rip him apart—this time for good.

"Morning," she said.

He grinned. "Good morning. Did you sleep well?"

"With what little sleep I got, yes." Her smile widened as her eyes twinkled. "Not that I'm complaining. And you?"

"Yes." Though he rarely slept. As a Dragon King he didn't need to, not even in human form. Not to mention he had been in deep dragon sleep for several centuries.

She dropped the envelopes and turned back to the counter. "Coffee?"

"Sure. Three teaspoons of sugar, please."

Sophie glanced at him over her shoulder, the surprise evident on her face. "Three?"

"I like things sweet," he said with a shrug.

She laughed but added the sugar to his coffee before handing it to him. "That's two surprises this morning."

"Two? What was the first?"

"You still being here."

He waited until after she poured her coffee before he said, "I wasna supposed to return to you at all."

"Why did you?" she asked as she leaned back against the counter, her coffee mug held between her hands.

"You know why."

"Because we're good in bed together?" she asked before taking a sip of the steaming liquid.

Darius set his mug on the table and studied her. "Does that bother you, lass?"

"Definitely not. It's been a long time since I've had sex."

"How long?"

She glanced at the floor. "Too long. But that brings me to something I can't believe as a doctor that I didn't think about. Protection."

"Protection?" Darius was confused. Was she asking him to protect her from Ulrik?

"Yes. I don't want to get pregnant."

Darius could only stare at her as she spoke so matter-of-factly. It must have to do with the fact that she was a doctor and used to discussing such things.

He was battered by the memory of holding his son in his arms. Pregnant. It could happen, as he well knew. He clenched his teeth together and waited for the worst of the pain to pass so he could breathe easier.

Darius swallowed and shook away the memory that had pushed him to his mountain. "You needn't worry about any diseases. As for you getting pregnant . . ."

He couldn't even finish the sentence. Darius wanted to tell her it couldn't happen. He wished with all his might that were the truth.

The idea that she might very well be carrying his child made him begin to shake. He couldn't go through that again. He refused.

"Darius? Are you all right?"

He blinked and looked down to find Sophie next to him, her hand on his shoulder as she gazed at him with concern in her olive eyes. All right? He'd never be all right again.

"Aye," he lied.

"You didn't look all right a moment ago."

Darius waved away her words. "You didna upset me."

"Good." She dropped her hand from his arm and picked up her coffee that was beside his on the table. "I'm not good with social niceties, Darius. I'm sure I'm going to offend you with my bluntness. It's just how I am. Life is too short for deceptions and lies."

Deceptions and lies. Yes, he agreed. Yet he'd lived his entire existence from the moment of the war with the humans in shams and deceits. It was the only way he and the other Kings survived without another war.

It would've been so easy to take out the mortals. Nothing they had then—or now—could kill a Dragon King. They could have wiped the realm of any existence of humans, but they hadn't. All because of a vow.

That oath put them in a position where they had to hide who they were and make deception a way of life. Sophie would never understand that. Most humans wouldn't. If they only knew what the Dragon Kings had sacrificed for their existence.

"You drifted off again," Sophie said.

Darius raked a hand through his hair. "I apologize. I've a lot on my mind."

"The danger you spoke of the other night?"

"Aye." Darius took the opportunity that presented itself and said, "There's a man who would hurt you just from being associated with me. He's a murderer, Sophie. He was at the hospital the other day. I followed him there. You saw both of us."

Her head slowly nodded. "The man in the sweater."

"Yes." Darius grabbed her shoulders and looked into her eyes. "He might try to approach you. He'll seem innocent enough, but he's extremely cunning in—"

"He came by the hospital to see me yesterday," she interrupted him.

Darius felt as if he had been skewered with Dark magic. And to think he'd almost left Edinburgh and Sophie behind. "Tell me everything."

CHAPTER
FIFTEEN

Darius's distress was palpable. And now, so was Sophie's.

Murderer. That in itself frightened her. She had coffee with a killer and hadn't even known it. What would've happened had she left with Ulrik? Sophie didn't want to even think about that.

She hadn't felt creeped out by Ulrik, which she should've. Was she so used to ignoring people and being alone that she could no longer sense those kinds of things?

Sophie stared at Darius. She didn't need to wonder about him. From the first there had been something appealing about him. She was drawn to Darius—and there was no ignoring it.

It wasn't just physical either. It was mental and emotional.

With him, she felt normal. As if the catastrophe seven years earlier hadn't destroyed her and her life. Safe. That's something else he brought out. Sophie didn't worry about anyone or anything as long as Darius was near.

"Ulrik wanted to get me to work for him," she said.

Darius briefly closed his eyes. "Sophie, you're a strong woman who knows her own mind. I can no' tell you what to do, but I'm begging you to be careful. I'm no' exaggerating when I say Ulrik is dangerous."

"Tell me what he's done," she urged. When Darius hesitated, Sophie grew nervous. "Tell me, please. I spent time with him. He seemed nice, although the kind of man who is used to having his wealth get him whatever he wants."

"I can no' tell you details no matter how much I want to. You've no reason to trust me, but I'm asking that you do."

Sophie didn't trust people. But she did trust Darius. It surprised her and terrified her. "You say he's a murderer. Do you have proof?"

"None that I can show or tell you. Ulrik has no good intentions. He'll no hesitate to kill you or anyone around him to get what he wants."

"He could've killed me yesterday. He didn't."

Darius dropped his arms and turned away to pace in the living area. He raked a hand through his hair before he stopped and faced her. "He came to the hospital the first time because he saw us together the night in the alley."

"He watched us . . ." Sophie couldn't even finish the sentence she was so shocked. Yes she'd known they could be seen, but she hadn't really expected anyone to come forward and admit it.

Darius blew out a breath. "Because you were with me, he took an interest in you. I bet he's followed you or had you followed since that night."

Sophie felt sick to her stomach. Ulrik had admitted to following her. "He said as much."

"Shite." Darius dropped his chin to his chest for a moment before he looked back at her. "Stay away from him. He'll only hurt you. Few come away from their dealings with Ulrik with their lives."

"He wants me because we were together?"

Darius's face was lined with worry. "Aye."

"Then why not just kill me? He could've taken me from the hospital."

"He could've. He's got many people working for him. He didna hurt you yesterday because he wants me to know he was able to get close to you. I wasna there. I didna see it. That was his message to me."

"What? That he could get close to me?"

Darius nodded. "What ruse did he use to get near you?"

"He made mention of my philanthropic work tending to those who can't get to the hospital. Though he never did tell me what he wanted. Once I mentioned that I saw the pain he tried to hide, he made a few remarks and left."

"If we're lucky, you may have put yourself out of his path."

Sophie pulled out a chair at the table and sank heavily into it. "All of this because we had sex?"

"Ulrik has it in for me and my . . . group."

Now that was interesting. Sophie wanted to know more. "Why?"

"We saved him from a betrayal, but he didna see it that way. We then had to stop him when he began attacking others. The only way to end what he was doing was to banish him from our group."

"Banish him?" she repeated. She expected that from a medieval culture, but not in the here and now. Just what kind of group was Darius involved in? And did she want to be a part of it? "That's . . . extreme."

"Perhaps. It was our only option."

Now it was beginning to make sense. Ulrik's pain, his need to hurt Darius. "So Ulrik wants revenge?"

"Aye."

"And he goes after anyone you and your group are with?"

Darius gave a slight nod.

"What about Thorn and Lexi? Are they all right?"

"Ulrik targeted Lexi, but Thorn was able to save her."

Sophie leaned back in the chair while trying to grasp the situation. "This can't be real."

"I'm sorry to say it is. I wanted to leave to prove to Ulrik that—"

"I meant nothing to you," she spoke over him. "I understand. There's no need to explain."

"If he came to see you, then he didna believe what I told him."

"You spoke to him?" she asked in shock.

Darius looked a tad contrite. "Aye."

For some reason that made her angry as well as confused. "The man who is after you? You spoke to him? Why not just try to work it out?"

"Ulrik wants to hurt us by hurting those he believes we care about. I did talk to him, but there's only one way this will end, Sophie."

"How's that?"

"He blames all of us, but his true target is our leader. He and Con will eventually battle it out."

She stared wide-eyed at Darius. Had she just stepped into a movie? All of this was so surreal. "You're saying he's a sociopath?"

"I am."

"Why not stop him before he and Con can meet? Or why haven't he and Con gone ahead and battled it out as you say?"

Darius rubbed his hand over his chin. "We've a set of rules that must be followed."

"That somehow prevents you from going after Ulrik yourself?" Sophie asked. "That makes no sense. Especially if Ulrik is targeting anyone you and your group spend time with. You should be able to defend yourself."

"We do. Ulrik isna acting alone, though. The . . .

people . . . helping him are just as dangerous. We've been fighting them for some time now, and always Ulrik manages to get away."

"Then have Con call him out and get it over with."

Darius lifted one shoulder as his lips twisted. "Con is searching for Ulrik for just that reason."

"Ulrik is here. Call Con."

"Con is in the city. He knows what's going on."

No matter how many questions she asked and responses Darius made, Sophie was more perplexed than ever before. If only she was privy to the parts Darius was leaving out she might understand, but she had a feeling those secrets were better left unsaid.

"I'm confused. Why hasn't Con gotten in touch with Ulrik?"

"He's trying. It's no' as easy as it sounds. Ulrik has a plan. While he goes about it, he's going to hurt as many of us as he can. The final blow will be attacking Con."

"And the all-powerful government isn't going to move things along so people like me are safe? Tell me MI5 is involved."

"Oh, they're involved," he stated, his voice laced with irritation.

She wondered if Darius knew he revealed he didn't work for MI5. Sophie stared at her mug of coffee that was now lukewarm. She wouldn't be able to drink it anyway with her stomach in knots as it was.

"I didna mean to cause you any anguish. I just want you to be safe," he said.

Safe. It was such a relative thing. Was anyone ever truly safe? Even at a time when she believed she was never safer, she hadn't been. First the city had burned and dozens killed, with no answers as to the killers. Now there was Ulrik.

And Darius.

"You doona believe me?"

He said it with such confusion that Sophie almost smiled. "I'm trying to take it all in."

"So you doona believe me."

Sophie met his dark brown gaze. "It just seems so odd that Ulrik would come after me just because we had sex. Unless he knew you came here the night before last."

"He doesna. I made sure no one followed me. There were a couple of men watching your building, but I came in from the roof."

"The roof?" she asked in alarm. Was there ever going to be a time when she wasn't taken aback by what he said?

Probably not, and that's the appeal!

True. Dammit.

"It was the only way I could get in without them seeing me," Darius stated as if it was a common occurrence.

For him, she guessed it was. "And last night?"

"They were watching the roof."

She looked at him expectantly. "My window was open. You came in through my window. How?"

"I've skills."

That was one way of putting it. She knew for a fact he had many skills that he had proven to her time and again the previous night. "And Ulrik? Does he have those same skills?"

Darius's face mottled with anger. "Aye. I hadna thought of that. Precautions will need to be taken."

"Not if he doesn't believe you've returned. If he comes back to the hospital I can make him think you've moved on. We just had a one-night stand."

"He'll know I'm still here. Besides, I doona want you talking to him. I'll make sure I'm around the hospital in case he returns."

Sophie got to her feet and grinned. "It's worth a try. I won't have my life in danger because I enjoy having sex with you. I'm going to ensure Ulrik turns his attention away from me."

"Doona underestimate him, Sophie."

"That's one thing you don't have to worry about." She brought both of the mugs to the sink and dumped them. "I'd cook breakfast, but I have nothing in the flat."

"And I can no' get it for us since he may see me. I doona want Ulrik to know I'm here," Darius grumbled.

Sophie turned to face him and looked at his impressive chest with the head of the dragon seeming to look at her from his shoulder. "I'll go. If you want to stay, that is."

He visibly relaxed. "I want to stay."

"Good."

Sophie walked to the bedroom to change. She knew exactly why she wanted him to stay, and it was only partly due to his mastery in bed.

The biggest reason was because she was enjoying having someone in her life—someone like Darius. Even if that thread of danger she'd discerned from the beginning put her in the thick of it. She still wouldn't change anything.

Sophie pulled on a pair of jeans and a tan sweater before reaching for her boots. She brushed out her hair and put it in a loose braid that fell over her left shoulder. A quick brush of her teeth and she walked back into the kitchen where Darius sat at the table.

"I'll be back," she said as she put on her coat. Then she paused and looked at him. "What do you like?"

"Anything."

She laughed. "People say that, but they don't mean it. Is there anything you're allergic to or that you don't like?"

"Nay, lass. I'll eat whatever you put in front of me."

Sophie put her hand on the doorknob. "What about what you do like? Do you have a favorite?"

"Meat. I like meat."

"That I can make sure you have. I'll return soon."

"Sophie," Darius called, stopping her at the door.

She looked back at him. "Yeah?"

"Be careful," he cautioned. "Notice everything. And hurry back."

Sophie gave him a wink. "It'll be fine. I'm not going far."

"Perhaps you'd better stay. We can find something here."

"I have nothing. You said yourself if Ulrik wanted to take me yesterday he could've. He didn't. But I'll be on the lookout."

Darius rose and walked to her. He cupped her face in his hands and looked deep in her eyes. "Ulrik has men watching the building."

"I'll be quick," she promised as she rose up and gave him a quick kiss.

She closed the door behind her and hurried down the stairs with a smile on her face, her thoughts on Darius and the amazing feelings he awoke within her.

It wasn't until she walked out of her building that she realized how light her steps were. A night of having a man like Darius make love to her had certainly removed any stress. Her body was pleasantly sore, and it was no surprise that she still wanted him.

She lifted her face and looked at the bright blue sky without a cloud to be seen. It was colder than the day before, but she was going to enjoy the sunshine. It made her want to spend the day outside.

Sophie crossed the street to her favorite deli. She didn't know what reminded her that Darius had said men were watching her building. Whatever it was made her slow her steps and look in the glass of a shop as she passed. She noticed there was a man on the opposite side of the street looking at her.

Her heart skipped a beat. A small part of her had

thought Darius was just being overly cautious, but there was no denying what she saw.

Sophie observed the man. He wore glasses, a black jacket and jeans, and he was looking right at her.

She tried to pretend she didn't see him. When a group passed her, she made sure it appeared as if one of them ran into her, spinning her around.

It was the chance she needed to look behind her. Her gut clenched when she saw another similarly dressed man walking about fifteen paces behind her.

"Oy! Watch where you're going," she called out to the group to keep up the ruse.

Sophie turned and kept walking. Men had been watching her building. She'd trusted Darius, but it had been just a feeling. Now she knew for sure she could trust him.

She suddenly wished she'd remained at her flat. As soon as she reached the deli, she placed her order. While she waited, she walked around, subtly looking at everyone in the deli—and outside. The two men were waiting.

Sophie leaned over the counter to the older man she had paid after she had her order. "Is there a back exit?"

"No."

She glanced over her shoulder at the men standing at the window who had been following her. "You see the guy outside with the bald head and goatee? He's my ex, and he's been stalking me. I'd really like to get home without confronting him. Please. Is there another exit I can use?"

The old man glared at her follower and called someone else to work the register. Then he waved her around the counter. With a hand on her back, he led her through the kitchen to a storage room and the door to the back alley.

"He willna see you, lass," the man said.

Sophie patted his arm and shot him a grateful smile. "Thank you so much. You've saved the day."

To her surprise, he blushed to the roots of his salt-and-pepper hair. "Be safe."

Sophie exited the deli and hurried back to her flat, her heart pounding against her ribs. Her two followers were none the wiser, but she saw another man dressed just as they were standing across the street from her flat. As soon as he saw her, he brought his mobile phone to his ear and placed a call.

She pretended she saw nothing as she entered the building and made her way up to her flat. Sophie threw open the door and hurried inside, slamming the door shut and locking it with shaking hands.

"Sophie?" Darius said as he came from the bathroom putting on his shirt.

"I was followed by two men. There's a third outside," she said as she handed him the bag of food.

Darius gently grasped her hand with one of his large ones and took the food with the other. "They willna hurt you as long as I'm here."

And God help her, but Sophie believed him. How could she not? The sincerity was in his voice, it was in his eyes.

It was in the way he held her.

CHAPTER
SIXTEEN

Rhi fought to cling to the darkness. She was determined to remain asleep, because if she woke, she'd have to face everything she'd been running from.

"I know you can hear me," Rhys said.

His voice was low, just above a whisper, but he was close. She imagined he was sitting by the bed. Rhys, her faithful friend, who had seen her at her worst. The friend who never wavered in his support of her, even when other Dragon Kings—Darius—sided against her.

"You're hiding," Rhys continued. "You ken I know you, Rhi. I know you better than most. You're hiding in that sleep like I hid in the Dragonwood no' that long ago. You urged me to come out of hiding. Now I'm telling you to get your arse in gear and wake up. You're no' a weakling. Face whatever this is. I'll stand beside you in whatever way you need of me. You know I will."

Rhys always did have a way of shining the light on a particular situation.

He sighed loudly. "It's been three weeks. Three weeks. It's past time for you to wake. I came in yesterday, and I swear I caught Henry before he climbed in bed with you."

That made her want to smile. It was Rhys's way to make light of a volatile situation.

"Con might verra well throw you out."

Let him try, Rhi thought. She wasn't foolish enough to believe Rhys would allow that to happen. Rhys was grasping at anything to get her to open her eyes.

"Dammit," Rhys grumbled. "There's no reason for you to no' wake other than you're scared. When have you ever been scared?"

Every damn day. But Rhys didn't need to know that. They all thought her strong and undeterred by things. They were all wrong. She was just a very good actress.

"Is it Balladyn? Is he pressing you into becoming Dark? I'll be happy to kill him."

"You'll have to stand in line behind me."

Phelan. Of course he would come. How could she withstand both Phelan and Rhys? They were like brothers, and in some ways closer to her than her own brother had been.

There was movement on her other side and someone took her hand. Phelan. He gave her hand a squeeze. "What have you told her?" he asked Rhys.

"To wake her skinny arse up," Rhys stated.

Phelan chuckled softly. "You think that'll work? The Rhi who goes against any kind of order?"

Rhys grunted and said, "We've tried sweet-talking her, cajoling her, bribing her, and even ignoring her. I figure this was the only option left."

"There's another one."

No. Rhi knew what Phelan was thinking. All she could do was pray that Rhys wouldn't let the secret out.

"What's that?" Rhys asked.

"Bring her lover to her."

No. Nonononononononooooooooooooo.

There was a long pause before Rhys said, "I willna. She'd never forgive me."

"But she would wake."

"Maybe. Maybe no'. Too much has happened, Phelan. Rhi isna the same Fae from even a month ago. With the way she's been experiencing things, she might verra well sink further into the sleep instead of waking. Besides, she'd skin me alive if I let the name slip to you."

Phelan snorted. "He's been here, hasn't he?"

"Let it go."

"It was worth a try to discover who the asshole is. Why will none of you tell me?"

"Because Rhi doesna want you to know."

Phelan's grip on her hand tightened. "Why is that exactly?"

"You'd try to kill him, which you know is futile."

"So I've met him?"

There was a creak from a chair as Rhys stood. "Does it matter?"

"It does. He hurt Rhi. He continues to hurt her."

"Until she moves on."

There was a beat of silence. Phelan's voice was laced with surprise when he asked, "Is she moving on?"

"Many of us have urged her to do so."

"Because there's no hope of her lover returning to her?"

Rhys tugged on her hair. "Because unrequited love can kill, and Rhi is too important for that to happen. I'd like nothing more than for the fucktard to realize he lost something precious, but I think for Rhi's peace of mind she should stop loving him."

"I could never stop loving Aisley. Never," Phelan said.

"She's gone several thousands of years without her love being reciprocated. That changes a person, especially someone like Rhi. She feels things deeper than most. She's one of the most giving individuals I've ever met, and she deserves happiness."

"And if that happiness is with Ulrik?"

Was that a growl she heard from Rhys? Most definitely it was.

"She's no' that stupid."

Phelan made a sound at the back of his throat. "It was Ulrik that carried her out of Balladyn's dungeon. She's gone to see him a few times as well. Tell me you're no' worried there's something there."

"Aye. I'm no longer concerned about Henry though. He'll have his heart broken, but he'll find someone else eventually."

"Like Rhi?" Phelan asked. "What about Balladyn? Rhi told me that he loves her."

"I believe he does. He's the one I'm really worried about. They had a close connection before, during, and after Rhi's lover. I doona think it's coincidence Balladyn has come back into her life now."

Rhi hated to admit it, but she agreed. Why after all those millennia had she found Balladyn? Why had he just sought her out? There was no such thing as flukes, of that she was certain.

"He's Dark," Phelan stated.

"Tell me something I doona know," Rhys said sarcastically.

"If she goes with him, she'll turn Dark."

"There's a chance of that, aye, but she has you and me. There are others who could help pull her back from that."

"Nay, Rhys. I'm no' comfortable pushing her toward Balladyn."

"There may no' be a choice for us. Rhi desperately wants to be loved and have that love returned. Balladyn is

giving her that love. I doona believe any of us could withstand him if we were in her position."

Wow. So that's what they thought of her. Rhi wasn't
sure whether to be flattered or not. One moment they were
saying she was strong, and the next that she was too weak
to withstand Balladyn.

Never mind the fact that she hadn't thought about re-
sisting him. That wasn't true. She had—briefly. It just felt
so nice to have someone's arm around her, to see desire in
a male's gaze, and to be wanted.

"I'll talk to her."

Rhys chuckled and resumed his seat. "We can talk until
the sun explodes, but it willna do any good. Rhi has a mind
of her own. She'll do whatever she wants."

"I can no' lose her."

"Neither can I. None of us can. I'm no' sure she knows
that."

Rhi hadn't comprehended the depth of Rhys and Phelan's friendship until that moment. She wanted to sit up and
hug them simultaneously.

It was too much for her to take. She sank further into
the darkness and let the sleep take her, because she knew
it wouldn't be long before she had no choice but to wake.

Not yet though. Not yet.

Phelan gazed down at Rhi sleeping and rubbed the back
of his neck with his free hand. "Do you think her being
here is causing this?"

Rhys raised his aqua ringed dark blue eyes to his. "I
think if we brought her anywhere else Balladyn would be
there in a second. Or Ulrik."

"Can any magic reach Rhi where she's at?"

"I've tried. If it is, she's no' responding." Rhys sat back
in the chair and stared at Rhi.

"I'm no' going to sit and watch her any longer. I need
to do something."

"You are. You're here for her."

Phelan raised a brow. "And that has done so verra much."

"More than you know. Rhi has been on her own for a while. She claims to like it that way, but how often is she at Dreagan? I know she visits me at least once a week. How about you? How often do you see her?"

Phelan thought back over the last few months. "More now than before. The last time I saw her, she just hugged me. I knew something was wrong, but she wouldna tell me all of it."

"The fact she came to you says a lot. Rhi isna one to open up easily."

"So we wait?"

Rhys nodded. "We wait."

Phelan released Rhi's hand and pulled another chair closer. "I'll stay with her for a bit. Return to Lily."

Rhys rose and strode toward the entrance. He looked back at Rhi once before he stepped through the doorway and closed it behind him.

Phelan leaned his head back and stared at the ceiling. "Balladyn, Rhi? Really? Is it because he's told you he loves you? Should you turn to the first one who says that? After you've experienced the kind of love I have with Aisley, how can you settle for anything less?"

He sank down farther in the chair and laced his fingers over his stomach. "Then again, I suppose Balladyn could be another such love. I just hate the thought of him with you after he tortured you. I also hate the King who rejected your love so harshly. I hope one day you tell me who he is. I'd really love to punch him.

"No' that you'll ever tell me. Hell, Rhys wouldna even share the name. I'm beginning to think everyone is keeping it from me because of how I'll react. Which means I've already met the wanker. Just please tell me it isna

Con. The way you two hate each other leads me to think it's him.

"But the shared loathing could have to do with your lover. Con might have talked your lover into letting you go. If you discovered that, you would turn the full force of your ire on him."

Phelan blew out a breath. "I just wish I knew which it was."

Ulrik was in the hospital a mere ten minutes before he discovered Sophie had the day off. He was on his way out when he heard a whistle behind him. Ulrik halted and slowly turned around to find Sophie's blond friend smiling at him.

"Are you the one?" she asked.

Ulrik cocked his head to the side and smiled. "I'm a great many things, lass. Which are you referring to?"

She laughed and closed the distance between them. "I overheard you asking the nurses about Sophie. I saw you in here the other day with her. I'm wondering if you're the one who has been rocking her world, if you get my meaning."

"I understand you," he replied with his best smile. "What makes you think it's me?"

"Besides the fact you can wear a suit like nobody's business and you're incredibly good looking? You came here for her again." She stuck out her hand. "I'm Claire, by the way."

He took her hand in his and shook it. "Nice to meet you, Claire. I'm Ulrik."

Her hand returned to her side. "I know it's you. I just wanted to thank you for putting the smile on her face."

"Does she come in smiling often?"

"A few weeks ago she did, and you must be doing something right, because she did yesterday as well. I'm curious as to why you didn't know she was off today?"

"I got the days mixed up," Ulrik hurried to lie. "I must have written it down on my agenda wrong."

"Then you best get to her soon. I want another smile on her face the next time she comes in," Claire said with a wink and walked away.

Ulrik stalked out of the hospital with a smile. Soon Dr. Sophie Martin would be his, and Darius would watch another woman of his die.

CHAPTER
SEVENTEEN

Darius wanted to get out and track down Ulrik himself. But he also wanted to remain beside Sophie. He wasn't sure which one would be the best alternative to end the current situation.

Ulrik wouldn't fight him. Not really. Ulrik wanted Con, but along the way he would hurt as many Dragon Kings as he could. As well as anyone connected to them.

Darius looked at Sophie sitting on the couch surfing the telly. She looked bored. How many times had she checked the clock in the last half hour? At least a dozen, if not more.

"I hate days off," she said.

Darius pushed away from leaning against the wall near her windows so he could look out without being seen. "We all need them."

"Not me." She turned off the TV and tossed the remote onto her coffee table. "I have to be occupied, or I go a little daft."

"How much do you work?" he asked.

She shrugged and turned so that she was leaning her arm against the back of the couch to look at him. "I work all of my shifts."

"Which are?"

"Twelve to fourteen hours. Then I pick up others when I can. Every couple months I'm forced to take a few days off, because apparently it's not normal for a person to work several weeks in a row without a day off."

Darius walked to the couch and sat on the opposite end. Sophie turned with him, her expression telling him she was waiting for him to say something.

He considered her a moment. "All you want to do is work?"

"It fills the time better than watching a movie."

"When was the last time you watched a movie?" Darius himself might have only caught one or two since he walked from his mountain, but he'd enjoyed them.

Sophie looked at the ceiling and bit her lip. Then she said, "I know it's been four, possibly five, years."

Darius was shocked. Wasn't that abnormal for a human? Sure, some liked more leisure time than others, but to want none? There had to be a reason for that.

"I've astounded you," Sophie said with a laugh.

Darius rested his arm on the back of the sofa, bringing his fingers close to touching her. "That you have."

"So tell me something about you, since we're sharing."

Darius wasn't finished discussing her need to work every hour of every day. He wouldn't give up easily on it. She would find that out quickly enough. "What you see is what you get."

She barked with laughter. "I highly doubt that."

"You didna tell me anything I couldna have found out from someone at the hospital."

She narrowed her gaze teasingly before she smiled. "All right. I hate downtime of any kind. I don't exactly have insomnia, but I can only sleep for about four hours before I'm wide awake."

"You slept last night," he told her with a grin.

Sophie glanced away as she smiled. "That's because someone exhausted me."

"Perhaps that's what you need every night."

"I might never want to leave the bed."

Darius didn't think that would be a bad thing. In fact, the idea of having her in his bed every day appealed to him much more than he was comfortable with.

"I'm still waiting to hear something about you," she said.

He rubbed his jaw. What did he tell her? What *could* he tell her?

"Oh, come on. There has to be something," she teased.

Darius shook his head. "I love thunderstorms. I feel . . . free when they come." Or he used to. Even that had been curbed recently.

"Thunderstorms, huh?" she said, looking at him with interest. "I can see that."

There was a knock on her door that had Darius on his feet in a second. Sophie stood and put her hand out to halt him.

"It's all right. It's my friend, Claire. She always stops by on my days off."

He jumped to his feet and hurried around the sofa. "Doona tell her I'm here."

"What?" she asked in a hoarse whisper.

Darius looked pointedly at the window. "You're being watched. No one knows I'm here."

"Right," she said, worry filling her gaze.

Darius walked to the bedroom closet and pulled the door closed behind him. He left it open just enough that he could see out.

Sophie watched the door to her closet close before she opened the door.

"You are here," Claire said in surprise. "I thought you might be out, but I thought I'd drop by anyway."

Sophie moved aside to let Claire in. "Nope. I'm here. I'm always here. Why would you think I'd be out?"

"Because I met him. And let me tell you, Soph, he's gorgeous!"

Sophie pulled her gaze from her bedroom, her stomach falling to her feet. She knew Claire wasn't referring to Darius. She prayed it wasn't Ulrik. "Met who?"

"Seriously?" Claire asked as she barked with laughter. "You're going to play that card? The guy who's been wearing you out with that great sex you've been having."

Sophie's stomach clutched painfully. Oh God, no. "When?"

"This morning."

"What did he look like?" she asked hurriedly.

Claire rolled her eyes. "Girl, please. He's the drop-dead gorgeous guy who wears a suit better than a *GQ* model. With that long black hair and those gold eyes . . . yum is all I can say. You couldn't have picked a better-looking guy."

Actually she could have—Darius. But Sophie didn't say that. She didn't want to alert Claire that she had just described Ulrik in case it put her friend in danger.

"Don't you have anything to say?" Claire asked suspiciously. "Or are you angry at him for not remembering it was your day off?"

Shit. The situation just kept getting worse. "I'm not angry." Sophie hated lying to Claire, and she would tell her everything once Ulrik was out of her life. Until then, she would lie as much as she had to for Claire to be safe.

Claire nodded with a knowing smile. "You're going to make him pay for forgetting, aren't you? I'm also surprised he's not here. Do y'all have any plans tonight?"

"We play it by ear."

"That can be good," Claire said as she began to gather her things. "I know you've kept guys at arm's length, Soph, but it's good to see you getting out there again. It's been *years*."

She said the last word in a whisper, as if it was some great secret.

Sophie fought to keep her smile in place. Claire knew the reasons, but her friend had still constantly pushed her to forget the past. It was the past that had shaped Sophie into who she was now. It couldn't simply be forgotten like last week's lasagna.

"You're going to end it." Claire rolled her eyes, her lips pinched together. "Why? It might actually go somewhere. You just can't let go of the past and what that prick did to you."

Sophie often wondered how quickly Claire's mind could jump from one thought to another, but it was the perfect solution. "Yeah, I am. He's not right for me."

"First lay you've had in years." Claire looked her up and down, her hand on her hip. "I know you all too well, Soph. You'll send him packing before there's even a chance you might have feelings for him."

Sophie shrugged, not sure what to say. She wanted Ulrik to stay away from Claire. Sophie wondered if it would be better to tell Claire he was dangerous, but then if Ulrik returned to the hospital, Claire might act differently and alert Ulrik. More importantly, it might draw Ulrik's attention to her.

And if Ulrik was as threatening as Darius said, then that's the last thing Sophie wanted to do to her friend.

Claire looked away, her eyes bright with tears. "I worry about you, you know. You've no idea the men that look at you when you walk down the halls of the hospital. You could have any one of them, and I can't get a guy who isn't scum to look my way. Men are waiting for you to pay them the least little bit of attention."

"You're going to find a guy, Claire. I know it. You're too special not to have someone to spend your life with."

"I know." Claire wiped at her eyes and faced her once more, a bright smile in place.

Sophie walked to her friend and hugged her. "You've been a true friend."

Claire pulled back and looked at her with a deep frown marring her forehead. "What's going on, Soph?"

"Nothing," she said. But that wasn't true. There was something big, and Sophie couldn't stand to have her friend hurt.

"Tell me. Now," Claire demanded. She put her hands on her hips. "I've never seen you so unsettled. It's like you're waiting for something bad to happen."

Sophie licked her lips and glanced at her closet door. "Claire, the man I've been seeing isn't who came to the hospital today."

"What?" Claire's eyes were wide.

"Look, I don't want to scare you, but the man who came to the hospital is dangerous. He's . . ." What did she say? She wasn't even sure what he was involved in, so she didn't know what to tell Claire.

"The Mob?" Claire asked.

It sounded good, and there was enough fear in Claire's voice that Sophie nodded. "Yes. He wants me for something, but I'm not interested."

"Shit," Claire said and covered her mouth with her hand. "I told him it was your day off."

Sophie closed her eyes briefly. Ulrik had men watching her flat anyway. "It doesn't matter. Just steer clear of him if you see him."

"Perhaps we should go to the police."

"He's not done anything yet. I don't want him alerted that you know who he is," Sophie said.

Claire nodded numbly. "Yeah. Okay."

"It's important, Claire. Keep away from him, but if he seeks you out, put in one of those spectacular performances of yours and get as far from him as you can as quickly as possible."

"What the hell did you get involved with, Sophie?"

She shrugged, shaking her head. "I don't know."

"How did you get involved with this jerk?"

"He just found me. I'm separating myself without getting on his bad side."

Claire wrapped her arms around herself. "That's a good idea. Want me to stay here tonight?"

"Thanks, but I'll be all right. He won't come here." At least she hoped he wouldn't. And if he did, Darius was there.

"I think I'm going to go home then." She gave Sophie a quick hug. "I'm going to call later. If you don't pick up, I'm calling the authorities."

Sophie smiled, loving Claire even more. "Yes, ma'am."

"That's right," Claire said with a wink. She grabbed her purse and waved as she exited the flat.

Sophie locked the door behind her and put her forehead against the wood.

"Ulrik knows I'm here."

Sophie whirled around at the sound of Darius's voice. She hadn't heard him leave her closet, so to find him behind her was startling. "How do you know?"

"He went to the hospital. Claire spoke of your lover. Ulrik played along to get information."

She rubbed her eyes, suddenly very weary. "Will he hurt Claire?"

"Most likely no'. He's after me through you."

"So what now? What do I do?"

"You do nothing. I'm going after Ulrik."

Sophie put her hand on his chest to stop him as she looked into his chocolate eyes. "Why?"

He ran a finger along her cheek to her jaw. "The revenge Ulrik seeks doesna involve you. It never involved you. I'm going to make sure it stays that way."

"Will I see you again?"

He hesitated, which was answer enough. Sophie was angry at herself for even asking. She didn't get attached. She *shouldn't* get attached.

But it was already too late.

His arms wrapped around her. "Yes," he said.

With his dark gaze holding hers, he slowly lowered his head and kissed her. Sophie sank into the kiss, the slow, mesmerizing, sinful kiss that made her forget . . . everything.

When he ended it, she kept her eyes closed. When he placed a soft kiss on her forehead, she squeezed them tight. She didn't open them until the door closed behind him.

Sophie looked around her flat. She hadn't realized how quiet it was until Darius was gone. The morning hadn't been unbearable. She had been restless because he was so near and she wanted him back in the bed with her.

She let him think it was because she was bored since she hadn't been able to handle the truth. Now that she was once more alone, she remembered how much she hated days off.

Sophie walked to the couch and plopped down. She turned on the telly and sat back to watch a movie and pretend that she wasn't already missing Darius.

CHAPTER EIGHTEEN

It took longer than Darius wanted, but he made it out of Sophie's building without any of Ulrik's men seeing him. Darius waited until he was three blocks away before he ducked into an alley to see if anyone followed.

He then opened the telepathic link and said Con's name. The King of Kings answered immediately.

"We have an issue," Darius said.

"What kind of issue?"

"Ulrik knows I'm still here. He went to the hospital today to talk to Sophie."

There was a pause before Con asked, *"I gather she was with you?"*

"Aye."

"And?" Con asked testily.

Darius clenched his jaw. Now he understood why Thorn had been so hesitant to let Con know about Lexi. Con was single-minded in protecting the Kings. Except when it came to killing humans.

He would allow them to be killed by the Dark or even MI5 without blinking if it meant that the Dragon Kings' secret remained safe.

"Darius?"

"Ulrik wants her to work for him. He didna tell her in what capacity. I've warned her away from him and told her Ulrik was dangerous."

"Do you think she'll listen?"

That was the real question, wasn't it? Darius had overheard the conversation between Sophie and Claire. Whatever happened in her past had soured her from ever trusting. She had that in common with Ulrik.

"There's a chance she will."

"So she could fall into Ulrik's trap?"

"Aye. She could, but I think she's too smart for that."

"Does she know our secret?" Con demanded.

"She knows nothing."

Con sighed loudly through the link. *"Finally. Someone with some fucking sense."*

"It might be better if she did know. If I told her the whole story she'd understand why Ulrik is so dangerous."

Every King knew that Con was less than pleased at how many of them were finding mates. Darius understood Con's reluctance in accepting the changes. The first time Kings began to take mates, a female tried to betray Ulrik.

It was the catalyst in the war with the humans, sending their dragons away, and the Kings going into hiding for several centuries.

A repeat would be . . . catastrophic.

Darius was quite sure the Kings wouldn't willingly go to their mountains and hope the humans forgot about them again. There would be another war.

And the mortals would lose.

"You're no' going down the same road Warrick and Thorn did, are you?" Con asked.

Darius thought about Sophie and how he couldn't wait to have her in his arms again. Bedding her was all he wanted. Anything else was . . . futile.

"*Nay.*"

"*Excellent. Then there's no need to tell her anything.*"

Darius leaned a shoulder against the building. "*That doesna mean I'm going to sit by and watch Ulrik pull Sophie into his web of deceit. He's only after her because he saw us together. That's on me.*"

"*So you want to protect her?*" Con said with exaggerated sarcasm.

"*Do you really need to ask that? We gave a vow to safeguard the humans. I've put one in danger because I didna get her off the streets before I took her so that anyone could stumble upon us.*"

"*If you doona have feelings for the doctor, let Ulrik have her,*" Con said, breaking into his thoughts. "*We'd get to see exactly what Ulrik is up to.*"

"*Now who's daft?*" Darius muttered.

Con chuckled. "*I suppose that's a nay, then?*"

"*You know damn well it is. Ulrik will approach her again. I think it'll be wise for me to have a chat with him first.*"

There was a pregnant pause from Con. "*That could be a good move. Ulrik willna be expecting it. No' when I want all of you to stay far from him until it's time for our battle.*"

"*My thoughts as well. Does he know you're in the city?*"

"*It's possible. I've no' tried to hide myself.*"

Darius scratched his cheek. "*I'll play it by ear. If he doesna mention you, then I willna either.*"

"*What do you hope to accomplish? You push Ulrik to stay away from Sophie, and that will only spur him on harder to get her.*"

"*I know. I doona know what I'll say yet, but it willna be about Sophie.*"

Con's laugh was short and loud. "*Brilliant, Darius. Let's hope Ulrik will fall for it.*"

Darius didn't expect Ulrik to. He severed the link with

Con and walked from the alley. He made sure he was on the other side of the city before he stopped hiding and walked into the open.

For the next hour, Darius once more strolled the streets of the city. He kept his eye out for anyone who might be a Dark Fae, but there were none. It wasn't that he was unhappy about it, Darius was just confused as to why they'd departed Edinburgh so quickly.

He noticed the man following him almost as soon as it happened. Darius didn't try to get away. He wanted Ulrik to find him.

Darius made his way to Princes Street Gardens. The public park was in the center of the city and in the shadow of Edinburgh Castle.

Even in mid-November, the park teemed with people—locals and visitors alike. The beautifully colored flowers were gone as winter approached, but with the castle, fountains, and beauty of the park, it was a mecca.

Darius saw a vacant bench and sat. He leaned his head back with his eyes closed and let the sun shine upon his face. While he waited for Ulrik to find him, he dreamed of flying through the clouds, the sun so close that Darius had often thought he could touch it if he but tried.

But that only made him sad. Darius opened his eyes and lifted his head. He could make out the top of Scott Monument from his seat. The field of green grass before him had people scattered all over it thanks to the gorgeous day.

"I didna take you for a people watcher," Ulrik said as he walked up and sat.

Darius didn't look Ulrik's way. He kept his attention on the mortals. "You see all kinds. It's a form of entertainment."

"Why have you sought me out?"

"I didna."

Ulrik made a sound at the back of his throat. "You stopped hiding. I'm no' a fool. You wanted me to find you."

"So I did." Darius turned his head to look at him. "Why?"

He'd surprised Ulrik, just as he'd wanted. Darius needed to be careful though. Ulrik was a master at manipulation. Darius wanted to take advantage of the opportunity he had. "I found you here. Why no' remain in Edinburgh and keep an eye on you?"

Ulrik's lips lifted in a smile before he began to laugh. "Keep an eye on me, aye? Are you sure you're no' here for Dr. Martin?"

"I told you she means nothing."

"That's why you bedded her again?" Ulrik asked with raised brows.

Darius scooted farther down on the bench and extended his legs. "It doesna matter what I tell you, you willna believe me."

"I'd believe you if you told me you were with her."

"Fine," Darius said. "I was with her."

Ulrik's eyes narrowed. "You gave in too easily."

"I told you that you wouldna believe me."

Ulrik looked away and was silent for several minutes. Finally he asked, "Why lie? Why no' tell me the truth?"

"How do you know I'm no'?"

"My men didna see you enter her flat."

Darius nodded slowly. "So if they didna see it, then it's no' true."

"You're trying to play me."

Darius didn't hide his smile. "Am I?"

Ulrik's head swiveled to him. "You are. I think you care about the doctor. I think the idea that she might actually consider my offer infuriates you."

"I doona want her involved with you, but no' because I

have feelings for her. I'd feel this way about any mortal getting entangled with you. They all end up dead."

"How would you know? Have you tracked all the people who work for me? Nay, you've no'. You've no' because you doona have a clue as to who they are." Ulrik cut him a derisive look. "I treat my employees verra well."

"As long as they do what you want."

Ulrik shrugged, his look stating that was a given. "It's true that I put an end to anyone who attempts to betray me. Only those who are completely loyal remain. Con is the same way in regards to each of the Kings. All of you are just so used to it you doona realize it anymore."

"He doesna kill us."

"Of course he doesna. He just sends you to your mountain and tells you to sleep for a few thousand years."

Darius tried not to react, but he couldn't stop his body from stiffening. How had Ulrik found out? There was no way Ulrik should know of such things since it happened when Ulrik was battling the humans.

Ulrik's cocky smile made Darius want to physically remove it.

"Con would never kill a Dragon King. I'm proof of that," Ulrik stated. "It matters how many of us are here. Did he tell you that?"

It was the first Darius had heard of it. Of course the more Dragon Kings that were alive the better, but Ulrik made it seem as if there were more to it. Knowing Ulrik, it was a trick to make Darius doubt Con.

Then again, Constantine had a habit of keeping things to himself. The only other one who knew was Kellan as Keeper of the History.

"Of course he didna," Ulrik continued. "When does Con share that kind of information with the rest of the Kings unless it involves the continuation of Dreagan?"

"What's your point?"

Ulrik lifted a shoulder in a half-shrug. "I think the Kings should begin asking Con questions. Make him answer for his decisions as he's always made each of you answer for yours."

"Let me guess," Darius said with a flat look. "If you were King of Kings, things would be different?"

Ulrik threw him a smile. "Of course they would. I'm no' Con. He wanted to be King of Kings from the moment he was born. He didna stop until he achieved that position. Do you really think he'd give it up so easily? Why keep me alive if I could potentially challenge him one day?"

They were damn good questions, and it pissed Darius off. He wasn't here to have Ulrik put thoughts in his head. Yet that was exactly what was happening.

"The lengths Con went to in order to be King of Kings were extreme," Ulrik said. His smile vanished as if he were recalling days long past when he and Con were still friends. With a slight shake of his head to dislodge those memories, Ulrik was smiling again. "Perhaps you should ask Con why he's kept me alive. He says he's ready to battle me. Why then is he holed up in his suite no' far from here?"

"He willna fight you in front of the mortals."

Ulrik laughed as he got to his feet and adjusted his suit jacket to button the top button. "I never said I'd fight him in front of humans. I just said that I'd challenge him. And I *will* win."

CHAPTER
NINETEEN

Rhi? Can you hear me? Please hear me.

Balladyn's voice reached her deep into her sleep. The note of longing and worry was enough to yank her awake. She lay still until she was sure she was alone.

Rhi tried to gather the darkness around her to sleep once more, but Balladyn's voice shattered whatever tenuous hold she had on it.

She opened her eyes. It took blinking a few times before the room came into focus. She stared at the white ceiling and crown molding for a few seconds before she sat up.

The room was decorated in various shades of white and taupe. It was a soothing palette. One that made her want to curl up on her side and sleep some more.

Rhi.

She winced at Balladyn's call. Had Taraeth discovered he was the one who'd told her where Lexi was being held? Was Balladyn in trouble? That thought made her swing her legs over the side of the bed and stand.

Instantly, she felt the eyes of her watcher on her. Every

time she had woken he'd been there. Did he ever leave? And what the hell did he want with her?

Rhi got a look at herself in the mirror and grimaced. She was still in the same clothes from the battle, and the holes in her shirt from the Dark magic were doing nothing to make her look good.

With a snap of her fingers, Rhi replaced her clothes with pale denim jeans and a bright orange long-sleeved shirt that hugged her breasts and waist. She looked down at the brown booties and smiled.

Orange. She couldn't remember the last time she had worn orange. In fact, she'd worn nothing but black and white for some time. She hadn't exactly chosen orange, but she hadn't thought about her usual colors either.

There was a sound at the door. Rhi whirled around to see Rhys. He was looking at her choice of shirt with a smile about his lips.

"I was beginning to wonder if you were ever going to wake," he said as he walked into the room.

Rhi looked pointedly at the door. Rhys closed it without question and walked to her. Before Rhi could react, he enveloped her in a hug.

"We've been worried," he said.

She closed her eyes and returned the hug. There was something calming about a hug. Something that made all the stress melt away. "I'm sorry."

"Are you all right?"

"I don't really know," she admitted.

"And the sleep? Was it only the Dark magic?"

Since Rhi couldn't lie without experiencing extreme pain, she opted not to answer.

Rhys blew out a breath and leaned back. "It's what I suspected."

"I needed some time."

"I can respect that. I took some as well. We all need it, but that doesna mean you have to sink into such a sleep that we can no' reach you."

Rhi didn't bother to tell him that she'd heard some of the conversations. Others she had been too deep in the sleep to hear.

"I'm back now." What else was there to say really?

"Aye. So it seems."

Rhi looked away from Rhys's penetrating gaze. She looked down at her nails and knew one of the first things she was going to do was get a manicure. Might as well get a pedicure too. If her fingers looked that bad, then she could imagine how her feet looked.

She tossed her long hair over her shoulder. Just as she was about to teleport away with some snappy remark, she heard Balladyn say her name again.

That hesitation had Rhys beside her.

"What is it?" he asked.

She turned her face to him. "What's happened while I've been asleep?"

"Nothing much. All the Dark are out of Edinburgh. Out of most of the cities, actually."

"The Dragon Kings kicked ass, I suppose."

Before she finished speaking, he was shaking his head with a frown. "That's the odd thing. Darius is in Edinburgh now, and he was killing plenty of them. Then it became harder and harder to find Dark. The last time Thorn spoke to him was a few days ago and Darius had gone days without seeing a Dark."

Wasn't that interesting? Had Usaeil stepped up and done what a Queen of the Light should have done as soon as the shit hit the fan?

Rhi looked to where her watcher stood in the corner of the room. She knew he was Fae. Only a Fae could veil themselves in such a way, but as far as she knew, not even Usaeil could remain veiled as long as Rhi. And her watcher stayed that way almost indefinitely.

A Fae for sure. But Light or Dark?

More importantly, what did he want with her?

"What's going on with the Dark?" she asked off-handedly.

Rhys snorted loudly. "You mean what's going on with Balladyn?"

She looked at him and raised her brows, waiting for him to tell her.

Rhys gave a little shake of his head. "I understand you were close to him at one time. He tortured you, Rhi. Remember the Chains of Mordare?"

There were times she could still feel the weight of them on her wrists. She took a step toward Rhys. "I wore them," she said in a clipped tone. "I remember."

"Fine." Rhys threw up his hands in surrender. "As far as we've heard, Taraeth doesna know Balladyn told you where Lexi was."

"Was that so difficult?" she asked with a smirk.

A vein ticked in his temple. "More than you know."

"As for why I care about him, he helped us. At the risk of himself, he gave me the information I asked for."

"Because he wants you to trust him. Can you no' see that?" he beseeched.

There was a good chance Rhys was right.

Then there was the hope that someone loved her.

"I see it," she admitted in a low voice, unable to meet Rhys's gaze.

He grasped her arms and waited until she looked at him to say, "I'm sorry."

She looked at him askance, unsure of why he was apologizing. "Why?"

"Because I didna know the depth of the pain you experienced when . . . *he* . . . turned away from you."

Rhi didn't want to listen to this. She tried to pull away. Yet Rhys held fast.

"I understand now. Lily has given me a love I didna think possible. Even if I feel only a drop of what you experienced, I get it. I want you to find that kind of love again."

She looked anywhere but at Rhys. No way was she going to see the pity in his gaze. "A love of the ages, Rhys. Remember that? It's gone now. I can find happiness elsewhere."

"Aye. Just no' with Balladyn."

Anger spiked in her. She couldn't have her Dragon King lover. Now, she was being told she couldn't have Balladyn either. When could she have love? When could she be happy?

"I doona know when you'll be happy again," Rhys said in a soothing voice. "Calm down, Rhi. We're just talking."

"I am calm!"

"Rhi," he said as he caught her gaze. "There's no need to get angry."

She glared at him. "If you think I'm angry now, wait until I start glowing."

"You are."

"What?" she barked.

Rhys glanced down at her. "Glowing."

She looked at herself and saw the white light emanating all around her. A glimpse at the room showed everything was shaking.

There was a commotion at the door. Rhi looked over to find Phelan, Henry, and Kellan gawking at her. She closed her eyes and slowly pulled her anger back into a little ball within her.

"Out!" Rhys yelled over his shoulder. Then he enveloped her in a tight hug. "It's all right. I didna mean to make you mad. I'm just trying to look out for you."

She clung to him, tears threatening. What was wrong with her that an innocent remark could set her off in such a way? She was a danger to everyone.

"You're going to love again. I know it, Rhi," he said while stroking her hair. "You've been through too much no' to find someone."

"I don't want to be alone anymore, Rhys. It's . . ."

"Awful," he finished for her. "I know."

Rhi squeezed her eyes closed, but the tears still spilled down her cheeks.

"Stay here a wee bit longer," Rhys suggested. "Con is gone to Edinburgh, so he willna bother you."

Yes. A few more days might be just the thing.

But . . . there was Balladyn.

Rhi pulled out of Rhys's arms and wiped at her tears. "He's calling for me. I need to see what he wants."

"Balladyn."

It wasn't a question. "I'll be back soon."

"You've been asleep for over three weeks. You've missed a lot."

"And I need to catch up." She put a bright smile in place and winked. "Don't worry, stud. I'll be back soon."

Rhys blew out a breath once she left. "You can come in," he called to the others.

The door to the room opened and Henry, Phelan, and Kellan walked in.

"She's going to see Balladyn?" Henry said with an angry glint in his hazel eyes.

Rhys exchanged a glance with Kellan.

It was Kellan who said, "He gave us the information for Thorn to find Lexi. She owes him."

"You heard her," Phelan said. "She'll be back."

With a noise that sounded suspiciously like a growl, Henry turned on his heel and strode away.

"Shit," Phelan said. "He's got it bad for her."

Kellan crossed his arms over his chest, looking at the door where Henry had disappeared. "Aye. We need to turn Henry's attention onto someone else."

"Who? The only females here are mated to us," Rhys said.

Kellan twisted his lips. "We'll have to think of something fast."

"Speaking of fast," Phelan said. "What set Rhi off?"

Rhys glanced at the floor. "Me. I told her Balladyn wasn't for her."

"We heard her yelling," Kellan said.

Phelan nodded. "It broke my heart to hear her asking when she would get to love."

"Aye." Rhys felt Kellan's gaze on him. Both were thinking the same thing. That it was time to beat the shit out of a certain Dragon King until they discovered the truth of why he'd ended things with Rhi.

"Oh, I doona think so," Phelan said, looking between the two of them.

Kellan frowned. "What?"

"I see the way you're looking at Rhys. You want to go find Rhi's lover and hit him a few times. That's no' going to happen unless I'm with you," Phelan stated.

Rhys slapped him on the back. "It's no' a secret that will be held for eternity. And trust me, when you find out, you're going to wish you didna know."

CHAPTER
TWENTY

Rhi arrived at the desert and looked around for Balladyn. She was disappointed when he was nowhere to be seen. She hadn't bothered to track him, because she assumed this was where he would be. She didn't know how, but the desert had become the location where they always met.

It felt good to have the sun on her skin again. After weeks asleep, she craved the warmth of the sun and the way it made her skin prickle.

She didn't know how long she stood there before she felt the presence. It wasn't her watcher. He'd been there seconds after she teleported in. No, this was someone else.

Rhi turned around, ready to call up her sword if need be when her gaze landed on Balladyn. He was looking at her as if she couldn't be real.

"I saw you fall," he said. "I saw the magic hit you, and you didn't get up. I tried to get to you. You didn't rise after the blast, and I feared you were . . ."

"Dead? Not me," she said with a flip of her hair.

In the next moment, he was before her, one hand on her back and the other cradling her head as he kissed her deeply, fervently.

She felt his arousal against her stomach just as she felt his passion in their kiss. Rhi wrapped her arms around him and returned his kiss with a heavy dose of her own desire.

He took her head between his hands and ended the kiss to stare into her face. She looked into his red eyes and saw the concern he didn't try to hide.

"You could've died," he whispered.

She closed her eyes as he put his forehead against hers. This was a side of Balladyn she had never seen before, and it touched her greatly.

"Where have you been?"

She rubbed her hands along his arms. "Asleep."

"Did the Dark magic wound you that bad?"

"No." She didn't even think of lying to him. "Con healed me, but the darkness was my escape."

Balladyn straightened. "From me."

She tenderly touched his face. "From everything. Usaeil, the Dark, Ulrik, the darkness growing inside me, and yes, the feelings you're stirring within me. I needed a break from it all."

"I see."

"I'm here, aren't I?" she asked him with a grin. "If I wanted away from you, would I've come?"

He gave her a crooked smile. "Nay."

"Then ease your mind about that. I don't know what I want yet, so don't think this is me saying yes."

His smile grew, making his eyes crinkle in the corners. "You will. One day soon, you will."

Was it her imagination, or had the red of his eyes dimmed a little? Rhi only had that glance before he was kissing her again.

Sophie woke to the sound of her phone vibrating on the coffee table. She hurriedly reached for it to read the text from Claire.

She smiled and quickly typed a text letting Claire know that everything was all right. Sophie then sighed and dropped her head back on the couch.

Her thoughts were on Darius, not Ulrik. But then again, she was always thinking about Darius. The sex was amazing, but was it enough? Did it matter that he could give her a couple of orgasms?

A couple? Girl, it was a dozen!

A dozen or not, it didn't matter.

Sophie laughed at herself. Of course it signified. To have a man be able to touch her and bring her to the edge of release in a matter of seconds was a skill rarely found.

"As rare as the Arc of the Covenant," Sophie mumbled to herself.

It wasn't just the sex. She wished it was so she could schedule something every few weeks. Waking up that morning to find Darius still in bed had done something to her, changed her.

She rose to pour herself some wine. Noon had come and gone, and she couldn't watch another minute on the telly. With Ulrik's men out there, she wasn't keen on leaving her flat either. She also had no idea when Darius would be back.

He said he'd return. She hoped he would, but she was preparing herself for the fact that he wouldn't.

"It's better to expect the worst," she said as she sipped her wine.

She'd let Darius into her life—and her heart. Now Sophie feared it had been a mistake. What if he hurt her? What if he didn't return?

Sophie lifted her chin. She'd been through worse. She would get through whatever happened with Darius.

All the while she prayed that he came back to her. She liked the new outlook on life that he'd given her. Did he even know what he'd done for her? She didn't think so.

She was going insane thinking of what Darius might be doing and if he would come back to her. That's when Sophie found a deck of cards and played solitaire.

She was on her third game and shuffling when she remembered she had downloaded an app on her phone. She set the cards aside and curled up on the couch with her mobile to begin playing.

It took only a few games before she got bored. Sophie moved onto Bubble Witch 2, and played that until she ran out of lives. It was addictive, but she wasn't going to pay good money to buy more lives that would magically appear in ten minutes or so.

She began looking through all the apps on her phone that she never paid attention to and discovered that she had downloaded an e-book reader, and that there was a book there.

Sophie decided to give it a try since it was a romance, and she was suddenly interested in such things. Before she knew it, she was sucked into the book. What made her stop reading was when she put herself in the heroine's place and put Darius in the hero's.

She tossed the book down, staring at it as if it was the Devil incarnate.

"Never again," she whispered.

Wasn't that what she'd told herself? Why didn't it work to remind her not to fall for another man?

Sophie stood and walked around her flat. With nothing else to do, she began to clean. First she dusted. Then she vacuumed before she wiped down all of her cabinets and scrubbed her sink.

When that was done, she made her way into the bathroom and scoured the shower, tub, sink, and toilet. When she finished mopping the bathroom and kitchen, she wiped the back of her hand over her brow and sighed.

The flat might have needed a good scrubbing, but it

reminded her how much she hated to clean. It was easy to ignore when she was rarely in her flat, but having to spend the day looking at everything had gotten to be too much.

That wasn't entirely true. It was thinking about Darius and being bored that prompted her to clean. So the moral was not to be bored.

With that solved, Sophie put away all the cleaning supplies and put away the dry cleaning she'd picked up a few days earlier that was still hanging on the back of her closet door.

She finished putting the last piece away when there was a knock on her door. Sophie stared at it a moment before she walked from her room and hesitantly made her way to it.

She wanted it to be Darius so desperately that her stomach knotted.

"Sophie."

Her knees almost buckled when she heard Darius's voice. She rushed to the door and quickly unlocked it.

The door opened and he yanked her against him. Sophie savored his arms around her. He'd returned, just as he'd said he would. Now she knew for certain he was trustworthy.

When he stepped back, she saw his agitation by the way his jaw clenched and his body was tense. "What is it?"

"I spoke with Ulrik."

"And?" she asked as he walked inside and she closed the door behind him.

Darius turned to her and shrugged. "I didna get much from him."

That was his way of telling her that he wasn't going to divulge what he learned. Sophie tried not to be upset. He'd tell her if it involved her. Wouldn't he?

This was why she didn't get close to people. Because she always second-guessed them. She never believed they could be honest with her, and most times, she was spot-on.

Darius seemed to be the exception to the rule.

"You cleaned," Darius said as he looked around.

It was her turn to shrug. "I was bored."

The lines of strain vanished as he smiled at her. "You need a hobby, doc."

She had a hobby—him. Every time she made love to him, she softened. Almost as if the sturdy walls around her heart were waning. She already trusted him more than she did anyone else.

It never occurred to her that she might trust or think about loving another man again. And yet here she was. The fact she was even thinking of the word *love* was enough to alert her that things were going deeper and faster than she wanted.

"Is the building still being watched?" she asked.

Darius nodded. "It is."

"I don't like being cooped up in here, but I don't like being followed either."

"Then let's go out."

She gaped at him, a smile on her lips. "Are you serious?"

"Ulrik knows I'm with you. I'll still come and go without his men seeing me, but only because I doona want him to know when I'm here and when I'm no'."

"I do need to check on some of my home-based patients."

"Then get dressed, doc," he said.

In less than twenty minutes, she was showered, changed, and standing by the door with her medical bag.

"Do you want me to walk with you?" Darius asked.

She touched his face. "Yes, but I also want to prove to Ulrik that he doesn't scare me."

"Then I'll follow behind his men and make sure nothing happens."

Sophie wasn't sure how she'd gotten so lucky in finding

Darius. Well, really he found her, but she wasn't going to split hairs. The fact was, he was a damn good man. Each time he kept his word, he restored the faith she'd lost in others.

His arms wrapped around her as he pulled her against him for a long, slow kiss that made her burn for him. "Something to keep you warm," he whispered and placed a kiss behind her ear.

She couldn't stop smiling as he helped her into her coat and opened the door for her. As she took the stairs down, Darius found another way out.

When Sophie exited the building, she saw Ulrik's men, but she wasn't frightened. Because Darius was there. And she knew he wasn't going anywhere.

Her first patient was just a short walk away. Sophie buttoned her coat and turned to the right. She glanced at the sky to see that the sun was sinking rapidly and clouds were moving in. The snow that was predicted would likely fall that night.

She wanted to be back in her flat before then and curled in Darius's arms.

Darius jumped from the roof silently. He waited until two of Ulrik's men followed Sophie before he trailed them. One stayed behind to watch the building, but he never saw Darius.

Sophie disappeared around the corner, and Ulrik's men were quick to keep up. Darius hated that Sophie was involved in his war.

That's not what kept him returning to her though. That was all Sophie, from her soft skin and heady kisses to her husky laugh and inquisitive eyes.

He found himself wanting to tell her who he was as soon as she opened the door. After his talk with Ulrik, Darius knew things were only going to get worse. His hope that if he kept his distance from Sophie that it would turn Ulrik's attention away was gone.

Ulrik made his own conclusions, and he was now after Sophie with everything he had. Darius wished he was walking beside her. Even keeping her in sight didn't halt the thread of fear that wound tighter and tighter about his chest.

What would Sophie's reaction be if he told her the truth? Darius wanted to trust Sophie, and he did. Yet he reminded himself that his entire race was on the line. Not from extinction, because that wouldn't happen, but from discovery by the humans.

The video leak of the battle on Dreagan with the Dark Fae was bad enough. From what Thorn told him, helicopters and planes were flying over Dreagan day and night where there used to be a no-fly zone.

Darius didn't know how much longer the Kings could keep their secret from the rest of the world, but he knew that once it was revealed, there would be some mortals who didn't care one way or another.

Some would want to befriend the Kings.

Some would want to hunt them.

Some would want to experiment on them.

Some would want to cage them.

And some would want to annihilate them.

Which group would Sophie fall into? She was a practical person. By her reaction to his tattoo, she wasn't too fond of anything fantastical or paranormal.

He was the epitome of fantastical and paranormal.

And immortal.

Darius peered over the side of a building when he saw her enter a residence. She had her black bag so she was probably making house calls.

But what if she wasn't?

CHAPTER
TWENTY-ONE

Sophie felt better after she visited her fourth and last patient. She kept wanting to look behind her for Darius, but she managed to stop herself.

Despite the chill, or perhaps because of it, she opted to walk home. She paid no attention to the two men following her. It felt so good to trust someone again as she did Darius. How she'd missed it.

The streets of Edinburgh were much different than they had been weeks before. A visitor might look and think everything was normal, but the unexplained deaths, the attacks, and the fighting had affected the residents deeply.

The scars were there for those who knew how to look, and with a city that had seen much war, the wounds were new and still festered.

People were frightened. They still walked the streets, but everyone was more wary and watchful than before. Occasionally she'd pass a group of college-aged kids who were too drunk to realize there were still dangers out there.

Sophie didn't know how she knew that the threat still lurked. It was a feeling she had. As if those responsible for the deaths and destruction had merely hidden for a time. But they would be back.

She held back a shiver as best she could, wishing Darius was beside her. Edinburgh hadn't been prepared for the monsters the first time. Would they be the next?

There were weeks where everyone had red eyes. Sophie thought they were evil looking. Who wanted red eyes? She'd done a search on how to get red contacts, and though she found some, none were as vibrant red as what she saw in the city. It made her almost believe those red eyes were real.

Almost.

Then she reminded herself that she didn't believe in that sort of thing. Red eyes weren't a natural occurrence in humans. There were all sorts of enhancements that a person could get, but so many with red eyes? It had to be contacts.

Thank goodness they were no longer wearing them. Those red eyes gave her the creeps. Like she used to feel as a child when she thought there was a monster beneath her bed.

Sophie felt sorry for those poor people who actually believed in the paranormal. The legends throughout the British Isles were extensive, and it was easy to make them part of daily life. Fortunately, Sophie had never fallen for any sort of fairy tales.

Or she hadn't for long.

Her heels clicked on the sidewalk. Her coat was buttoned tight and her purse was on her shoulder. The black bag in her hand grew heavier as her fingers got colder.

She was a block from her flat when the first flakes of snow began to fall. They were scattered at first, but in a matter of seconds they were coming down so thick and fast they clung to her eyelashes.

Sophie knew the men were still following her, but she

didn't care. All she wanted was to get inside her flat and warm up in bed. With Darius.

All she could think about was Darius. It made her want to laugh and dance in the snow. How free she felt!

She quickened her steps and hurried up to her place. Sophie slammed the door behind her and locked it. Then she set down her keys, purse, and bag and fumbled with numb fingers unbuttoning her coat.

No sooner had she hung up her coat than strong arms came around her. She leaned back against Darius. This she could get used to.

"Thank you," she said.

He turned her around and smiled. "My pleasure, lass."

She shivered and moved closer to him.

"You're frozen," he said with a frown.

"Then warm me up."

He lifted her in his arms and pivoted to walk to the bedroom. "I doona have to be told twice."

In a flurry of hands and fingers, their clothes were removed and they fell into bed, mindless with passion. There was no foreplay, no teasing.

She needed him. As if sensing it, Darius leaned over her, entering her with one thrust.

Sophie sighed, her body eagerly accepting him. This was what she needed. Darius.

In every capacity.

Sophie woke to a grumbling stomach. Food had been the last thing on her mind when she'd returned home. She glanced at the clock beside her bed to see it was just after three in the morning.

She rolled out of bed and grabbed her robe, tying it around her. A glance at Darius showed him asleep, his hair mussed.

It made her smile. She wanted him around, and that terrified her to the very pits of her soul. There was nothing she could do though. He was already a part of her life—and she liked that.

On her way to the kitchen, Sophie looked at her flat. It was sparse. A spray of dried lavender hung near the entrance of the bathroom, but other than that, there were no personal touches to the room.

Granted, it was a bathroom, but she had been in the flat for five years. By now those personal touches should've made their way even into this room.

She walked to the kitchen. It was as impersonal and cold as the bathroom. Sophie turned and looked at the rest of the flat trying to find something that would make it a home and not just a place to live.

Other than the spray of lavender, her white comforter, and her choice of white couches, there was absolutely nothing.

That's how her life had been. Sparse.

But not anymore. Darius brought in color and life. And it was refreshing and glorious.

Sophie paused when she saw an envelope that had been pushed from underneath the door. She picked up the envelope and saw her name written in black marker.

She glanced at the bedroom, but Darius still slept. So she opened the envelope.

To her shock, it was a dinner invitation from Ulrik for the next night. It said nothing more than where to meet and when.

She eyed the phone number at the end of the invitation.

"Sophie?"

She turned at the sound of Darius's voice. His gaze immediately lowered to the envelope as he sat up in bed.

"From Ulrik?" he asked.

She nodded and walked to the bedroom where she handed him the envelope. He read it quickly, anger tightening his face.

"What do we do?" she asked.

Darius took her hand and kissed it. "He's near. I need to follow him."

"Go," she urged.

He rose and dressed. Just before he left out her window, he paused and said, "I'll be back soon."

Darius saw Ulrik check his watch and give a nod to his men watching Sophie before getting into his ice silver McLaren 12C Spider and driving away. He managed to stay even with him moving from roof to roof.

It wasn't until Ulrik's route took him toward The Balmoral Hotel that Darius sent Con a shout through their mental link. Con didn't respond. Darius tried again as Ulrik pulled up alongside the hotel and tossed the keys to a valet.

"*Con!*" Darius tried for a third time. "*I'm following Ulrik. He's at a hotel.*"

When Con still didn't respond, Darius jumped to the ground and strolled across the street to the hotel. He walked into the lobby and glanced around. Ulrik was making his way to the bar area.

He waited for Ulrik to sit at a table before Darius selected a position in the lobby so he could watch him. Darius wondered who could be meeting with Ulrik when a tall figure with blond hair walked straight to Ulrik.

"Con," Darius whispered.

What the hell was going on?

Ulrik smirked at Con who took the chair opposite Ulrik and ordered a drink when a waitress walked up. Con's typical emotionless expression stared back.

If Darius didn't know him so well, he'd think Con didn't

feel anything. Except that Darius saw how straight and tense Con sat.

So this was a meeting—in public. Who wanted it, and who decided to meet here? Was it to keep Con in check? After what Ulrik said earlier about never stating he wanted to fight Con in front of mortals, Darius was having trouble discerning who wanted what.

It should be easy. Ulrik was the villain. Con was the one who kept the Dragon Kings together throughout all the countless centuries.

Good and bad. Bad and good.

Could either one be designated with such basic words? Sure, Con had done questionable things, but all in the name of keeping the Kings secret from the humans.

Ulrik had done detestable, heinous things. But he'd also brought Lily back from the dead for Rhys.

Con's attempt to wreck some of the Kings and their mates caused friction at Dreagan. But Con had moved heaven and earth for them.

Ulrik wanted revenge for being banished. He'd used a Druid—Darcy—in order to do it, and tried to kill her after. It was only Con who managed to keep her alive and heal her.

Good and bad.

Bad and good.

The lines were blurring more each day. Darius feared that one day none of the Kings would be able to look at Con and still believe him to be the good guy. Con's need to protect Dreagan and keep the Kings together while fighting the Dark, Ulrik, and now the mortals was backing him into a corner.

There was only one other time Con had been backed in such a way, and Ulrik's banishment and the binding of his dragon magic had been a result.

What would happen this time?

CHAPTER
TWENTY-TWO

Con set his fingers on his glass of whisky and looked across the table at Ulrik. "You came."

"As if I wouldna."

Dozens of millennia had passed since he'd seen Ulrik other than just in pictures. But his old friend hadn't changed. He still looked as roguish and clever as ever.

Con used to envy Ulrik his easygoing nature, but now all Con wanted was to put an end to Ulrik's reign of terror.

With his black suit jacket open to reveal a deep red shirt, and his black hair long and loose, Ulrik looked as devilish as Con knew him to be.

Ulrik chuckled and took a drink of whisky. He slowly set the glass down, a small smile playing about his mouth. "We can sit all night staring at each other, dreaming of what we'll do when the time comes for us to battle. Or you can spit out whatever it is you want to say."

"Leave Edinburgh."

Ulrik's black brows rose on his forehead. "No' going to happen."

"I can force you."

"You actually think you can. How . . . cute."

Every time Ulrik laughed, it felt like talons flaying Con's back. He was King of Kings. Ulrik needed to be reminded of that. Now.

Just before Con stood and showed Ulrik who was in charge, a woman's laugh from across the room broke into his cloud of fury, reminding him where he was. Muscle by muscle, Con relaxed.

"I bet that was difficult," Ulrik said before taking another drink. "You're the one who wanted a public place. I would've been happy to meet you out in a field somewhere."

"Really?" It was Con's turn to smirk. "I didna think it was good timing with your plans and all."

"At this point, I figure what the hell. It's going to happen one way or another."

"Aye. It is." Con fisted his left hand that was beneath the table. The urge to reach across and punch Ulrik was strong. Very strong.

"Am I late?"

Just when Con didn't think the night could get any worse. He glared to his left where Rhi stood in a slinky burgundy dress that molded to her curves. Her black hair was pulled up in some kind of messy do that looked as if it had been carelessly thrown up. A few waves framed her face, giving her a sensual look that had every eye in the bar drawn to her.

Her silver Fae eyes cut to Con. "Thank you for healing my wound."

"When did you wake?"

She feigned a bright smile and lowered her voice. "You're welcome, Rhi. I was happy to help since you risked your own ass to help us yet again."

"Rhi," Ulrik interrupted as he stood and pulled out her chair.

Con didn't miss the way Ulrik looked at her or how fidgety Rhi became under his gaze. He began to wonder if the two of them were lovers.

As much as Rhi knew about the goings-on at Dreagan, she could be the mole leaking information to Ulrik. Then again, it was Ulrik's magic that had nearly killed her in the last battle.

There was a missing part here. Con could sense it, but he couldn't figure out what it was. He'd suspected it for some time, but now he had confirmation of it.

"You nearly killed Rhi," Con said. "How can you smile at her now as if it never happened?"

Ulrik took his seat once more and waved over a waiter for Rhi's drink order. "Do you really need to ask that?"

"I'm alive," Rhi stated calmly before Con could say anything else. "I have one of you to thank for the wound, and another for the healing. Let's move on."

Con waited until the attendant set a French martini in front of Rhi before he asked, "What are you doing here, Rhi?"

"I called her," Ulrik said. "I thought it only fair we have a mediator. Or at the verra least, someone who can attest to what is said tonight. I know how you . . . twist . . . things to suit you."

Con was growing more irate as the minutes passed. "This was between the two of us."

"No' true. The Keeper of History has knowledge of this, even as we speak. Kellan writes the truth as it happens because he's compelled to."

"Kellan would never try to hide anything. And neither would I."

Ulrik shrugged. "Whatever you say."

Rhi rolled her eyes. "Both of you have tried to injure me. Both of you have tried to recruit me. I help who I want, when I want. Just think of me as Switzerland."

"I can do that," Ulrik stated.

Con bowed his head in agreement when Rhi looked his way.

"Great. Then get on with it," she said as she leaned back in her chair with her drink.

Con and Ulrik stared at each other in silence for several minutes. Rhi's gaze was either on her drink or looking around the room.

"Why did you want this meeting?" Ulrik asked again.

Con drew in a deep breath and slowly released it. "You used to be honorable."

"And you used to be a good guy."

"You used to think of others."

"You used to have my back," Ulrik said. "We can do this all night."

Con tried another tack. "You want to take out your vengeance on me. Then focus. *On me.*"

"Oh, I am focused. You're usually much sharper than this. Is it the bad fortune that's now hovering over Dreagan?"

"Leave the Kings and humans out of our war."

Ulrik's smile was cold and furious. "Did you leave them out when you killed her? Did you leave them out when you bound my magic and banished me?"

"You left me no choice."

"You always had a choice," Ulrik said with a sneer. "You made the wrong ones, and now you'll pay for it. All of you."

Whether Ulrik wanted to or not, he'd let a bit of his plan slip. "What's your endgame? You want your revenge. Let's say you get it and become King of Kings. Will you forgive the others? Or will you kill them as well?"

"Does it really matter? If I win, you'll be dead and unable to do anything. If you win, I'll be dead and nothing changes."

"Leave the Kings alone."

Ulrik sat forward in his chair to lean both forearms on the table. His was smiling, but there was no humor in his gaze. "I hurt them, and it in turn hurts you. Have you no' figured it out yet, *old friend*? I'm going to rip your world apart bit by bit. I'm going to take away everything you hold dear and count on, everything you look to in order to get through each day until there is nothing left."

Con had suspected as much.

"I want nothing more than for you to walk this world for millennia in human form, unable to shift, as I did. But I'm no' that stupid as to leave you alive. I'm going to sever your head from your body and take the position I should've taken from you long ago," Ulrik said in a low tone.

Con shook his head in a slow motion. "I ordered you to fight me when I claimed the position. You were too afraid."

At this, Ulrik let out a loud laugh that had everyone in the bar area turning to them. Con remained where he was, his gaze never leaving Ulrik.

When Ulrik quit laughing, he ran a hand over his mouth and pinned Con with a look. "I find it amusing how you remember things. I wasna afraid of fighting you. I was afraid of *beating* you, you insufferable, conceited bastard. I didna want to be King of Kings, but you so feared I'd change my mind that you tried to order me to challenge you. Tell me, Constantine, who was afraid of what?"

There was no sense in answering. No matter what Con said, Ulrik would never admit that he was wrong and Con was right. "I learned long ago it doesna pay to argue with a madman."

"Madman?" Ulrik said, looking amused. "When this is all over, we'll see who the real madman is. If all you wanted was to tell me to stay away from the Kings, then you've wasted your time and allowed me to know that you care about them so much you'll set up a meeting with me."

He rose to leave, but Con wasn't finished. He asked, "If you wanted to hurt them, why did you save Lily?"

That stopped Ulrik in his tracks. He swung his gaze back to Con and snorted. "You think I saved her? Do you honestly believe that a life with a Dragon King is better than death?"

"I think you didna want Rhys to suffer as you did."

Ulrik's silver gaze hardened. "Doona pretend to understand what I endured. I know better than anyone that there is no soul mate out there for us. Humans and dragons were no' meant to be together. The mortals who mated with the Kings will learn soon enough how long the years become. What will you do, Con, when the mates begin to go insane from the endlessness of time?"

It was a question Con had been asking himself from the moment Hal took Cassie as his mate, and again each time a King found love.

He had no doubt the Kings loved. But the humans? Did they love like a Dragon King? The mortals proved time and again that they married and loved as easily as they divorced and cheated. Few took vows seriously, and he feared that all of his Dragon Kings who mated would discover that for themselves.

"Ah," Ulrik said as he put his hands on the table and leaned forward. "You'll do what you do best, will you no'? You'll kill the mates, saving the Kings from having to do it themselves."

Con lifted his chin. "I always do the difficult tasks."

"Nay. You take the easy way out. You did it with me, and you've done it with the others at Dreagan. You allow them to mate the humans, knowing what's ahead. Instead of telling them what could happen, you hope for the best and prepare for the worst."

"I'm a King."

"You're shit on the bottom of a shoe," Ulrik said

contemptuously. "A real leader would've told them the truth. A true leader would've forbid the mating until the mortals had been with the Kings for several years to understand what life was like."

Con wasn't going to justify his actions to anyone, least of all Ulrik. Con had his reasons for the decisions he made, and in the end, he'd be the one to answer for all of them—good and bad.

"And what of Rhi?" Ulrik asked.

Con ground his teeth together. Why did Ulrik have to bring her into it? It was bad enough she was at the table listening to their conversation, her gaze moving between the two of them.

"Nope, handsome," Rhi told Ulrik as she finished her drink and set it on the table. "Leave me out of it. I can handle my own with Con. I don't need you fighting my battles for me."

As if he hadn't heard her, Ulrik ask, "Did you know he was in Balladyn's dungeon? He saw you chained and looking like death, but he didna release you."

Rhi's gaze narrowed on Con as she smiled tightly. "That's not surprising."

Ulrik straightened and buttoned his suit jacket. Without another word he walked away.

Con waited until Ulrik was out of earshot before he looked at Rhi. "Why did you answer his summons?"

"Summons?" she repeated with a laugh that held a heavy dose of sarcasm. "You have so much to learn about me if you think I can be *summoned*."

"That's right. You only answer certain people at certain times."

She looked away, a flash of pain on her face. Con wanted to hurt her, and he had. It should make him feel better. Then again, Ulrik always brought out the worst in him.

"Ulrik wanted the conversation on record," Rhi said.

"I thought it was a good idea. It doesn't matter who wins between the two of you, now the Kings will know what happened here."

"And you'll be willing to state the truth?" he asked doubtfully.

Rhi uncrossed her legs and gave him a smile. "I don't do it for you or Ulrik. I do it for the other Kings who are my friends."

"He was wrong, by the way. I was coming to help you in the dungeon."

Rhi pushed back her chair from the table. "I know you want nothing more than to never see me again. Perhaps you'll get your wish one day."

As she walked away Con tossed back his whisky. None of this had gone as he intended. It felt as if everything and everyone now stood against him.

But then again, Con had always been alone—standing against evil and those who would hurt the Kings.

He rose, intending to return to his suite. Except when he looked up Darius stood before him.

CHAPTER
TWENTY-THREE

Darius didn't know what to say at first. To watch Ulrik, Con, and Rhi all sit at a table and talk without anyone getting killed seemed almost surreal.

"Darius," Con said and resumed his seat. He motioned to one of the other chairs. "I didna know you were here."

"I called to you." Darius took the chair Ulrik vacated and pushed aside the empty glass. Darius shook his head when a waiter began to walk up.

Con nodded as if he just now remembered. "I was focused on my meeting."

"And if it had been important?" Darius asked. "Say, that the Dark surround the hotel?"

Con's black gaze grew cold. "I would've handled it."

"You ignored me when I was trying to tell you I was tracking Ulrik."

Con blew out a breath. "The simple truth is that I didna want anyone to know I was meeting with Ulrik. I wanted to talk him out of coming after all of you and focus on me."

That sounded exactly like something Con would do. Darius looked around the room at all the mortals going about their everyday, mundane lives. "He's no' going to do that."

"Nay, he's no'. He knows by hurting all of you, it upsets me. He wants to rip away my world."

Darius rubbed his eyes with his thumb and forefinger. "That means Dreagan."

"Aye. I ken."

He lifted his head and looked at Con. "What are we going to do?"

"Prepare. We're dragons, Darius. They can no' kill us. We've hidden for so long and gotten away with our secret. But," he said, pausing for a heartbeat. "We may be heading to a time where we can no longer hide."

"We'll never be able to leave Dreagan. We'll have to remain and keep others out."

Con shrugged and lifted his empty glass to the waitress for another. "We do what we must. The Dark have outed us. Some of the humans doona believe the video, but others do."

"Those that want proof."

Con gave a nod to the attendant when a new glass of whisky was set in front of him. Once she was gone, he said, "We might as well get used to the attention, but I'm beginning to think we look beyond that."

Darius, like the rest of the Kings, had been so wrapped up in not being able to shift and fly that they nearly missed the obvious. "Ulrik wants our attention diverted."

"Precisely. I wanted a face-to-face with him to see if he'd divulge anything."

"Did he?"

Con's lips twisted. "Of course no'. But what he didna say was almost as good. I wasna able to get him to leave all of you alone, but we did learn this part."

"That gives us an edge. It's only a wee bit, but it's still an edge."

"My thoughts exactly."

Darius eyed Con. "And what was Rhi doing here?"

"Ulrik asked her to come as a mediator of sorts. She listened and will be able to call either one of us a liar if we say something that isna true."

Darius ran a hand through his hair. "That could benefit us."

Con merely made a sound at the back of his throat.

"You shouldna have been here alone. You should've let me know what was happening."

"I'm King of Kings. I doona need a babysitter," Con stated.

Darius blew out a breath, his thoughts turning back to Sophie.

"What is it?" Con asked.

Darius sat back in his chair. "Ulrik sent Sophie a letter tonight asking her to dinner tomorrow."

"He wants her alone."

"I think so. He went to the hospital today looking for her, but she wasna there."

Con nodded, a frown forming. "Ulrik most likely wants to see if you'll show up, but his target is still Sophie."

"He wants to hurt her as he has tried with the others."

"And nearly succeeded with Darcy."

"Why do that after saving Lily?" It was the subtle tightening in Con's shoulders that told Darius something was wrong. "We all know he was the one who saved her."

Con waved away his words. "Ulrik's behavior suggests that he's lost his mind."

"No' the man I spoke with today or the day before. What are you no' telling me?"

"Nothing," Con said. "Let's get back to the letter. Are you going to send Sophie?"

Darius shook his head. "I'll no' use her as bait. It could backfire. I'll no' take that chance."

"We might find out something useful."

"No' going to happen," Darius stated with finality. He wasn't going to put Sophie's life in any more jeopardy than it already was.

"She could learn something that saves us."

"Most likely he'll either kill her or turn her. Whatever information we find we do it ourselves either by over-hearing something or by Ryder doing his magic with the computers."

"Tell me about Sophie," Con commanded.

Darius lifted a shoulder. "She was hurt years ago. I suspect it happened when she still lived in London. She doesna date, and she has only one friend that I know of."

"She keeps people at a distance."

He looked up at Con. "Aye."

"Much like you."

"I keep humans at arm's length, and you know why."

Con cocked his head to the side. "All of this can easily be discovered. All we need to do is have Ryder dig into Sophie's past."

"Nay." Darius was surprised at the vehemence with which the word flew from his mouth.

Con raised a brow. "Why?"

"There's no need. I doona require her history."

"Maybe no', but it makes things easier."

"Nay."

Con held up both his hands. "If you're no' going to send her to the dinner, then what?"

"I'm going to go."

"He willna be happy. He could take it out on Sophie somehow," Con cautioned.

Darius smiled tightly. "He can try."

"Ulrik likes to think he's in charge. Give him that," Con said with a grin. "At least for the time being."

* * *

Rhi was walking down the streets of Edinburgh with her mute—and veiled—watcher following her yet again.

"This is getting old," she said aloud. "I know you're there."

Silence. She should've guessed.

"Why don't you just tell me what you want? If you're spying for Usaeil, she can kiss my perfect ass, because I'm not going back to the Queen's Guard."

More silence.

She halted and turned around. Though she couldn't pinpoint exactly where he was, she felt his gaze and knew he was behind her. "When I was a child, I didn't like my brother following me around to keep me out of mischief, and I assure you that I'm becoming furious with it now. Reveal yourself and tell me what you want, or go away. The next time, I won't be so nice."

Still nothing.

With a roll of her eyes, Rhi teleported away.

Daire didn't follow Rhi immediately. He dropped his veil as Cael stepped from the nearby shadows. Daire watched the leader of the Reapers and raised a brow.

Cael shot him a look of interest. Then asked in the Irish accent all Fae had, "Have you spoken with her?"

"You know I haven't," Daire answered. "I watch, which is what Death ordered me to do."

Cael gave a nod of acceptance. "Rhi is as strong as Death suspected."

"When is Death ever wrong?"

"Never."

"Then why do you sound surprised?" Daire asked curiously. Every Reaper followed the orders of Death—or died. It was that simple.

Every Reaper was chosen specifically by Death. The

seven of them brought something unique to the group that was judge, jury, and executioner of the Fae.

"Rhi could be trouble," Cael finally answered.

Daire flattened his lips as he recalled her with Balladyn. "More than you know."

"She's been with that Dark Fae again."

"He wants her. And she . . ." Daire trailed off, unsure of how to put into words what he now knew about Rhi.

Though he'd never tell her or anyone else, he felt sorry for her. She'd been gravely wronged by her Dragon King lover. Despite that she'd continued to love him throughout the centuries, waiting for him to return to her.

But he never would.

Daire wondered if Rhi finally realized that herself. Perhaps that's why she was turning more and more to Balladyn. And Daire couldn't blame her.

A person needing love and desire would find it anywhere they could. Balladyn was giving Rhi exactly what she needed, and Balladyn knew it. The Dark Fae had waited patiently for Rhi. He wasn't waiting anymore.

"Daire?" Cael called his name.

Daire looked into Cael's silver eyes. "I applaud Balladyn for having the balls to go after Rhi."

"You know what'll happen if they get together?" Cael asked in a voice filled with shock. "Rhi will turn Dark."

"You don't know that. None of us do. She could return him to a Light Fae."

"If their love is true," Cael pointed out.

That was the catch. True love. Some scoffed at the idea, but it was out there. Most humans settled for the first person that came into their lives that they could see themselves with. Others didn't know true love was standing right before them and kept looking.

"Point taken," Daire admitted.

Cael ran a hand through his long black hair. "Stay with her. I don't know what Death has in store for Rhi, but it's important."

"And if she goes off with Balladyn?"

Cael's silver eyes narrowed. "Let's hope that doesn't happen. Though I can't be certain, I've a feeling that if Rhi does, it'll change things drastically."

"She will. Eventually."

"Let's hope it's not today."

Daire veiled himself as soon as Cael teleported away. It didn't take Daire long to find Rhi. She was back on her island standing shin-deep in the turquoise water.

Her arms were crossed with her long black hair lifting in the breeze. She wore a gray bikini that barely covered her shapely ass.

That was twice now she'd worn a color other than black. Daire began to wonder if she was shaking off the darkness that surrounded her.

He saw it because when Rhi was alone she no longer tried to hide it. The darkness was growing, slowly, but growing nonetheless. Even now it surrounded her like a haze.

But this time it seemed . . . dimmed.

Daire moved to stand next to a tree. He hadn't been happy about his assignment at first. Who wanted to follow a sassy Light around instead of battling the Dark with the rest of the Reapers?

Death had chosen him, however. The more Daire was around Rhi, the more he saw glimpses of greatness. It came naturally for Rhi to take charge, but she fought it. She didn't want the responsibility.

Just as Ulrik hadn't wanted it with the Dragon Kings. Ulrik was regretting that decision now. Would Rhi?

Suddenly the haze vanished—as did Rhi's bikini. Rhi

slowly turned and faced him. Daire's breath locked in his lungs when he took in the sight before him.

"If you're going to watch, I figure you should get to see all of me," Rhi said.

Damn his body, but it responded to her.

"Come on, stud. Don't you want this?" she asked in a husky tone and held out her arms, her breasts out.

He was Fae, of course he wanted it. Desperately. But he was to watch and only watch.

"Or do you get off on spying? What about with Balladyn?"

No, Daire definitely didn't like seeing her with Balladyn and the way the Dark held her possessively.

She walked out of the water to stand in front of him. "I'm offering myself to you. All you have to do is drop the veil."

Daire looked away from her splendidly made body and took two steps back. Somehow she always knew he was there—and where he was. She shouldn't be able to do that.

"I could kill you right now."

She could try, but Daire wasn't that easy to kill. Something Rhi would most likely find out soon enough. She was getting angry with him following her, and she was obstinate enough to try and skewer him.

Daire was actually looking forward to it.

CHAPTER
TWENTY-FOUR

Sophie blew out a breath as she turned one way then the other in front of the mirror. The black dress was one of her favorites. Anytime she wore it, she felt sexy.

And she needed something to bolster her courage.

Her hair was down and pulled over one shoulder. Sophie wore only a pair of gold chandelier earrings, a gold ring, and a set of gold bangle bracelets.

She glanced down at her black stilettos with the heel in gold and gave a nod of approval. Understated, but sophisticated. A perfect combination for meeting with a man like Ulrik.

Sophie was nervous. And not just because she was going to meet Ulrik, but because she had yet to tell Darius. When he'd returned the night before, he was the one to send the response from her phone to Ulrik.

Then there had been no talking with all the kissing and touching. After they'd made love, she'd fallen asleep in his arms.

Waking up next to him was only making it easier to allow the feelings for him to grow. She closed her eyes.

Who was she kidding? They weren't growing. They were there—full blown and glorious.

And it scared the hell out of her.

The last time she'd opened herself in such a way had been the worst time in her life. Darius showed her time and again that he was trustworthy and a man of his word. But he was embroiled in something dangerous.

She was about to put herself in the line of fire without even knowing the secrets Darius kept. That proved how she'd come to care for him.

Even with all the intrigue, secrets, and peril, Sophie wanted a life with him. She wanted to have friends again, to decorate her house, to cook, to have dinner parties.

She wanted to be a part of something important.

She needed it.

In a short amount of time Darius managed to get closer than anyone had in seven years. What was it about him? Why didn't she turn her back on him as she did others? Why did she keep seeking him out?

He had a past, but it didn't define him as hers and Ulrik's did. No, whatever had happened to Darius left him shuttered and aloof.

But he still sought out others because he had no other choice. The complete opposite of her.

"*I'm no' a good man.*"

Even now replaying his words in her head made her wish to know more about him.

He didn't think he was a good man, but he was. Why, then, did he think he wasn't? She was curious to know the reason. Though she might never discover the truth.

Sophie opened her eyes to the mirror and saw Darius standing behind her. She whirled around, a smile in place. He opened his arms and held her close as he kissed her.

"You look stunning," he murmured. "Going somewhere?"

She took a deep breath. "To meet Ulrik."

"Nay."

Definitive. Authoritative. She normally detested men like that, but Darius wasn't doing it to control her. He was doing it to protect her. Sophie recognized that and it made her smile.

"You grin?" he asked in confusion.

Sophie gazed up at him and nodded. "Because I know why you don't want me to do it."

"Aye. You'll no' get anywhere near that bastard."

"But I have to," she insisted.

Darius dropped his arms and stepped away from her, raking his hand through his hair. "No."

"Yes." She walked to stand in front of him. "You know it's the right thing to do. I can get information from him."

"What you'll be doing is playing right into his hands. He knows you'll be there as bait."

Now she hadn't thought about that.

"I know him," Darius continued. "He's smart, Sophie. Smarter than even you. He's thought all of this through, in every conceivable scenario, and he's going to make sure he has the advantage."

She swallowed, more nervous now than before. "Even in a crowded restaurant?"

"Even there. It's too dangerous." He tugged her back into his arms. "But I appreciate you wanting to help."

Sophie rested her head against his chest and soaked in his warmth and strength. "He wanted me, so I thought it would be the right move."

"No' this time, lass," he whispered and kissed her temple. "No' with you."

Never had Sophie ever felt so cherished, wanted, or needed than she did in that moment. She wished they could stay just as they were, without interference from the outside world or anyone.

Then it suddenly hit her. She raised her head to look at him. "You're going to talk to Ulrik."

Darius looked down at her with his deep brown eyes and slid his fingers in her hair. "I am."

"I can't lose you."

He silenced her with a kiss. "That willna happen. I promise."

"Everyone dies. What if you get injured? Let me be there so I can reach you quickly in case something happens," she urged.

He was so calm about their speaking of him getting injured. That either meant it happened often, or he wasn't afraid. Since she knew every inch of his body, she knew there were no wounds from knives or bullets.

That was odd for someone in his kind of work. In fact, there wasn't a single scar anywhere on his skin. Everyone had scars.

"You're not afraid of being hurt," Sophie said.

He shook his head. "Doona do this. No' now."

"Why? What aren't you telling me?"

"We both have secrets, Sophie."

"That's true." And maybe it was time she came clean with hers. "But I don't want there to be any more secrets between us."

"Sophie," he began.

But she stopped him by saying, "I was engaged once."

Darius couldn't have uttered another sound had his life depended on it. Of all the things he'd thought Sophie might be hiding, that wasn't it.

He let her go when she walked out of his arms to the sofa. She sat on the edge of the cushion and stared out her window, seemingly weighted down by the past.

Darius ached for her, because he knew how that felt all too well.

"You never asked about my past. Did you find out as Ulrik did?"

"Nay."

She looked down at her hands clasped in her lap. "In the seven years I've been in Edinburgh, I've told exactly one person my story."

"Claire," Darius guessed.

"I didn't want to be friends with Claire, but she was relentless," she said with a laugh. "I had no choice where she was concerned. It's sad, isn't it, that I only have one friend? Seven years, and I don't even know my neighbors."

He walked around the sofa and sat beside her. "You have a life and a verra important career. You're a healer, Sophie. Every day people put their lives in your hands. So what if you doona know your neighbors."

"Yeah," she murmured. Then she turned her head to him. "I was in a relationship for ten years with another doctor. We were engaged and living together.

"I was in love with him. He made me laugh every day, and everyone liked him. He was the life of the party. We did everything together, spent every minute as one. Or so I thought."

When she paused, Darius knew she was going back through her memories. It killed him to know she'd suffered so, because he'd already guessed what she hadn't yet said.

"There was a new doctor Scott was helping out," Sophie continued. "She was nice. I liked her. Not that I spent much time with her. What I didn't know was that they began having an affair months earlier. All those texts from work were actually from her."

"The ultimate betrayal," Darius murmured.

"To give someone your love, devotion, trust, and your soul only to have them trample on it as if it meant nothing. That was awful, but it didn't stop there. He shagged her in our bed and took pictures. They made me out for a fool, and I never expected any of it."

The solid, beautiful doctor was vulnerable, and he hated seeing her like that. Darius wanted to avenge her in some way. Because no one should have to suffer from such a fate. "Shall I kill him?"

Sophie smiled softly. "Had I known you a few years ago, I might've asked you to rough him up, but now . . . I just want to forget all of it. I don't care about Scott or what he's doing."

He reached over and placed his hand atop hers. "He was an idiot to let you go."

"I kept what Scott did close to keep it from ever happening again. I expected to live my life alone. Then you walked out of the shadows."

Darius felt his blood heat when he saw the desire in her eyes. Did the woman not know what she did to him? Surely by now she had to, and perhaps that was the point. "For you."

She threaded her fingers with his. "I think that's why I understand Ulrik's need for revenge, because I got mine."

Darius's brows rose. "How?"

"I convinced another doctor to get Scott's lover to have sex with him in his car. I was snapping photos of all of it, which I promptly sent to Scott. Their relationship blew up spectacularly all over the hospital."

"Did your retribution feel good?"

"For a time. Then I felt slimy for setting it up. It would've eventually happened. Once a cheater always a cheater, right?"

"You just facilitated things," Darius said.

She chuckled wryly. "He tried to come back to me about a year later. It felt so good to tell him to kiss off and slam the door in his face. I've been broken for a long time, but I didn't realize it until quite recently. Until you."

"I'm sorry you had to endure such a thing. You didna deserve that."

"Does anyone?" she asked.

"Nay."

Her olive gaze searched his. "Where does that leave us? Whatever it is that we are."

Darius wanted to be with her—craved it actually. But he'd already been down that road. He'd already lost his mate. "I'm no' sure."

"All right."

She began to pull her hand away, but Darius stopped her. There was a question in her eyes—and there was hope.

He let his gaze roam over the lace of the dress that covered her arms just past her elbows and from her neck down to her breasts, showing just enough of their swells to make his cock twitch with longing.

Her flame red hair was vibrant against the black, beckoning him to take a fistful of it and hold her steady while he kissed her.

"I've kept my secret from you to keep you safe," he said.

"I want to know. All of it."

"I doona think you do."

She shifted so she faced him fully. "I've seen all kinds of trauma in the hospital. I can handle whatever it is you're trying to protect me from."

Darius wasn't so sure. Then again, he'd known all along she would learn who he was. Perhaps it was time. It would also keep her away from Ulrik, which was exactly what needed to happen.

It would be neigh impossible to convince her of the Dragon Kings and Fae without proof. Sophie was practical. She'd already admitted she didn't believe in any kind of fantasy things like dragons.

How would a complete nonbeliever in such things

react when she saw one? It wouldn't be good, of that Darius was certain.

"I can take it," Sophie said with a firm nod.

Darius rubbed his jaw, trying to think where to start. How did he tell someone he was immortal and had been around since the beginning of time?

"I doona work for the government," he stated. "The group I speak of is all I have left. They're my family, my home."

"All right," she said with a nod.

Darius rose and paced slowly. He glanced at Sophie to find her watching him closely. "There's no other way to say it than to just say it."

"So spit it out."

He halted and faced her. "My dragon tat isna there because I chose it. It's there because it's what I am."

She gazed at him silently for a moment before she said, "I don't understand."

"I'm a Dragon King, Sophie."

"Okay," she said, drawing out the last syllable. "Is that some kind of gang or something?"

Darius wished Con or someone else were here to explain it to her, because he was mucking it up badly. "Let me start at the beginning. This realm formed when time began, and with time came dragons."

"Realm?" she repeated with a small frown.

He was losing her, he could tell. But he had to finish. "There were millions of us. Every size and all colors. It wasna just birds in the sky, but dragons as well. We were divided by colors, and within each faction was a leader—a king. The most powerful of the kings became King of Kings."

Sophie barely batted an eye as she listened.

"For eons we lived here and ruled this planet. Then one day, humans were here. Suddenly each of the Dragon

Kings shifted into the form of a mortal. That's how we were able to communicate with them."

"So you became a human?"

"We were able to shift at will." Darius sat on the arm of the sofa. "We moved dragons out of territories so the mortals would have somewhere to live. Tensions were always high, but we managed it and kept the peace. Some of us Kings even took humans as lovers. Ulrik was such a King."

Sophie's eyes widened, but she didn't speak.

"He was going to take her as his mate. It's a ceremony in which the mortal would then become immortal, living as long as her King did. But it wasna to be."

Darius squeezed the bridge of his nose. "Con, the King of Kings, discovered Ulrik's woman was going to attempt to kill him. It was a foolish plan, because the only thing that can kill a Dragon King is another Dragon King. But she didna know that. All she wanted to do was instigate a war.

"Con sent Ulrik away on some mission. While he was gone, we cornered the woman and killed her. When Ulrik returned he was furious. With her, with us. With the world. He turned that hate to the humans."

"What did Ulrik do?" Sophie asked in a soft voice.

"He started a war. Mortals killed dragons, and dragons killed mortals. When the humans came, each King vowed to protect them. We had to stop Ulrik, except he wouldna listen to reason. Nothing we said made a dent in his anger. The dragons had magic, and we were stronger. We could've won the war with the mortals, but it was our vow that prevented us from joining Ulrik.

"To help put an end to the war, we sent our dragons away. We all thought it would be for a short time, just until the mortals calmed down. Four of Ulrik's Silvers wouldna leave his side. We captured them and put them into a magical sleep. Then we went after Ulrik."

Darius dropped his chin to his chest and closed his eyes. "We stripped him of his magic, preventing him from shifting into a dragon so that he was destined to walk the world as the very thing he hated."

"A human."

He nodded, not looking at Sophie. "We banished him from Dreagan. Afterward, we all went to our mountains and slept away centuries, waiting for a time when we passed into myth. After a few hundred years, we awoke and took our places beside you. We hide our true selves, only taking to the skies during the night. Or at least we used to. All that has changed with Ulrik's revenge and his allegiance with another group."

Silence met him. After a while, Darius lifted his head and found Sophie staring at him. Her face was ashen, her eyes glazed over.

"I ken it's a lot to take in, but it's all true. I've never lied to you. And I never will."

"That story is preposterous," she said. Then she closed her eyes and shook her head as she turned away. "I trust you, and you haven't lied to me. I don't want to believe any of this. It doesn't make sense." She looked at him then. "Can you show me?"

"If I shifted now, I'd destroy your flat. But there is something I can do. If you'll allow."

She gave a quick nod. Darius moved to sit beside her, then he took her hands in his. As he held her gaze, he thought of the time before humans, a time of dragons. Then he pushed that thought into Sophie's mind with his dragon magic.

Sophie wanted to believe Darius, but how could she? Everyone knew dragons weren't real. If there were dragons, someone somewhere would've seen something. Nothing could be hidden in this technological age. Nothing.

She felt something push against her mind while she gazed into Darius's chocolate eyes. Then it was there, the memory playing in her head as if it were her own.

Dragons. Thousands of dragons. There were massive ones flying in the sky. Tiny ones who built their homes in the sides of cliffs, and even ones who called the oceans home. Just as he'd said, they were every size, every color. And they were beautifully magnificent.

The memory faded away. Sophie blinked, looking at Darius anew. "That was you?"

"With my dragon magic."

Magic? Was she really going to believe in that and dragons?

"Now do you understand why I didna want to tell you?" Darius asked.

Sophie took a deep breath. "I do."

"That's who I am." He hesitated, swallowing. "But it isna my past. I was also going to take a mate."

Those few words hurt Sophie more than she'd thought possible. That's how she knew she'd fallen head over heels for Darius.

"We doona carry diseases, but we can impregnate a mortal. There is something incompatible between our two species. Most of the women miscarry within weeks. But each month that passed, her belly grew. I held out hope my child would be the exception to the rule."

Sophie tried to swallow, but her mouth was too dry. She held Darius's hands tighter.

"She went into labor. Every Dragon King held his breath to see if the bairn would live. A few women managed to carry the infants to term, but all of them were stillborn. My child was strong. He was going to beat the odds."

Tears gathered in Sophie's eyes, but she refused to let them spill.

"There was a problem with the birth," Darius continued, his voice flat. "There was so verra much blood. We tried to help her, but nothing worked. Con could've healed her. He would've. If he'd been there. She was so weak she could barely birth our child. She died as he came into the world."

Sophie felt a tear drop onto her cheek. Darius's chest expanded before he released a breath, sadness filling his gaze.

"My son followed her a few minutes later. I lost them both in one night."

There were no words to heal the wounds inside Darius, and Sophie didn't even try. She wrapped her arms around his neck and simply held him. The way his arms tightened about her, almost crushing her, told her how much he was hurting.

And she hurt with him.

CHAPTER
TWENTY-FIVE

Darius stood on the roof and stared at the Portuguese restaurant that Ulrik had recently entered. His emotions were still raw from his talk with Sophie. The rage roiling inside him at Ulrik's attempt to get her alone overflowed.

The stone crumbled beneath Darius's hands. He released his hold and leaned back from the edge of the roof. His emotions needed to be brought under control if he was going to proceed with his plan.

It wasn't easy when all he wanted to do was race back to Sophie and make love to her. What was wrong with him? Was it because he'd shared his past? Surely not.

It was one thing to slake his lust with her willing body. It was quite another when he craved her to such a degree that he was willing to do anything to have her in his arms.

Darius didn't want to imagine how this night might have gone had he and Sophie not trusted each other. She could be here instead of him—and maybe not as bait. Ulrik was persuasive. He might've talked her into joining him.

That made Darius extremely thankful. It also reminded

him that it was time for him to get down there and confront Ulrik.

He jumped silently from the roof to an alley. He bypassed
Ulrik's men—who were entirely too overconfident—and
snuck close to the restaurant.

There was a grunt then the sound of someone hitting
the ground. Darius turned, only to find Con walking
toward him.

"Did you just knock out one of Ulrik's men?" Darius
asked.

Con smiled brightly. "I may have knocked all six unconscious. Including the MI5 agents following me."

Darius had to chuckle. "You didna save one of Ulrik's
men for me?"

"You're the one who walked right past them."

That had Darius narrowing his eyes on Con. "How long
have you been here?"

"Awhile."

"How did you know the restaurant?"

Con shrugged, his jacket opening to reveal the blue
shirt beneath. None of them got cold, but in order not to
draw interest, the Kings wore coats in the winter. Sometimes.

"I found you earlier," Con said. "I said your name, but
you didna hear me. I gather the building you snuck out of
is the doc's?"

"Ballocks."

"You were focused on Sophie."

Darius sighed. "She wanted to use herself as bait.
I talked her out of it."

"And?" Con pressed.

"She shared her past."

Con's lips pinched. "I gather you shared yours. Did you
also share our secret?"

"Aye." Darius wasn't going to apologize for it. He'd made a decision, and he'd stand by it.

"So. She's your mate."

That took Darius aback. "I've already had my mate. And lost her before the mating ceremony."

"Are you sure?"

Darius had known Con would try this tactic. "Am I sure I've already had my mate? Aye."

"You're going to great lengths to protect Sophie. Makes me wonder if she isna your mate," Con argued.

"I'm concerned Ulrik will try to harm another innocent." But that wasn't all, and he knew it. Con was asking if Sophie might be his mate when he himself had had that same thought a fleeting time or two.

Con's gaze shifted through the window to where Ulrik sat behind the curtain. "What's your plan?"

"He thinks Sophie is coming."

Con cut him a look. "He has her watched. He knows she's no'."

"It doesna matter."

"You should've let her come."

Darius gave Con a dark glare. "He'll have been expecting her to be used as bait."

"You're saying we can no' outwit him?"

"I'm saying he's way ahead of us. He's been planning this a verra long time, as is evident in every move he makes. Even when we try to change the game, he manages to stay ahead."

Con stared at Ulrik for a long time in silence. "We must win this war. And sometimes innocents must be sacrificed for the others to win."

Darius was flabbergasted. "You can no' be serious. You want to willingly put Sophie in his trap? A woman who helped us when we needed it?"

"She isna the first innocent, and she willna be the last." Con glanced at him once more. "Go to Dreagan."

"Nay."

Con's head slowly turned to him. "I thought you said she wasna your mate. Why are you fighting so hard for her?"

"I'm no'." Darius shook his head as he laughed. "We made a vow, remember? That same promise sent our dragons away and had us hiding for centuries. You now want to disregard that?"

"No' at all."

Darius seriously considered punching him. "You're testing my patience."

"I wanted to see your reaction. I agree with your assessment of the situation. Find out what you can from Ulrik and report back. I'll keep an eye on Sophie in the meantime," he said and then turned on his heel and walked away.

Darius frowned after him. Would the night get any weirder? At this point he was having a difficult time determining which way was up.

But there was one thing he did know, and that was that Ulrik needed to be stopped.

CHAPTER
TWENTY-SIX

Darius walked into the dimly lit restaurant. Within moments, he was taken to the back where sheer curtains divided the table from the main dining area.

The curtain was pulled to one side by the maître d'. Ulrik stood, meeting his gaze. Darius noted Ulrik didn't seem surprised to find him there.

Darius pulled out his chair and eyed Ulrik in his black suit and light gold dress shirt that made his eyes stand out. A black tie that looked to have some kind of small gold design on it finished it off.

His hair was pulled back in a queue, and those gold eyes were directed squarely at him.

"Darius," he said in his smooth voice as he resumed his seat. "How . . . unsurprising."

Darius grabbed the bottle of red wine from the bucket and poured himself a glass. "Let's dispense with all the threats and declarations. Why no' just tell me why you willna leave Dr. Martin alone?"

"Because you've no' left her alone."

He sat back, his wineglass in hand as he observed

Ulrik. "Do you really expect me to believe that you'd have left her alone if I'd departed the city?"

"Of course no'."

"She's a healer, Ulrik. All she did was help Thorn and Lexi."

Ulrik's smile was slow. "You've always been choosy about your females. The doctor is a good choice. Brilliant, beautiful, and stalwart."

"Your point?"

"She's important to you."

Darius was going to have to tread carefully. "I'm here because I'm the one in Edinburgh."

At this Ulrik made a sound. "So is Con. He could've come in your place. But instead it's you."

"Con is dealing with something else. You two have already had your discussion."

"So have you and I. Why repeat it?"

Darius set down his untouched wine on the table. "You want to come after me, then do it. Stop using others."

"Tell me, Darius. Did you enjoy telling Rhi that it was over between her and—"

"Stop," he said over Ulrik. "You're no' going to rile me."

Ulrik's smile widened. "I already have."

How satisfying it would be if Darius shifted and torched the entire restaurant, reminding Ulrik that he was still trapped in his human form.

That might've happened hundreds of years ago, but not now. Especially with the video leaked of them. Darius had no choice but to remain as a human and deal with Ulrik without causing a scene.

Difficult considering Darius wanted to cause a very big scene.

"Nothing to say?" Ulrik taunted with a grin.

Darius rested on arm on the table. "I think you're too afraid to go after us yourself. You've been too long without your magic and power. You doona remember what it's like to have that, so you put your energy into hurting the humans. Still holding that grudge, I see."

"And you're no'?" Ulrik grunted, all pretense of a smile gone. "Can you honestly tell me you doona look at them and wonder what our lives would be like if I'd wiped them from existence?"

"I doona deny it, but it makes little difference. We made a vow, Ulrik. A promise that as Dragon Kings we doona break."

"Con has made many promises. Trust me when I say he's broken most of them."

As close as Con and Ulrik had been, Ulrik would've been privy to much of what Con did. But he could be saying that in an attempt to turn Darius from Con and the others. "Nice try."

Ulrik raised a black brow. "There's one thing I've no' done during all of this, old friend, and that's lie."

Darius spent a few moments thinking through everything that had happened up until that moment. "Did you bring Lily back to life?"

"Are you going to go through everything you think I've done and ask me to give you an answer?"

"You've never answered anyone about that. I'm asking now."

"Lily was dead. Then she wasna."

"That's your answer?" Darius asked in confusion.

Ulrik shrugged slightly. "That's all you're going to get."

He was the only one who could bring someone back from the dead, which meant it was him. But why couldn't he just admit it? "And Darcy?"

"It had to be done," Ulrik said, his gold eyes going even colder than before.

Another admission, without actually saying the words. Ulrik wasn't lying. Shite.

"If I'm no' lying, then who is?" Ulrik asked.

"You're trying to undermine Con."

"He's doing that without my help." Ulrik rose and buttoned his suit jacket. "Whether you know it or no', you've showed your hand where Sophie is concerned. You care for her. Greatly."

Darius got to his feet and glared at Ulrik. "I'm the one in the city. It's up to me to protect her."

"And apparently share her bed."

"We all have needs."

Ulrik slid a hand in his pants pocket and walked around the table. He paused when he was even with Darius. "I'll have Sophie as mine. One way or another."

"I'll kill you myself if you lay a hand on her."

"Ask yourself why Con was so intent on me challenging him when he first became King of Kings. It's because he knows I can take him. And if I can take him, I can do the same to you."

"With only half your magic?" Darius asked with a sneer.

But Ulrik merely grinned before he walked away.

Darius wanted to chase after him and put an end to Ulrik that night. Con might be pissed, but he'd get over it.

He closed his eyes and brought his rage under control. Con wouldn't just be pissed. He might very well lock Darius up for eternity for going after Ulrik.

The one thing Con had demanded was that Ulrik was his—and his alone.

Though Darius didn't have to make Ulrik's life easy.

He rushed out of the restaurant, but there was no Ulrik. The bastard had disappeared again. "How is he doing that?" Darius asked himself.

"*Con,*" he said through their link. As soon as he felt Con

allow him inside his head, Darius said, *"My meeting with Ulrik is finished. He vanished again."*

"There must be a Dark nearby to take him," Con said. *"What happened?"*

Darius began his walk back to Sophie's flat. *"Ulrik vows he hasna lied to us."*

"And?"

"I tried to tell him to come after us himself instead of using the mortals. I attempted to goad him by saying he was weak, which is why he didna go after us."

"Did it work?" Con asked.

Darius sighed. *"No' as I'd hoped. Especially when I mentioned our vow to protect the humans. He told me that you've broken many promises."*

"In other words, his killing of the mortals is justified in his mind."

"Essentially."

"No one has bothered Sophie. Ulrik's men are still here, and they doona look like they'll be leaving anytime soon."

"I'll be there soon."

Darius cut the connection. It didn't go unnoticed by him that Con hadn't admitted or denied that he'd broken promises. In fact, Con had glossed right over that.

By the time Darius reached Sophie's building, he couldn't wait to hold her. He got in once more without being seen by Ulrik's men.

Darius leaned back against the wall on the far side of the living area. He watched her move about the flat. The black dress was gone, replaced with sweats and an oversized blue plaid button down.

She suddenly looked up and smiled, happy to see him. Sophie set aside the towel in her hands. "How did it go?"

"As expected. He gave me nothing I could use."

She bit her bottom lip. "Did you dissuade him from me?"

"The opposite, unfortunately."

"Hmm," she said with a nod and an absent look in her eyes as her gaze lowered. Then she looked back at him. "Why did you come into my life?"

Darius didn't move an inch. She'd been thinking, and that was worrisome. "Lily was sick."

"And she was being pursued by bad men, which is why Thorn couldn't take her to the hospital."

"That wasna a lie."

"I know. Was it Ulrik after her?" When he didn't immediately answer, she continued. "You've already told me who you are. I'm in this," she motioned her hands in a circle, "whatever this is. I didn't ask questions that night. I'm asking now."

Darius watched Sophie. She had no idea how stunning she looked standing in the light with her shoulders back, her chin raised, and defiance in her gaze. In that instant, Darius could well imagine her as one of the Celtic warriors of old.

He wasn't entirely certain that she believed him about who he was, but she hadn't run away from him or told him he was daft. Nor did he believe she continued to welcome him because he was keeping her safe from Ulrik.

Her emotions were genuine. She wanted him there as much as he wanted to be there. Darius was consumed with wanting Sophie. His body was attuned to hers in a way he hadn't known was even possible.

"Are you ready for this?" he asked.

She swallowed, nodding. "I need to know. For myself. For you."

Darius didn't go to her, though every fiber of his being demanded he feel her warmth against him. Instead, he kept his distance to not crowd her.

"Some of the myths and legends repeated are derived from truth."

"Which ones are truth?"

"Derived," he corrected her. Then he took a deep breath. "The Fae."

Sophie walked to the sofa and curled up facing him. She sat quietly, waiting for him to continue.

"The Fae are no' the dainty winged creatures pushed on the public. They look just like you or me, except they are so beautiful they doona look real. There are two classes of Fae—the Light and the Dark."

Sophie said, "I gather the Light are good, and the Dark evil."

"Aye. You might've seen some Dark in the city the night it burned and the weeks leading up to it."

"The ones with red eyes," she said in astonishment.

Darius gave a nod. "With silver in their black hair. The more silver, the more evil they've done."

"What evil? I saw people flock to them."

"Humans are drawn to them. They can no' help themselves. The Dark will have sex with them, pleasuring the mortals beyond belief. But it's done to mask what the Dark are really after."

Sophie shuddered. "Which is?"

"Souls. Every time they have sex with a human, they drain their souls."

"Dear God," she mumbled.

Darius hooked his thumbs in his belt loops. "The Light are just as beautiful. They have black hair and silver eyes as a general rule. However, all Fae can use glamour to change their appearance."

"Oh, that's great," Sophie said sarcastically.

"Once you know what to look for, you can spot a Fae whether they use glamour or no'. The Light remain that way because when they do have sex with a mortal, it's just the once."

Sophie's lips twisted. "Have they always been here? Like you?"

"The Fae arrived thousands of years ago. They have their own realm that's been mostly destroyed by their constant civil wars. We fought them. The Fae Wars occurred without any humans knowing of it."

"That must've been a long time ago," Sophie said with a slight grin.

Darius smiled. "Oh, aye. A verra long time ago."

"Didn't you push them out?"

"The Light eventually sided with us, and we made the Dark sign a treaty that kept them out of Scotland. They were never supposed to call this realm home, and yet they have. They did it quietly under our noses in Ireland."

Sophie's mouth parted. "Ireland?"

Darius threw up his hands. "We trusted them to keep their word. They didna, and it's come back on us. We're now in a war with them. The attack on Edinburgh was one of many across the U.K. The Dark were trying to keep us thinned out so they could get to us."

"They didn't get to Lexi, did they?"

"Despite our best efforts, they did. But Thorn and Con, along with a Light Fae named Rhi, got her back. She and Thorn live at Dreagan."

Sophie sighed loudly. "Why are the Dark after you?"

"They have an alliance with Ulrik. They're working together, each one attacking us at a different time."

"So you're constantly taking a hit one way or another," she said with a nod. "It's a good tactic."

Darius had to agree. "That's Ulrik."

"Most of the world has seen the video the Dark taped of us and then released. Have you?"

Sophie gave him a wry look. "I don't turn on the telly nor do I pay attention to the news."

"Look it up," Darius told her.

She rose and found her mobile phone. Within minutes she found the video and watched it three times before she looked up at him. "This is real?"

"It is. Those are the Dark we're fighting."

Sophie set down the phone and looked at him. "What else is here?"

"There are Druids, but they're humans. Just humans with magic. Oh. There are also Warriors. They're immortal as well and have a primeval god inside them. They're good people though. And our allies."

"All this time," she said as she slowly walked to him. "Magic, immortality, and dragons. I feel like this is a dream."

Darius tugged a lock of her red hair. "It's no'. It's all verra real. I'm so sorry you got pulled into this."

"I'm not."

Darius stared into her eyes, the gold flecks vibrant in the olive color. He couldn't have been more surprised by her words. "Your life is in danger."

"It is. And I'm frightened. Then I think of you. You've changed me, Darius. You broke through the walls I built around myself."

He should be telling her not to think of their relationship. If that's what they had. He didn't know anymore. He'd honestly believed he'd had his mate—and lost her. Now, he wasn't so sure.

The consuming hunger for Sophie overruled everything. If he didn't have her, he was going to go up in flames.

"Do you want me?" she asked.

"I've wanted you from the moment I first walked up to you outside the hospital. You've known from the night I took you on the street that I craved you."

Her eyes glittered with desire.

"What do you want?" he asked.

"You," she said right before she threw her arms around him.

Darius easily caught her. He held her tight as they kissed each other hungrily, as if neither of them could get enough of the other.

He set her on the counter and yanked off his shirt. She smiled as she tugged down her sweatpants. When he spotted the red silk panties covering her sex he moaned in pleasure.

"Don't make me wait."

"Nay," he said even as they both unfastened his jeans and tugged them down.

He entered her with one thrust, her loud moan echoing through the flat.

This was where he felt peace—deep inside her.

CHAPTER
TWENTY-SEVEN

Con lowered his gaze to the top of the roof where he stood. He'd known when he came to watch Sophie's place that Darius would confirm his suspicions. The proof was right there before him.

Con sensed it when he'd told Darius to remain in the city and learn what Ulrik wanted with Sophie. He'd known Darius had it bad for the doctor, but Con had hoped it was merely sexual.

Watching them talk showed Con a great deal. Whether Darius wanted to acknowledge it or not, there was something more there than just physical attraction between the two of them.

Con's gut clenched in dread, because he had a feeling another King had found his mate. Though Darius never wanted to listen, Con had tried repeatedly to tell him the mother of his child hadn't been Darius's mate. But Darius had been too torn up over their deaths to listen.

Now he was experiencing it firsthand.

Con stiffened when he felt a hand on his back that caressed over his shoulder to his chest.

"Hello, lover," whispered a feminine voice with an Irish accent.

Usaeil.

Con stood still as she walked around to his front, trailing her hand down his chest. She wore a sexy smile and a short white dress that dipped so low he could see she wasn't wearing a bra.

"You're no' supposed to be here," he told her.

She tsked. "I'm the Queen of the Light. I can do whatever I want."

"Then perhaps you need to kill off your persona of an actress."

Her chuckle was husky. "You're supposed to be happy to see me."

"I am."

"Really?" Her hand dipped down to cup his balls and run her hand along the length of his limp cock. "I'm beginning to think you're lying."

Con grasped her hands to stop her. "It's November, Usaeil. If humans see you, they'll wonder why you're in that dress without a coat."

"Who cares?"

"I told you we could only have this affair if it was kept private. You showed up at my hotel, and now here. Private, Usaeil. That means it's kept from everyone."

"You're King of Kings, and I'm queen," she said as she yanked her wrists out of his grip, her silver eyes narrowed in anger. "Why do you care if anyone knows?"

"I doona have to explain anything to you."

"You do if you want to share my bed."

He simply stared at her, refusing to speak.

Usaeil's gaze widened as her mouth fell open in shock. "No one refuses me."

"There's a first time for everything."

Her hand connected with his face with a loud crack. "You don't have any idea what you've done."

Con slowly turned his face back to her. "I told you my requirements if you wanted me to share your bed. You agreed."

"We've progressed past that," she argued, hurt filling her face.

"Nay, we have no'."

"I'm ready to tell all the Light, Con. Why no' unite our two races?"

"Because the Kings were never supposed to be matched with the Fae."

She jerked her head, flinging her long black hair from her shoulder. "What of Kiril and Shara?"

"An exception."

"What of Rhi and—"

He leaned his face down to hers and snarled, "Doona even say it."

Her smile was cold and calculating. "The great King of Kings afraid of others discovering he's fecking a Fae."

"I'm no' afraid." No, what Con felt was much deeper.

Usaeil looked over her shoulder to the window where she could see Darius and Sophie making love on the counter. She began to chuckle. It grew into a laugh as she turned to him. "Oh, you are so very sad, Constantine."

"There is too much disheveled right now. You should be with your people or gathering your army. I've heard the whispers about the Reapers. Are they back?"

"Don't you dare try to tell me how to handle the Light." Her nostrils flared. With a snap of her fingers, the dress disappeared so she stood naked. "You can pretend you don't want me, but we both know I can have you on your knees."

"I'll never get to my knees for you," Con stated.

His gaze lowered to her body, and his cock hardened. But damn if he wouldn't refuse her.

Con wrapped his hand around her throat and squeezed. It only made her smile. He was about to throw her down and take her when a flash of white hair caught his attention. Con leaned close to her and whispered, "Wait for me in your bed. I want you naked and wet."

"I'm always ready for you, lover," she said with a quick kiss before she vanished.

Con focused on the spot where he'd seen the white hair. There, just inside the shadows he saw a man. He was tall and formidable looking, and just as Darius described, he had long white hair.

The man had his back to Con so he couldn't see his eyes, but he was Fae. Light or Dark remained to be seen. Perhaps it was time for Con to go talk to him.

"I never got the voyeurism thing," came a sarcastic Irish voice from behind him.

Con closed his eyes and prayed for patience. What had he done to merit a visit from Usaeil and Rhi within minutes of each other?

Then it hit Con. Had Usaeil not left, Rhi would've seen them. The implications of that had Con reeling. Usaeil said she didn't care who discovered them, but he knew that was also a lie. She very much minded if Rhi knew. Because, if Rhi knew then—

"It's also not polite to ignore people," Rhi said.

Con opened his eyes, but the white-haired Fae was gone. Again. He whirled around to find Rhi sitting on the edge of the roof with her legs dangling over the side as she looked at her nails.

It took Con a moment to realize she wasn't wearing black for the second time. She had on a beige sweater infused with gold threads. The dark denim clung to her legs like a second skin and showcased how long and lean they were.

"What are you doing here?"

"I love these chats of ours," she said and threw him a sugary sweet fake smile. She batted her long lashes. "I always leave so warm and fuzzy."

"Rhi," he said in warning.

As if he hadn't spoken with a tone that always got him what he wanted, Rhi said, "I figured Darius needed to blow off some steam after all those years of sleep, but by the way he's touching and kissing that mortal, this is much more than a quick shag."

As if Con didn't already know that. "I'll worry about my men."

"You've done a bang-up job so far." She swung her legs around before she lifted her face to the sky. "There are plenty enough clouds. I thought you'd be up there."

"I can no'. You know that."

"Right. I did." Again she flashed him another mocking smile.

She was goading him. Con normally was able to shake off her sarcastic remarks and antagonistic ways, but not tonight. Too much was happening at once. He was being pulled in a million directions, and he wasn't sure which one to give his attention.

"Do you want them to be unhappy?"

He was taken aback by her softly spoken question. Con studied her profile as she watched the street below them. He knew without asking that she referred to the Dragon Kings.

Though he'd vowed to protect the mortals, that didn't mean he worried over their happiness.

"You know I don't."

She lifted silver eyes to him. Gone was the derision. For

a split second, she revealed her true self. "I don't know that. And neither do they."

"I doona want them hurt." Con didn't try to pretend he had no idea what she was referring to. It was all about the Kings and finding mates. Everything always seemed to get brought back to that.

"It's part of life whether you're Fae, dragon, or mortal. You're acting like a parent who doesn't want their child to learn to ride a bike because they might fall and scrape a knee."

"This is much more than a scraped knee, Rhi."

Her smile was a little sad and forlorn. "Can you honestly tell me that none of the Dragon Kings has never betrayed another? Or lied? Or killed? Or stolen?"

"Only when it was necessary."

"Are you God now? To decide the fate of a human when you turn a blind eye to your own race or make excuses."

She said it all without any heat, which was the only reason he didn't get angry. "I doona judge the mortals."

Rhi swung her legs around until she planted her feet on the roof and stood. She shook her head at him, smiling at his words. "Trust your men. Let them decide their fates, and if anything happens, be there to help them. But take my advice, don't stand in their way or try to prevent them."

Con was wary. It wasn't like Rhi to want to pass on such assistance to him. It was good, which pissed him off. He should've known that and not had a Fae offer him such reasoning.

"I do this for them, not for you," she said. She looked him up and down as if he were dirt on her shoe.

Con crossed his arms over his chest and grinned. "You owe me."

She gawked at him. "Owe? *I* owe *you*? What have you been smoking?"

"I saved your life."

Rhi's shoulders began to shake as she laughed. "Oh, honey," she replied in a mocking tone. "I was there of my own free will to help Thorn. You didn't ask me, and I didn't ask your permission."

"I still saved your life."

"How many times have I helped the Kings? I think you owed me that and many more before I'm ever indebted to you."

He couldn't stop his triumphant smile as he figured out what bothered her. "It irritates you that I was the one who healed your wounds."

"You preening peacock," she said in outrage. "I didn't need you."

The smile fell from Con's face as he let his arms drop to his sides. "You actually did, Rhi. The wound was severe."

"And you didn't let me die? One less annoyance in your life."

She was right. It would've been easy enough to let her die, but it had never entered his mind.

"Rhys must have been there making you heal me," she said with a smirk. "I bet that stung."

Con let her think what she would. She didn't need to know that he'd healed her on his own without any demands from the Kings.

"I guess I should be thankful it wasn't just the two of us or I'd be haunting your ass right now." She flicked her hair over her shoulder as she finished talking.

"Next time you might no' be so fortunate."

She gave him a pitying look. "If you think that'll happen, you are as dumb as I think you are. That blast of magic was lucky."

"Ulrik hit you with it."

She looked to the sky and shrugged. "I know. It's war."

"Since when do you remain friends with someone who tried to kill you?"

"I'm not friends with him. But he's a hell of a kisser," she said with a wink.

Con suspected she and Ulrik had hooked up, but to have confirmation sent a wave of fury through him. "Which side are you on, Rhi? Ours or Ulrik's?"

"You're such a dumbass, Con," she said before she teleported away.

CHAPTER
TWENTY-EIGHT

Darius replayed his and Sophie's conversation in his head over and over again while she slept in his arms. Each time they made love it was new and wonderful. And each time he felt the connection between them strengthen.

That's what she feared—and so did he.

Sophie was a good person. She helped those in need, and she was a talented doctor. If she could be untouched by his world, then that was all the better.

He'd told her everything because she asked—and because he wanted her to know. But once Ulrik was dealt with, Darius would have Guy come in and erase every memory with him in it.

It was how he intended to leave things when he departed the city and her life once and for all. The longer he remained the harder it would be for him to leave.

He was developing feelings for her. Sophie was blessed with a gift of healing. He couldn't take her away from that.

"Do you ever sleep?" Sophie asked.

He looked down to find her eyes open and staring at him. Darius smiled and said, "A little at a time. I doona need much. Why are you no' asleep?"

"I should be. You wore me out again," she said with a grin. "I'm just thinking of everything."

"And?"

"Thank you for telling me."

He kissed her, rolling her onto her back. Seconds later he heard Con's voice in his head. Darius sat up and sighed.

"What is it?" Sophie asked.

"Con."

She raised her brows. "Um . . . what?"

"As dragons, we have a mental link that allows us to communicate. Con is calling me."

Sophie shook her head and rose to walk to the bathroom. "Better answer," she said with a wink.

"*Aye*," Darius said.

"*I need you at the hotel.*"

"*I doona want to leave Sophie alone. Ulrik willna stop until he has her.*"

"*You willna be here long.*"

Sophie walked back into the bedroom to see Darius sitting on the edge of the bed, his head in his hands. "What's wrong?"

"Con wants to see me."

"It must be important then."

Darius lifted his head and slapped his hand on his leg as he let it fall. "I doona want to leave you alone."

"I'll go to the hospital. There are plenty of people around. Ulrik won't be able to get to me."

Darius nodded. "Get dressed. I'll take you myself."

Sophie cleaned herself up and dressed. Minutes later they were walking from the building. She gaped at Darius when he hailed a taxi. "Don't you care the men will see you?"

"Ulrik already knows I've been here. It no longer matters," Darius said as he opened the taxi door.

Sophie slid into the car with Darius following. He

wrapped an arm around her and held her close. She rested her head on his shoulder and smiled.

All too soon they reached the hospital. Darius paid the driver and escorted her inside the building. There he stopped her and held her face between his hands as he kissed her slowly.

She felt her heart melt. When she opened her eyes, he was staring at her.

"Doona go with anyone you doona know. Keep someone with you at all times. I'll be back as soon as I can. I promise."

"I know," she said and rose up to give him another quick kiss. "You be careful."

Darius smiled. "I'm always careful, doc."

She laughed as he turned and walked away. Now her worry began for Darius.

CHAPTER
TWENTY-NINE

Darius walked into the hotel and spotted Con standing in the lobby talking to a leggy brunette who couldn't stop touching him. As soon as Con saw him, he said a few words to the woman and walked away.

"You ruined her night," Darius said.

Con shrugged. "She'll find someone else soon enough. Come."

They walked to the lift and rode it up to the top floor. Darius followed Con into the penthouse suite that occupied the entire floor.

His steps slowed when he heard voices coming from the living area. They rounded the corner and Darius saw Kiril and Rhys. Kiril sat on one sofa while Rhys took the other. They each had a glass of whisky in hand and were good-naturedly debating something Darius didn't even attempt to discover.

"You look well sated," Kiril said as he stood when they entered. Kiril's shamrock green eyes watched him carefully.

Darius took the offered glass of whisky from Con. "Mind your own business."

Rhys raised his glass to Darius, his aqua ringed dark blue eyes serious. "Ulrik up to his old tricks again?"

"New trick," Constantine stated.

Kiril's brows rose high on his forehead. "Oh? Do tell."

Darius was surprised Con hadn't already filled them in, but he was just as shocked to discover they were in Edinburgh.

"I asked them to lend a hand when you met Ulrik tonight," Con explained before Darius could ask.

Darius tossed back his whisky and let it warm his throat and stomach as it slid down. He needed an entire bottle of whisky, not just a dram.

Kiril sat on the rounded arm of the sofa, concern in his gaze as he shoved aside a lock of wheat-colored hair from his brow. "Is Sophie in danger?"

"Aye. Ulrik is after her to hurt me."

Con jumped in and said, "I asked Darius to remain in the city because Ulrik showed up at the hospital where Sophie works. He was there for her."

"Makes sense," Rhys said.

Darius walked to the sideboard and poured another glass of whisky for himself. "What Con isna telling you is that Sophie and I slept together."

The silence behind him was deafening. Darius drank down his second glass and poured a third.

"Go on," Kiril insisted.

Darius lifted his glass and faced the others. "Ulrik has her watched. She's followed everywhere she goes."

"He knew you were visiting her?" Kiril asked.

Darius nodded his head. "He knew I was still in town."

Rhys frowned as he scooted to the edge of the sofa. "What do you mean 'still' here?"

"He saw Sophie and me," Darius said.

Kiril's face scrunched. "You mean he spied on you two through her window?"

Con didn't say a word as he walked to the window and looked over the pre-dawn skyline.

"Nay," Darius said. "We . . . it was out in the open."

"That's a wee bit better, but he still watched," Kiril stated with disgust.

Rhys set his empty glass on the coffee table. "So Ulrik is interested in her because of you."

"I tried to tell him she was simply a way to ease my body, but he didna believe me."

Darius glanced down at the gold-colored whisky before he drank it. "When Sophie first helped us with Lexi, she didna ask any questions. She asked tonight."

"And you told her," Con said without turning around.

Rhys glanced at Con before he focused on Darius once more. "What happened?"

"She's accepted it," Darius said.

"At least she doesna think you're crazy," Rhys said.

Kiril ducked his head. "His biscuits are no' quite baked."

"His pilot light has gone out," Rhys quipped.

Kiril shook his head as he looked at Rhys. "He's a few grapes short of a fruit salad."

"He's no' the crunchiest crisp in the bag."

"He's a few leaves short of a bush."

"Not all the dots are on the dice."

"He's lost contact with the mothership."

"He's a few marshmallows short of a bowl of Lucky Charms."

"He's no' the fastest ship in the fleet."

"He's a few sheep short of a flock."

Darius closed his eyes and prayed for patience as the two kept going.

Kiril snickered and said, "He's a few bristles short of a broom."

"Nay, he's knitting with only one needle."

Con cleared his throat, but you could see his grin in the reflection of the window. "Give over, men."

Rhys bowed with a bright smile. "We'll be here all night."

By that time even Darius was smiling as he eyed them. He walked past Kiril and sat on the opposite end of the sofa. "Sophie knows Ulrik is dangerous. I brought her to the hospital before I came."

Kiril's smile dropped. "He can still get to her."

"But no' as easily," Darius said.

Rhys ran a hand through his long, dark brown hair. "Ulrik has an endgame. He's tried various ways to get to the women we're with."

"He's no' given up before. He willna now," Con said.

Kiril eyed him. "Sophie is important to you, aye?"

"It appears that way." Con turned from the window and faced them.

Rhys speared Darius with a look. "Aye."

Darius knew exactly what he was alluding to. "I've had my mate."

"Maybe you were wrong," Kiril said.

Con walked slowly around the room. "Regardless, Ulrik wants to hurt me through all of you. Denying what he thinks is a potential mate to a King is just one more blow."

Rhys's face grew stern. "What are we going to do?"

"What is there to do besides get Sophie away to Dreagan?" Kiril asked.

Darius shook his head. "Nay. She has a career here. She does important work. I'll no' take her away and ruin her life. We must protect her here."

The three exchanged looks.

"You're different," Rhys stated.

Kiril nodded twice. "He is."

Darius glanced at Con who seemed to be studying him.

He was different. He'd known it for some time, and he knew the reason was Sophie.

He'd been broken. All the Dragon Kings were in some form or another, but he more so than some.

"Did you tell her about your past?" Rhys asked.

Darius looked at his hand that he curled into a fist. "I did. She also told me hers."

Kiril let out a soft whistle. "You've never spoken of it with us. The mere mention of it sent you to your mountain for centuries."

Con sat on the opposite sofa from Darius and rested his ankle on his knee. "How far do you think Ulrik will take this with the doctor?"

Darius leaned forward and scrubbed both hands down his face. He looked at the three of them through his fingers before he dropped his hands and rested his elbows on his thighs. "Ulrik is confident. Verra confident."

"He's been that way for some time," Rhys said.

Darius shook his head. "No' like this. He could challenge Con tonight, but he's no'."

"Darius is correct," Con admitted. "Ulrik told me he wants to strip me of everything."

Rhys jumped to his feet and glared at Con. "You spoke with him? When?"

"Why did you no' tell us?" Kiril demanded.

"I doona answer to any of you," Con said in a cool tone.

Darius didn't get angry as Rhys and Kiril did. Instead he said, "You do. Just as we answer to you."

"We're no' asking who you're sharing your bed with," Kiril said.

Rhys threw Kiril a dumbfounded look. "You may no' be, but I sure the hell am."

Darius watched Con closely. There was something to the rumors swirling around Dreagan about Con's disappearances then. He had a lover, just as Rhys had long suspected, and it was obviously someone Con refused to speak of.

"I didna tell you of my conversation with Ulrik because of this exact reaction," Con said over Rhys who had continued to talk.

The room quieted. Only then did Con turn his head and look at Rhys. "This has nothing to do with who I take to my bed. This is about Ulrik."

"Nay. This is about trust," Kiril said.

Con's blond brows rose. "Do you no' trust me?"

"I doona trust you no' to attack Ulrik if he came in this room," Rhys said.

Con pointed to Darius. "He saw the meeting. Ask him how it went."

Three pairs of eyes turned to him. Darius frowned at Con before he looked to Rhys and Kiril. "They spoke in the bar below. Ulrik invited Rhi to be a witness. She sat with them without saying much. Con and Ulrik had a discussion without a finger being lifted against the other."

"You shouldna have been there alone," Kiril said to Con.

Con took a drink of his whisky and said, "I wasna. Darius was there."

"So you knew about the meeting?" Rhys asked.

Darius shook his head as he said, "Nay. I was following Ulrik and happened upon it."

"Ulrik could've had men there, Con," Kiril said.

Con rested his arm along the back of the sofa cushions. "He didna."

"There's no point in hashing this out," Darius said. "The meeting took place. It's done and over with. What we have now is what was said there, what Ulrik said to me, and what we know he told Con."

Rhys turned away and murmured a "fuck me" as he walked to get more whisky. He returned a moment later and refilled everyone's glasses.

Kiril resumed his seat on the sofa, his face lined with worry. "Mortals are untrusting of anything they doona understand."

"Meaning us," Rhys said.

Darius scratched the side of his head. "If Sophie hadna trusted me, this could all be going verra differently. She didna believe in anything magical."

"Are you sure she does now?" Con asked.

Darius nodded. He was more than sure.

Rhys looked at each of them. "All Ulrik tries to do is kill the women. He'll do something stupid. We need to be prepared."

CHAPTER THIRTY

Rhi wasn't sure why she'd come to Con's suite. Well, there was the whole spying without him knowing about it thing. He always managed to know when she was in his office at Dreagan, but so far, in the hotel, he had yet to notice.

Or if he did, he kept it to himself.

"Rhi was there?" Rhys said with a look of skepticism. "Ulrik nearly killed her, and she agreed to go? I doona understand."

Con gave a halfhearted shrug. "Doona even try. It's no' worth it. There's a record of our conversation with her now. That's all that matters."

"She can help us then," Kiril said.

"Will she?"

Of course Con would ask that. Rhi flipped him off. What a jerk, but then she'd always known he was.

"She will," Rhys said. "Rhi has always been there for us."

There was a pause and Darius said, "Recently she has been . . . absent."

"So was I." Rhys got up and paced in front of the sofas. "After all she went through, she deserves some slack."

Kiril lifted his whisky glass. "I second Rhys. She risked her life to help Shara and me. How many other times has she put herself on the line for us?"

"Too many to name," Rhys said.

Rhi smiled at Rhys and Kiril, but that smile faded as she turned to Darius. Was he remembering that day, so many thousands of years ago that changed her world forever?

She couldn't look at him without thinking about it. And though it was unfair of her, she focused all her hate on him because she couldn't even think of hating her lover.

That lasted a while, but eventually that anger turned to the one who'd sent Darius. Even now she didn't understand why Darius had agreed to bring her such disturbing news. Did he hate her that much?

He was one of a few Kings who was never thrilled with their romance. Darius must have enjoyed watching her world crumble away.

Were there other Kings who felt the same? Did they use her for what she could do to help them? Was that all she was good for?

She knew Con would be delighted if she never showed her face again. Rhi looked at the four Dragon Kings in the room. She knew without a doubt she could count on Rhys for anything.

The rest of the Dragon Kings she wasn't so sure about. Yes, she'd helped Kellan, Tristan, Kiril, Laith, Warrick, and Thorn, but would they ever help her if the situations were reversed?

Rhi leaned back against the wall and turned her head to where her watcher stood not five feet from her. No matter where she traveled, veiled or not, he was able to find her. What did he think of what he was hearing?

Why did she even care?

"Rhi is struggling," Darius said. "Hell, we all are right now."

Kiril nodded slowly. "And it's only going to get worse."

"How are your mates holding up?" Con asked Rhys and Kiril.

Kiril exchanged a glance with Rhys. "Shara is Fae. She's more than fine. She's concerned and worried, but she's good."

"You know Lily," Rhys said with a smile.

Rhi felt her heart clench. To see such devotion in Rhys's gaze when he spoke of his love. How Rhi missed having that kind of connection to someone, both physically and emotionally.

"She's been through so much already," Rhys continued. "She'll weather this as she has everything else."

Con gave a nod. "Good. I'd like to know the moment any of the mates become restless or upset."

"Why?" Kiril asked.

Darius kept his gaze on the ground because he knew about the exchange between Con and Ulrik regarding the mates. Rhi wasn't going to be the one to tell the Kings what could happen to their mates. Ulrik was correct in that Con should've told them, but Con hadn't.

Why? It would've been a good argument to prevent the Kings from taking mates. Then again, there wasn't much Con did that Rhi did understand. He was an enigma, and she'd learned long ago that he followed no one's rules but his own.

"Things could get bad for all of us," Con said. "The mates are used to being safe on Dreagan. That may no' be the case for much longer."

"What are you no' telling us?" Rhys demanded.

"We need to keep focused on Ulrik and Sophie," Con said. "We can discuss this later."

Rhi could see Darius felt something profound for Sophie. He wanted to protect her as all Kings did, but there was something more going on. She'd seen it herself earlier when she came upon Con watching them together.

That was the same type of crazy, primal magnetism that wouldn't be denied.

Rhi had once felt that same kind of lure. She ached to feel it once more.

Something touched her hair. She stilled as she realized her watcher had come near. It was as close as he had been to her—that she knew of. She could reach out and punch him in the stomach if she wanted, but she didn't.

It felt . . . nice . . . to have him there. Maybe he had become a sort of comfort since he was always around. He saw everything, heard every word. The only thing he didn't know was what was in her head, and even that she wasn't sure she kept from him.

The only other person who had ever been this close to her was her lover. She physically ached at not having that closeness.

She missed his scent.

She missed his arms around her.

She missed being wanted and touched.

She missed holding hands and cuddling.

She missed sharing meals and laughter and memories.

She missed the secret smiles only two people who have been intimate share.

She missed him, yearned for him and their love.

Rhi pulled herself out of her thoughts and realized she'd missed much of the conversation where Darius spoke of Sophie's routine.

For another half hour the four of them bandied around ideas about Ulrik and how they could get ahead of him. The problem with all of their plans was that it involved not allowing the humans to know of them.

That's where Ulrik continued to stay ahead. He didn't care who discovered he was a Dragon King. Since he wasn't concerned about keeping such a drastic secret, that gave him an advantage no one at Dreagan had. With that kind of lead, there was nothing the Kings could do to out-maneuver him.

Rhi would have to tell Rhys that later. He would listen to her and take it to Con. Not that the Kings would do anything with that information.

Darius, Kiril, and Rhys remained and ordered room service as they opened another bottle of Dreagan whisky and continued their talk of Ulrik. Con rose and walked from the room.

Rhi followed him past the grand piano, the dining table that could seat twelve, another living area, and into one of the three bedrooms.

Since Con had taken this one, it was obviously the master. The sheer size of it was impressive, including the large bed covered in an off-white comforter with navy accents around the room.

Con continued past the bed to the double doors that led out onto a balcony. Curious, Rhi followed him, surprised at how large the balcony was.

He leaned upon the iron railing instead of taking one of the many chairs. For several seconds he stared out over the city with his hands clasped together.

Then he said, "You can show yourself any time now."

Rhi looked to her right where her watcher stood. She knew Con didn't know of him, but she also didn't want Con to discover someone else had been listening to their conversation.

She unveiled herself and stepped out onto the balcony. He didn't so much as look her way. Rhi sank into one of the chairs and surveyed him.

Con looked relaxed on the outside, but she imagined

inside he was anything but. He'd learned to master his emotions. That threw many people off because they assumed his reactions reflected what he was thinking. That was never the case when it came to Con.

So she wasn't surprised when his voice, laced with cold anger said, "I'm tired of you spying on me."

"I wasn't here for you."

His head slowly swiveled to her. "Rhys is well settled now."

"You always think you know what I'm doing. How many times do we have to go through this before you realize you know nothing?"

In the next instant he was yanking her out of the chair, his forearm pressed to her throat as he pinned her against the wall.

Rhi smiled after her initial surprise at his sudden movement. Con usually had words for her. This was the first time he'd gotten physical, which proved how on edge he was. "What are you afraid of?"

"You betraying us. Rhys sings your praises constantly," he said as his face neared hers. "He can no' see that you doona have the same loyalties as before."

She raised her chin, defying him with her eyes. "You're wrong."

"Then tell me the truth, Rhi. Why did you come when Ulrik called? He nearly killed you."

"I did tell you the truth. You know I can't lie," she said as he pressed his arm harder against her throat.

His lips peeled back in a grin. "Do I? Perhaps you learned to control the pain enough to be able to lie."

"I didn't," she said and shoved him away from her.

His gaze drifted down her body for an instant before he looked back at her. "Now this?"

Rhi looked at her hands to see them glowing. Con always had a way of making her so angry that she lost control. She closed the distance between them and placed her hand on his chest.

She let the power of her magic that made her glow flow from her palm into her hand and through his chest. His jaw tightened as her glowing increased, but he didn't back away.

The chairs around her began to rattle on the concrete, reminding Rhi she was in the middle of a city. She had to pull herself together or she could kill many mortals.

She gave him a hard shove with her magic before she dropped her hand. The glowing subsided as she got control of her fury. She looked Con up and down.

"I went to the meeting because Ulrik asked. I went because of the friends I have at Dreagan. I went because I wanted to be there. I went to do your stupid ass a favor. Next time I'll decline."

She started to turn away when his hand wrapped around her arm to hold her. Rhi looked down at his fingers, then at his face.

"I doona trust you."

"You never have," she responded coolly. "This is nothing new."

He yanked her close so that their faces were inches apart. "If you betray us, there's nowhere you can hide where I won't find you. And kill you."

She smiled, briefly debating putting her lips to his and seeing his reaction. Right before she teleported away, she said, "Kiss my grits."

CHAPTER
THIRTY-ONE

Sophie made her rounds, taking her time to talk to patients and looking over charts. Being back at the hospital gave her a sense of belonging as it always did.

Then she thought of Darius and how, with him, she also felt as if she belonged, as if she was with the other half of herself.

She kept her mind occupied with patients, medicine, and anything else that would keep her from thinking of Darius. Yet he crept into her thoughts at the oddest moments.

Like while she was writing down instructions on a chart and she thought about his fingers and how his touch was both gentle and commanding.

Or like when she was rushing into a patient's room who was screaming in pain and she imagined how calm and collected Darius would be in such a situation.

Perhaps it was just because she was worried about him. This thing with Ulrik was big. Darius didn't make light of the situation, but he tried to play it off.

The video she'd seen of the men and dragons shifting, fighting, and breathing fire proved they were formidable opponents. But Ulrik was also a Dragon King. That's what made her so anxious.

Darius said only a Dragon King could kill a Dragon King. And Ulrik was after her to get to Darius. Did he want to kill Darius for his revenge?

The idea of Darius being slain made her stomach roll viciously. She hadn't wanted to believe his tale of dragons and immortality, but she found herself doing just that—accepting and acknowledging all of it.

How much her thinking had changed since meeting Darius was evident in everything she did. She smiled more. She even thought of the future again, allowing those dreams to return once more.

Sophie walked into her office and shut the door. The happiness she sought was on hold though. Because of Ulrik and the Dark Fae. She sat at her computer and did a search on the Fae first.

The plethora of links about the Fae boggled her mind. It would take her years to go through each one, trying to sort out all of it.

She then searched red-eyed Fae. Pictures of the men and women she'd seen when the city had been burning filled the screen. All were uploaded from mobile devices to Facebook, Twitter, Pinterest, and the like.

As she scrolled through them, she was shocked to see how many people were with the Dark. Sophie didn't want to think how many of those people were now dead.

The deaths leading up to Halloween had been in the papers and on the telly. Not even Sophie could keep from learning about them, but she hadn't paid much attention to the reports.

She went through them now, reading every account she could find. Sophie was shocked at the number of deaths. It was luck—and her stubbornness to shut out the world—that kept her away from the Dark.

It was a wake-up call for sure. She needed to know what was going on in the world, and she needed to be a part of it as well. Otherwise, why was she even there?

For a long while Sophie stared at the computer, wondering at the providence that kept her safe from the Dark.

After a moment, she did another search—this one for Dragon Kings. Various things popped up from movies to books and even comics, but nothing on the actual men. Then she searched Dreagan.

Links to the video popped up, and then immediately disappeared, as if someone were deleting them as fast as they showed up. Sophie imagined it was someone at Dreagan working to keep their secret.

She spent a few minutes learning what she could about Dreagan. Since she wasn't a whisky drinker, she didn't know much about it. The only thing she knew was that it was the Scotch everyone wanted. It was quite a boon when a restaurant was granted the ability to serve it.

Sophie read about the beginnings of the distillery. The website stated it began in the fifteenth century and continued ever since, production never stopping. Over six hundred years of distilling. It was impressive.

She sat back as she finished reading the Dreagan website. Her mind wandered to the people there. Darius hadn't told her how many Kings lived there, but she imagined it was quite a few.

And women? Had any of the others taken mates? Surely they had. If any of them looked as handsome as Darius, then they wouldn't be alone for long. After all, Lexi had Thorn, who was almost as gorgeous as Darius.

As she let her mind wonder about the Dragon Kings and all they'd endured, an image of Ulrik filled her mind. Darius had said nothing about a surname, but Ulrik had given her one.

Sophie sat up and quickly typed the name Ulrik Dunn

into the search engine. A row of pictures popped up, but none of them were the Ulrik she knew. She narrowed down the search to Scotland, but that didn't help at all.

No matter how hard she dug, she could find nothing on Ulrik Dunn.

Obviously the surname Ulrik had given her was fake. Despite the fact he was forced to remain as a human, he was hiding just as effectively as those on Dreagan.

Sophie leaned back in her chair and wondered where Darius was and what he was doing. She prayed he was safe. Dragon or not, he could still be hurt.

"*I'm no' a good man.*"

She pondered those words he'd first given her, because he'd shown her he was definitely a good man. Time and again he'd demonstrated.

He might not believe he was good, but then it was up to her to show him that he was. It would mean Sophie was putting herself in the middle of a war—a war she was involved in now.

There was a knock on the office door and then Claire poked her head in. "Hey. You all right?"

"Just taking a few minutes to myself. What is it?"

"That man is back," Claire said, a hint of fear in her eyes.

Sophie's gut clenched. Ulrik was there. Now. "Tell him I'm busy."

Claire glanced over her shoulder before she stepped into the office. She closed the door behind her and leaned against it. "Tell me what's going on."

"I can't."

"Yes, you can," Claire stated with a hard look. "You're mixed up with something, and I'm worried."

"Not by choice." Sophie pressed her hand to her forehead for a moment. Then she rose and walked around her desk. "Ulrik is an enemy of Darius."

"Your new lover," Claire said to clarify.

Sophie nodded. "Ulrik tried to use me against Darius."

"What the hell are you involved in, Soph?"

She shrugged, not willing to say more.

"We should call the police."

"Darius is taking care of it." The last thing Sophie could allow to happen was for Claire to contact the authorities.

Claire snorted. "That's not enough."

"You have to trust me, Claire. This is for the best."

"Nothing good ever comes from those kinds of decisions. You don't trust anyone, and you're putting your life in Darius's hands?"

"I am."

Claire's eyes widened. "My God. You actually have."

Sophie glanced away from her friend. "Surprising, I know."

"I'd love to be happy for you, but I'm more concerned with this threat from Ulrik."

"As long as I stay away from Ulrik, he can't get to me."

"Why didn't you tell me this before?" Claire asked, hurt filling her brown eyes.

"When you came to my flat, Darius was there. Ulrik's men were watching my place, and we didn't want to put you in a position where they might question you."

Claire crossed her arms over her chest and nodded. "All right. That makes sense. But Darius isn't here now. What do we do?"

"I stay clear of Ulrik until Darius returns to take me back to my flat."

"Then I'll get rid of Ulrik and make sure the other nurses know as well."

Sophie walked to her and took her hand. "Thank you, Claire. I'm lucky to have a friend like you."

"I want to meet the man who's made you change so and give him a hug," Claire said with a wink.

As Claire started to leave, Sophie stopped her. "Be careful of Ulrik. He's dangerous, Claire."

"So I guess I can cross him off the Potential Date List," she said with a wry look. "Are there any good men out there?"

Sophie knew that in fact, there were. "Yes."

Claire chuckled. "Let's get rid of Mr. Good-looking-but-dangerous, and then you're going to tell me all about Darius and Ulrik."

Sophie didn't have time to respond before Claire was gone. She locked her office door and returned to her desk. With renewed spirit, she began another search for Ulrik in Edinburgh.

The list that came up was long, but nothing came of it. She then looked through pictures. Again, nothing.

Sophie expanded her search to other large cities in Scotland. Ulrik was a man of money. He had to have holdings somewhere. He didn't seem the type to hide away in some small town. He'd be close to a city somewhere. He was also a Highlander, which meant he spent most of his time in Scotland.

It was on her sixth try when she typed in Perth along with Ulrik's name that she saw a listing for an antiques store called The Silver Dragon. She knew she'd found what she was looking for then.

Sophie dug more into the antiques store and discovered it had been around for several decades, passed through a family, though she was never able to locate the surname of the family.

After another half hour of searching for more, she finally gave up. Ulrik went to a tremendous amount of trouble to conceal anything pertinent about himself.

She pushed away from her desk and stood. Sophie was walking to the door when her mobile phone rang. Taking it from her pocket of her white coat, she saw it was a message from Ulrik.

HIDING IN YOUR OFFICE? THAT'S NOT NICE.

Her gut clenched at the words. She wanted Darius. And she wanted as far from Ulrik as she could get. How did he know she was in her office?

She didn't bother to answer his text. Sophie dropped the phone back into her pocket and closed the blinds at the window. If he was watching her, then she was going to close off any avenue he had.

Ten minutes later there was a knock at the door, then Claire's voice. Sophie hurried to unlock it and allow her friend inside.

"Everyone knows," Claire said. "Including the hospital administrator. I saw Ulrik walk away from the hospital myself."

Sophie took out her mobile and handed it to Claire to show her the text.

"Shit." Claire took Sophie's hand and walked her to the chairs in front of her desk. She gently pushed Sophie before taking the other seat. "It's time you spit it all out."

"The gist of it all is that Ulrik wants to get revenge against Darius."

"Through hurting you." Claire's lips twisted in agitation. "How far do you think Ulrik would take it?"

"As far as he needs."

"Bloody hell, Soph. Wouldn't it be easier to let the police handle this and get away from all of it?"

She smiled sadly and shook her head. "It might, but it's not what I want to do."

"Stubborn," Claire mumbled. Then she took a deep breath and tried another tack. "What has Ulrik done to threaten you?"

"Nothing."

Claire looked at her funny. "Nothing?"

"He came to the hospital and had coffee with me. It was before I knew who he was."

"What did he say?"

"Only that he wanted me for something, but he never said what. That's when Darius told me who he was. He invited me to dinner, but I didn't go. Darius went in my place."

"Ballsy," Claire said in approval. "What happened?"

Sophie shrugged. "Ulrik told Darius he'd get me one way or another."

"I think that's threat enough. Add in the text, and you definitely need to stay away from him." Claire glanced at her watch. "My break is almost over, and you can't stay in here all day. You have rounds."

"I know."

Claire got to her feet. "Looks like I'm your shadow today, doctor."

CHAPTER
THIRTY-TWO

Darius searched but hadn't found a single one of Ulrik's men at the hospital. That wasn't to say there weren't any there. Ulrik had proven to have a vast collection of people, and they were most likely walking beside Sophie without her even realizing it.

It wasn't like Ulrik to give the appearance of giving up. His death strike would come swiftly. Darius just had to figure out when that might be so he could save Sophie.

Darius walked to the corner of the street. He remained there watching the hospital. Sophie only had a little more time before her shift was over.

With a sigh he turned around, then stilled as his gaze landed on Rhi.

The Light Fae wore a long black coat with a white fur collar. The coat was open, showing a black shirt, jeans, and black boots. Her hands were in the coat pockets as she stood staring at him in the snow.

For a moment, he wasn't sure if Rhi was there to talk or to fight. Both knew she couldn't kill him, but that wouldn't stop her from inflicting some major hurt.

Her beautiful Fae face was devoid of expression. In

many ways, the silent way she stood watching him reminded him of Con. He squared off and met her silver gaze.

Thousands of years ago, Rhi caught the Dragon Kings' attention because of her skill as a warrior. She'd been the brightest light of her people. Her beauty, her happiness, and her loyalty captivated everyone who saw her.

It was no wonder that a King was drawn to her. In truth, he hadn't been the only one. All of them had wanted Rhi, but she'd only had eyes for one of them.

Everyone knew Rhi hated Darius. She'd hate whoever told her such devastating news, even if it had been Rhys doing the deed. But it hadn't been Rhys. It had been him.

Rhi made a point of never being alone with Darius, so he was unsure of what she wanted. It was true she'd been erratic of late. Rhys was positive of her loyalty, but Darius wasn't.

Rhi had helped Ulrik and was known to visit Balladyn—two of their enemies. She wasn't herself, and hadn't been since Balladyn tortured her. For all they knew, she could be turning Dark.

A gust of wind howled through the buildings and into them, but neither he nor Rhi moved despite the force. Her black hair lifted before falling back into place.

Darius released a breath. "If you've something to say, then say it."

She remained as silent as a statue.

He shifted his feet. Rhi was never one to hold her tongue on any occasion. The fact she was now told him either she was that angry. Or that calculating.

"You still hold anger toward me," Darius said with a nod. "I ken that."

"You know nothing."

Her tone was calm, too calm for the Rhi that he knew. Darius studied her. "Granted, I doona know you as Rhys or others do."

"You've never known me. Nor did you approve of me."

Ah. The root of the issue. "Need I remind you about the Fae Wars?"

"The Fae Wars," she said with a laugh devoid of humor. "Your dragons were sent away because of the war with the mortals, and yet many of the Kings take them as mates. You've been bedding one as well."

Darius lost any hint of composure as he stalked to Rhi and punched a finger into her shoulder. "Leave Sophie out of this."

"I'm not doing anything to her," Rhi replied coolly.

He frowned. Where was Rhi's temper? Darius lowered his hand to his side. "Are you helping Ulrik?"

There was a flash of irritation in her silver eyes. "Would you believe anything I said?"

"Aye. You can no' lie."

She rolled her eyes. "That's the only reason you'd believe me? Not because I've sacrificed many times in order to help the Kings."

"I wasna there. I only know the stories."

"Odd how quick you are to believe the stories that I'm helping Ulrik, but you're hesitant to accept the ones about me aiding the Kings as truth."

Darius shrugged. She had a point, but he wasn't going to admit that. "Answer my question."

"Why should I?"

"Then why are you here?"

Her gaze swung to the hospital. "I was curious."

"Doona be," he said and stepped into her line of vision. "Sophie is no concern of yours. Stay out of her life."

"Why? She knows all about me."

Darius ground his teeth together. How did Rhi know that?

Rhi smiled at his silence.

He narrowed his gaze on her. "Have you sided with Ulrik?"

"I haven't, but you don't believe that. Stop asking questions if you won't believe the answers."

"Then why are you here?"

"You."

That took him aback. Darius didn't need to ask why she sought him. The reason was crystal clear.

"Nothing to say?" she asked with a raise of her black brows.

Darius shrugged. "What is there to say? What's done is done."

"You make it sound as if you carried a jug of milk from the store. It was much more than that."

"We had this conversation long ago," Darius said. Actually they hadn't. It had been one similar, but she'd been too hurt and shocked by his words to ask anything specific.

Darius had known this day would come as long as Rhi was friendly with the Kings. He'd be lying if he said he hadn't hoped she would sever all ties with them.

Rhi leveled a baleful look with her silver eyes. "I've often wondered what type of slime would willingly help out a friend and deliver such . . . heinous words with such joy."

"You just said it. A friend."

"A friend," Rhi repeated softly and glanced at the ground. "He should've told me himself."

Darius didn't respond. Anything he said might be taken the wrong way. It was better to let things continue as they were.

"No reply. I didn't expect anything else."

The more she spoke, the more her Irish accent deepened. Darius would never tell her, but she had every right to be furious over how things went down. What he'd done, he did for another King. Period.

"You really don't get it, do you?" Rhi asked with a snort. "One day, Darius, you're going to be in a similar situation, and you'll have words delivered to you via your lover's friend. Then you'll know how it feels."

"I doona owe you any kind of explanation."

"Don't you?" she asked with a raised brow. "Why did you offer to tell me my relationship with him was over?"

Darius shrugged. "I saw a friend in need. I did what he couldna."

"He's a coward."

Darius didn't bother to reply. There was nothing that he could say. If she had seen him that day, she'd know that his decision had been the hardest thing he'd ever done. He had been torn in two about it.

It's why Darius offered to go to Rhi. Because if Darius hadn't, the relationship wouldn't have ended. Darius hadn't understood the attraction between his friend and Rhi—until he met Sophie.

"I've hated you a long time," Rhi said.

"I know."

"But I've recently realized that though you're the biggest ass for taking such pleasure in telling me that news, the real blame lies with him."

Darius frowned. He hadn't delighted in telling Rhi it was over. It had been horrible. He might not have particularly cared for her, but he hadn't wanted to hurt her. Now that he knew all she'd done to help the Kings, he felt even worse.

He breathed a sigh of relief when Rhi teleported away. He dropped his chin to his chest, her words echoing in his head. Rhi's threat worried him—because his feelings for Sophie were deepening by the minute.

He looked at the snow covering the streets, imprints from shoes marring the pristine white. Temperatures dipped lower as mortals huddled in their coats, scarves, and gloves. They paid him no heed as they hurried from one place to another seeking warmth.

Darius made a round of the hospital as he waited for Sophie. She enticed him to a degree that he was still wrestling with. It had been less than twenty-four hours since he had tasted her, been inside her. Felt her pleasure.

And he ached for more.

It was a yearning that went deep inside him. One that he couldn't shake no matter how hard he tried—and he had tried.

Darius passed an alley and glanced inside. He halted when he spotted the white-haired man talking to three other Fae—two of which were Dark.

He turned down the alley intending to take them all on. It didn't matter that one of the Fae was Light. If he was talking to a Dark, then he was considered an enemy.

As one, all four looked at Darius. And then vanished without a word.

Darius stared at the spot where he'd seen them. The white-haired Fae had looked right at him. It wasn't red eyes Darius saw, but white. Just like his hair.

He didn't retreat, because he had a feeling the Fae weren't gone. Darius sent a small push of his dragon magic toward the spot where the Fae had been. It encountered something, but then that too quickly disappeared.

"Who are you?" Darius demanded.

He stood there several minutes, waiting for them to show themselves, attack, or even give him an answer. But nothing happened.

Darius blew out a frustrated breath and returned to walking the perimeter of the hospital.

"That was close," Fintan said from the rooftop.

Cael looked down at Darius and nodded.

Fintan gawked at him. "You wanted the Dragon King to see us?"

"I wanted to see his reaction," Cael explained.

"Why?"

Cael scratched his chin. "I don't know exactly."

"That makes no sense if you doona want the Kings involved in our business."

"I know this." Cael turned his head to look in Fintan's white eyes.

"What does Death say?"

"Nothing."

Fintan made a sound at the back of his throat. "It's a mistake. The Kings have their own war, as do we. We don't need to be combining them."

"Don't we?" Cael's head swung back to Darius. "We've a common enemy."

"We know our enemy is Dark. That doesn't mean it's the same as the Kings'. Who, I might add, also have Ulrik as an enemy. One of their own."

"You're not telling me anything I've not told myself. I don't know what the right move is, but I've a feeling that eventually the Kings will need us as much as we're going to need them."

Fintan crossed his arms over his chest. "Can they know of us?"

"Good question."

"They're not Fae, which means they don't have to be killed if they learn who we are. But neither are they human."

"What they are are the first inhabitants of this realm. It's theirs. The mortals and the Fae are living here by the Kings' permission."

Fintan chuckled wryly. "Let's hope they don't kick us out."

"Yes. Let's hope."

CHAPTER
THIRTY-THREE

Sophie walked out the back entrance of the hospital. She saw no sign of Darius as she carefully picked her way through the snow.

Then out of the shadows near the spot where they'd first made love, moved a figure. He stepped into the light of the streetlamp, a smile on his face.

"Hello," she said.

"Hello, yourself."

Sophie hurried to him. His arms wrapped around her, holding her tight. She closed her eyes, enjoying his warmth and his arms.

"How was your day?" she asked, then laughed.

He leaned back. "What's so funny?"

"It seems odd to be asking you such a mundane question when you are anything but."

Darius gave her a quick, hard kiss. "Neither are you, doc." He took her medical bag from her and laced his free hand with hers. "As for my day, it was quiet."

"That's good. Right?"

He nodded as he glanced at her before returning his gaze to observing everything around them.

Sophie had to smile. Her life used to be simple. Boring to most, but she'd been content. Or at least she'd thought she was content.

Then Darius strode into her life with the force of a whisper and altered *everything*.

"What about your day?" Darius asked.

"The usual." Then she halted as she remembered Ulrik's visit. She quickly recounted the event, including what she'd told Claire.

Darius's face was grim. "Claire can no' know of us, Sophie."

"I know."

"We've survived because few know our secret."

"Why did you tell me? You could've lied."

He touched her face, his fingers warm despite the weather. "I wanted you to know who I was. The real me."

"I won't until I see the form you were born to."

His lips softened into a smile. "If I shift, it's because I'm protecting you. Let's hope it doesna come to that."

"Ulrik isn't going to give up, is he?"

"Nay."

"You can't be with me every second of every day."

He glanced at the ground. "There's a place I could take you to keep you safe."

She knew it was Dreagan without having to ask. As much as she wanted to be with him, she didn't want to give up her career. It never entered her mind that she might have to choose one over the other.

"Aye," he said with a nod. "I figured you'd wish to remain."

"I love what I do. I have commitments here."

He placed a finger over her lips. "You doona need to explain. I ken what you do is important. I'd no' want to take that away from you. If you doona want to go with me, then I'm going to have to be with you at all times."

Sophie was going to enjoy that. The question was, would Darius? He wanted to fight Ulrik. He couldn't do that when he was babysitting her.

"You could still use me as bait."

"Out of the question," Darius said with finality. "Come. We need to get you out of this weather."

Sophie followed, her mind now wondering where things were going to go with her and Darius once Ulrik was dealt with. Would Darius leave? Would he ask her to go with him?

Would she say yes?

Sophie glanced at him as he walked beside her, his tall form throwing off vibes that had people giving them a wide berth.

She didn't want him to leave. Ever. But she couldn't leave her job either.

But she knew one thing for certain—she was in love with Darius.

CHAPTER
THIRTY-FOUR

Rhi stood in the store gazing at all the bottles of nail polish from her favorite brand—OPI. There were many she hadn't gotten while she'd been in her funk.

That wasn't entirely true. She'd bought every shade of black, silver, and white there was. And really, it was surprising how many ways they could concoct a black to make it look different.

Since she was wearing color now, she needed to begin adding in all the bottles she didn't have. The problem was she couldn't decide on anything.

She changed three times because she kept putting on black. If she was going to make everyone think she was the old Rhi again, then she needed to dress the part. Except, she wasn't the old Rhi—or the new Rhi that had been around lately. She didn't know who she was.

Rhi chose a shimmering golden red OPI nail polish titled Go with the Lava Flow. Some days she felt like wearing black, and then she surprised herself by wearing color like she did when she woke at Dreagan.

She knew she wanted so much more than she'd had for

the past few millennia. She also felt like something big was coming. Almost as if she were in limbo, waiting.

That was the crux of the problem since Rhi hated waiting for anything.

Next, she moved to the blues and selected another color from the Hawaii collection. The lagoon blue name was This Color Is Making Waves.

She was about to turn away when the bright green caught her eye. Just as she went to grab it, she spotted a purple that reminded her of the reefs she swam near her island. Rhi picked up the bottle and read the title—Lost My Bikini in Molokini—and laughed.

Rhi made her way to the counter and paid for the three bottles. It felt very . . . human. Of course, she used magic to get the money, but no one needed to know that.

Then she teleported to her salon where her nail tech, Jesse, waited. Rhi closed her eyes and sat back in the chair as Jesse began her manicure. Rhi wanted to relax, but her mind kept going round and round between Balladyn, Ulrik, Con, and her confrontation with Darius.

She hadn't had the guts to ask Darius if her lover had been talked into severing their relationship. And did it really matter? If her lover allowed himself to be talked into anything then he'd never really loved her.

But their love had been deep and powerful.

Why had he let that go so easily? Why hadn't he fought for her, for them?

Rhi felt her watcher's eyes on her and began to relax. He hadn't harmed her—and there had been many opportunities. She also didn't feel as though he were there for any malicious intent.

It had annoyed her at first that he was always there, and she'd even been frightened of it. Now, she felt almost safe. No, that was the wrong word. She felt . . . protected. As if he were a sentry guarding her.

She opened her eyes and looked to her left where he stood. Rhi imagined him leaning against the wall. He'd seen her as very few had. Did he think her flighty? Vain? Stubborn? Arrogant?

All too soon her nails were done. Rhi moved to the massaging chair where Jesse put her feet in hot water to soak them. Her watcher remained on her left while her pedicure began.

Her mind drifted to Balladyn. She could have a relationship with him. He waited for her. Rhi had been alone for so long that she craved a man's hand on her back, his adoring gaze on her face, and his lips on hers.

She wanted to run her hands through his hair and wrap her arms around his neck as she lifted her face for his kiss. She wanted to caress his body and face. She wanted to be filled with such desire that she couldn't form a coherent thought.

She wanted to make love all night and feel pleasure so profound that it wiped away the past with one swipe.

Balladyn loved her. She saw it in his red eyes each time he looked at her. Rhi felt something for him, that she couldn't deny.

If only she could stop loving her Dragon King. First, she needed to stop calling him "hers." He hadn't been hers in . . . ages.

He'd moved on. For one, he was a male. For another, he was a Dragon King. Women flocked to them in droves, and he had needs.

It made her gut clench when she thought of him with someone else. She'd been chaste all this time, waiting for the possibility that he might want her again.

How utterly stupid. Why had she thought he might realize his mistake? His words—delivered via Darius—had been plain enough.

"Our time together was good, but it's over. It's time we go our separate ways."

By the stars! She was a complete nincompoop to think he might still love her. How many times lately had she seen him at Dreagan? How many times had he looked right through her? How many times had he pretended she wasn't even there?

He'd faked whatever love was between them. Rhi had known it for centuries, but she hadn't wanted to face it. No longer would she blindly hold onto something that was only a passing affair for him.

She'd never felt such love for another before him, but she had held a torch for him long enough. It was time to close the lid on that part of her past.

Rhi took a deep breath, and felt a huge weight lift off her chest. She was worth so much more than pining over a King who'd used her. She deserved happiness and the love of a man who would cherish her.

There was an itch on her cheek. She scratched it, only to realize it was a tear slowly making its way down her face. Rhi sniffed. That was the last time she would cry over the lost love of her King.

When her toes were done, Rhi paid Jesse and exited the salon to walk down the street. The next block over she teleported to her island. Rhi set her three new polishes on the shelf with the others, careful to put them with their colors. Then she strolled out of the hut and into the sun.

She held out her hands to look at her nails in the sun and smiled as she saw Jesse had chosen the lagoon blue polish. It had just enough shimmer to catch the sun. The thin gold line curving along her nail tips added a touch of color. With a snap of her fingers, Rhi's clothes were gone, replaced with a gold metallic bikini.

Was it her imagination, or was her watcher smiling?

She turned to look over her right shoulder to where she knew he stood. There was no use talking to him. He wouldn't answer her. Besides, there was no need for words between them.

Rhi sank onto the sand and lay back, letting the rays of the sun heat her skin. She stared at the vivid blue of the sky and wondered how it would feel to be with someone again, to not be lonely.

Because she was lonely. Oh, she told everyone this was the way she wanted it, but it was one big fat moose dick of a lie.

Each time she went to Dreagan and saw one of the Kings with his mate sharing smiles, holding hands, kissing, or just laughing, it was like a knife to her heart.

She closed her eyes and let her mind drift to anywhere but thoughts of her King and her broken heart. Her eyes snapped open when she felt something brush her hand.

Rhi turned her head to look at her right hand. There was an indent in the sand as if someone sat beside her and rested his hand alongside hers.

Her watcher. He was so close she felt his warmth. Rhi smiled and closed her eyes once more.

Daire wanted to touch her. He could sense Rhi's lonesomeness. She did a valiant job of hiding it from everyone. Except when she was alone. Then she let the mask fall away. She allowed him to see the pain and heartache she suffered daily.

Yet something occurred at the salon when she was getting her nails done. There was a kind of peace that descended over Rhi, almost as if she'd come to some kind of decision. There was still sorrow in her silver eyes, but it had lessened. Even on her island, her smiles came easier today. He was curious about what she'd decided. Was it about Balladyn?

Daire had an uneasy feeling about the Dark Fae. Balladyn cared about Rhi, that much was obvious. But what would his association with Rhi do to her?

Though Daire didn't know why Death was interested in Rhi, it must be important for Daire to be following her around everywhere. And Daire was fairly certain Death didn't want Rhi becoming Dark.

For the next hour Daire sat beside Rhi while she lay in the sun. He watched the waves crash upon the beach, the turquoise waters vibrant against the golden sand.

Everything around him was dazzling in both color and beauty, including Rhi. It was no wonder she had chosen such a place. It was where a Light Fae would be drawn with all the colorful flora surrounding them.

He turned his head to look at her. Long black lashes lay still against her cheek, though he didn't think she was sleeping. If Rhi knew how important a piece she was in the upcoming war she wouldn't be lying in the sun now.

Con was suspicious of Rhi when he should be courting her favor. Rhi was a formidable ally, and she had proven time and again that she would fight alongside the Kings.

Balladyn should push a little harder to win Rhi to his side. Balladyn could easily take the throne from Taraeth, but to lead the Dark and win against the Kings, he would need Rhi.

As for Ulrik, Daire suspected the banished King knew exactly how important Rhi was to this game. Ulrik had been there when Rhi needed him, and on occasion he had asked Rhi for help. Ulrik was smart in that he wasn't pulling Rhi one way or another. Which might very well win him her allegiance if Con didn't wise up.

He saw by Rhi's even breathing that she was asleep. Daire reached out and gently pulled a lock of hair from her cheek. Her head turned toward him as if seeking his touch.

His hands itched to caress her cheek, to smell the sun upon her skin. But he was a Reaper, destined to be alone. His only companions were the other Reapers. If Rhi or any Fae discovered the Reapers, they were immediately put to death. It was one of Death's strict rules involving the Reapers.

Daire wondered what Rhi would think of them and what they did. Knowing Rhi, she would approve. Then she might ask to join them.

That made Daire smile. Though they had both Dark and Light Fae in the Reapers, there had never been a female. He wasn't sure why Death only chose males, but it wasn't for him to ask.

He was reaching out to run the backs of his fingers along Rhi's cheek when Balladyn appeared. Daire was glad he'd remained veiled. He jumped to his feet and backed away even as he watched Balladyn look at her as if he had found the greatest treasure in all the realms.

That's when Daire realized that Balladyn truly loved her. The kind of love that all mortals dreamed of, but few actually found. The kind of love that Rhi thought she'd had with her King.

"Rhi," Balladyn whispered as he knelt beside her. He put his hands on either side of her head and leaned down to place his lips upon hers.

Her lids fluttered open to gaze up at Balladyn.

His smile was slow as it pulled up the corners of his lips. "You smell like sunshine and salt."

"You're not supposed to be here," she replied.

"As if I can stay away from you. I ache to be near you. Don't you understand that I crave your touch? I hunger for your kisses?"

She placed her hands on his arms and slowly caressed upward to his neck. "Show me," she bade in a husky voice.

Daire couldn't look away from the kiss that began slow and turned passionate. He continued to watch when Balladyn lowered himself onto her and gathered her in his arms before rolling to his back and taking her with him.

He held his breath when Rhi sat up and untied the top of her gold bikini before tossing it away. Daire gazed at her full breasts and hard, dusky nipples.

But he turned away when Balladyn sat up and wrapped his lips around one of the turgid peaks. Daire didn't want to be there, but he couldn't leave. He was tasked with watching Rhi—even when that meant remaining as she made love to Balladyn.

CHAPTER
THIRTY-FIVE

Sleep never came for Sophie, even within Darius's arms. She couldn't stop thinking of everything. It was shocking and exhilarating to find she'd fallen in love again, but on the heels of that was the terror of knowing she was in the middle of a war that had no end in sight.

Ulrik wasn't going to stop until she was dead. Sophie didn't want to die. She had too much to live for now—one big one was Darius.

She tightened her arm around him as they lay on their sides, her front to his back. Though she didn't ask, she had a suspicion that he wasn't sleeping, but she let him pretend. It gave her time to think.

Because when they were awake, they couldn't keep their hands off each other.

That kind of passion was heady, spine-tingling, and oh so amazing. Now that she'd experienced it, she'd never settle for anything less than that.

Career or Darius?

She didn't want to have to make that decision. All she could do was pray that she was worrying over nothing, that Darius lived in Edinburgh.

That brought her up short.

"What is it?" Darius asked sleepily.

She leaned over to see his face, but his eyes were still closed. "Where do you live?"

"Dreagan."

"I meant here in the city."

He opened his eyes and then turned over, wrapping an arm around her. "There's a warehouse we use if I need somewhere to go. We doona need to sleep or eat as you do."

"So when this thing with Ulrik is done, you'll go back to Dreagan?"

"Aye."

Just as she'd feared. So she definitely did have something to worry about. That is if he wanted her with him. He may not feel the same as she.

"I'll no' leave until Ulrik is dealt with."

"How long has this been going on with him?"

"It began a few years ago."

"Years?" she asked.

Darius wound her hair around his thick hand. "We can no' just attack him, Sophie. He doesna have all of his magic. It would be like an adult attacking a child."

"So you want to wait until he has all of his magic? That makes no sense. He's threatening friends of the Kings, and you want to wait?"

"He has to challenge Con. He's no' done that yet."

"You could take him."

Darius's jaw clenched. "I'd like nothing more than to do just that, but I've orders from my King."

"You're a King yourself."

He sat up to lean against the headboard. "It doesna work that way."

"It should." She faced him, crossing her legs.

"Think of us like the military. Con is our general. He makes the decisions, and we carry them out."

She shook her head. "You're not the military. You're a Dragon King."

"With no dragons to lead," he said quietly.

Sophie winced as she realized her voice had grown louder.

He took her hand in his. "The last time someone disobeyed Con was when Ulrik went after the humans. We may disagree with him, which happens often, but we doona go against a direct order."

"Even if it means saving someone?"

"I'll no' let anything happen to you."

She sighed. "I know that."

"What is this really about?"

Sophie tried to shrug it off, but he tightened his grip on her hand when she would've pulled it away.

"Tell me," he urged in a firm voice.

"What is this between us?"

It was his turn to fidget. "I doona know."

"I need to know something. If this is just a fling, then it needs to end now."

"It's no' a fling," he assured her.

That relieved some of her anxiety, but not all of it. "I like what I'm feeling. I don't want it to end."

"Even though I'm a dragon?"

"A Dragon King," she corrected with a smile. "And the answer is yes."

He ran a hand through his disheveled blond locks. "You doona know what you're getting involved in, doc. We're bombarded on all sides with Ulrik, the Dark, and MI5. We have more enemies than allies, and we're always battling someone."

"That sounds like the emergency room."

"We live on Dreagan. All of us."

She knew he was telling her that if they remained together, she'd have to live at Dreagan.

"You have a career here. Your path is set before you. If you remain with me, that'll change."

Sophie's confusion over what she wanted kept her quiet. She'd worked so hard to get to where she was at the hospital. She was in line to be Chief of Staff, a goal she'd set before entering medical school.

Then again, she had a man who healed her wounds and her heart. A man who loved and cared for her as if she were a precious piece of him.

When she compared her life with Scott to Darius, the differences were black and white. She would've never been truly happy with Scott. Though she hated that time of her life, it had happened for a reason. Now she knew what that reason was—Darius.

The sound of her alarm pulled her out of her thoughts. Sophie rose and headed to the bathroom, her mind still a jumble as she readied for the day.

Darius tried to get Sophie to take a taxi to work, but she was determined to walk, despite the temperatures. Snow was falling, but she walked with determined steps. Once more Darius didn't see Ulrik's men. They no longer watched her building—and that was disconcerting.

Ulrik wouldn't pull away. He was planning something. It was enough to set Darius on edge. He didn't want to worry Sophie though, so he didn't mention it.

As they reached a café just a block from the hospital, Sophie said, "I need some coffee."

He had his hand on her back as he opened the door to the café and waited for her to enter. Darius quickly scanned the restaurant, but he saw no sign of Dark. The mercenaries Ulrik hired Darius could easily handle.

They were standing in line to order when Darius felt the hairs on the back of his neck prickle. He peered out the windows of the café and spied three Dark Fae. Two used glamour, but the third flaunted his short black and silver hair and red eyes with a smile.

The trio approached from different directions, and their focus was the café. Darius was eager to take out the Dark, but not in front of witnesses. Nor was Darius keen on leaving Sophie alone for even a second.

Darius sent out a call through the dragon link to Con, Rhys, and Kiril. They would be here soon. Until then, Darius would remain by Sophie's side.

"That's a Dark," she whispered, her voice shaking as she caught sight of the Fae.

"Aye."

Her breath hitched as she caught sight of the other two. "I thought they were gone from the city."

"So did I."

This was some kind of trap. Darius knew it in the pit of his soul. If he left Sophie, Ulrik would be there in a heartbeat.

Each of the Dark soon had humans take notice of them. Moments later the Dark not using glamour smiled directly at Darius through the café window and led two women into an alley.

"He's going to take their souls," Sophie said in shock.

Darius fisted his hands. That's exactly what the Dark was doing. He was also attempting to draw Darius out.

"You must save them."

He glanced down at Sophie and shook his head. "It's what they want."

"My life isn't worth more than those two women," Sophie argued. "Help them."

Darius was resolute in remaining where he was. Then the other two Fae each walked off with mortals. The idea of any of the humans dying angered Darius, but it wouldn't make him leave Sophie.

Then four more Dark appeared.

"Oh, God," Sophie whispered urgently.

Darius knew Con and the others would take care of the Dark. All he had to do was stay with Sophie.

"You can't let them die," she said, giving his arm a shake.

Darius turned to her. "If I leave, Ulrik or one of his men will try to take you."

"Let them." She lifted her chin in defiance.

"They willna care who they hurt to get to you."

Sophie pointed outside. "You say I'm a healer. Do you have any idea what it's doing to me knowing what is happening to those people out there? They're dying because of me. And you can stop it."

"With the chance of losing you."

"It's a chance I'm willing to take."

"I'm no'," Darius stated. "Besides, Con and the others will be here soon. They'll take care of the Dark."

At that moment, Sophie's face crumpled as she gazed out one of the windows. The first Dark who'd walked off came into view. He merely smiled at them and motioned over another woman.

"Go save them right now, or I'll walk out there myself," Sophie demanded.

Darius hated being stuck between a rock and a hard place. If he didn't save the mortals, Sophie would never forgive him. If he went to help, she might be taken.

"Please," she begged.

Darius knew it was wrong, but he was going to help. He grasped Sophie's arms. "Fight with all you have if they come for you."

"I will."

"I'll be back soon."

She grinned and rose up to give him a quick kiss. "I know. Now, go be a hero and save those people."

Darius strode out of the café toward the Dark nearest him.

CHAPTER
THIRTY-SIX

Sophie walked to the nearest window to watch Darius. Everyone else in the café was oblivious to what was going on. She looked at them, knowing that had been her not that long ago.

But now that she knew what was out there she couldn't stand by and allow anything to happen. She had to save them. It was in her nature. She was a healer, and that meant whether it was her hands working to heal or she sent someone else, she was still working to save those around her.

She put her hands on the window trying to get a view of Darius as he headed into an alley where one Dark had disappeared. Two others followed him.

It felt like an eternity before Darius emerged from an alley leading a woman looking dazed. She let out a sigh and just stopped herself from clapping and whistling at her man.

Darius turned the woman away from the other Dark and gave her a push. Then he moved onto the next Dark. Sophie's line of sight into the side street where the second Dark was allowed her to witness Darius fight. She stood in awe as he quickly landed several lethal punches.

She had to stop herself from rushing out to him when she saw what looked like bubbles form from the Dark's hand before he threw them right at Darius.

When Darius's body jerked, she knew whatever those bubbles were had to be painful. In spite of the obvious pain he was in, Darius kept attacking the Dark.

The burn marks on Darius's shirt reminded Sophie of the video she'd watched. Those Dark had thrown those same bubbles. Magic. That's what it was, and it was hurting Darius.

"He's impressive, is he no'?"

Sophie's heart fell to her feet as she recognized Ulrik's voice behind her. She slowly turned to face him. Today he wore a pair of jeans and a charcoal gray sweater that accentuated his wide shoulders and thick chest.

"Con will be here soon." She wasn't sure why she told Ulrik that, but it was the first thing that came to mind.

He merely grinned. "Even better."

"It doesn't matter what you do to me, it'll never stop the Kings."

"Ah, so Darius told you." Ulrik moved closer to the window. "I wondered if he'd share those secrets. Con must be furious."

"I'm not going to tell anyone."

Ulrik turned his gold eyes to her. "What it tells me—and Con—is that Darius is falling in love with you. If he hasn't already."

That news made her want to shout with joy. If she wasn't so terrified of the man standing beside her. Sophie kept her back to the window. She wanted to see if anyone else came toward her so she'd be prepared.

"You see," Ulrik continued. "The Kings only tell those they trust, and since they doona trust easily, it means that Darius has feelings for you. And those Kings who share such secrets generally take the females as their mates."

Mate. Yes, Sophie could see herself as Darius's. It made her giddy to think that she could have everything she'd long thought would never happen.

"If that look is any indication, you like the idea." Ulrik grunted. "I'd think twice about it."

Sophie cut him a harsh look. "Because I was hurt in the past?"

"Because we've felt the worst life has to offer and were left knowing that it can never happen to us again."

Sophie had never looked for it. Then it was suddenly there. She could've ignored the feelings for Darius, but instead, he gave her the courage to open her heart once more. "It's true I once shunned anything that would've healed me, because I wanted those gaping wounds as a reminder of how stupidly naïve I'd been."

"So Darius changed your thinking? Hope is a dangerous thing, Sophie."

"It's also healing. It can give someone courage." And she needed a lot right now.

Darius had been right in knowing Ulrik would come for her. She had no idea if Con and the others were there yet or how Darius fared in the battle—and she didn't dare look.

"There's your friend Claire," Ulrik said. "She's filled with such hope that it's difficult to look at her. It's verra sad, really."

Sophie's throat clogged. Ulrik was now threatening Claire. She wanted to claw his eyes out, because Claire had done nothing but be her friend.

"It'd be a shame if something happened to her."

Sophie turned to face him. "I pity you."

"Pity me?" he asked with a grin.

"Yes. I thought you and I were alike because of our pain, but I just realized we're nothing alike. You comment on my feelings as if they're a joke. The fact is, it doesn't matter that you were cut so deeply by the betrayal that the wounds haven't healed, because you won't allow them to. You hold hate, revenge, and bitterness close in order to get through each day."

He raised a brow, no longer smiling. "You should know."

"That's right," she said, her anger pushing her forward. "I speak from experience. I did exactly that for years. It's the only way I survived in the beginning. I was suffocating under the weight of my betrayal. That hate was my life raft. Just as it is yours."

"Doona pretend to know me, mortal."

She knew by his fierce look that she was pushing him. Her fear should've halted any more words, but all she could think of was Darius. He would never stop—and neither would she.

"You cling to revenge," she continued. "It's all you have. You've no friends, no home, and no family."

He stepped close until his nose was nearly touching hers. "Careful, doc. You're treading on dangerous ground."

"Is this where you kill me?"

Ulrik laughed softly. "You should've walked away from Darius when you had the chance. Instead, you continued to play with fire. It's time both of you discovered the consequences."

Sophie elbowed him in the stomach and made a run for the door. She caught a glimpse of Darius fighting two Dark in an alley right before her vision went black.

Darius finished off the Dark he was fighting. Before he could go back out onto the street, more surrounded him. The Dark were making up for being absent the last few days. If he didn't know better, he'd think they were keeping him from getting back to Sophie.

He broke a Dark's neck, letting the body fall to the

ground as he realized that was exactly what they were doing.

Darius didn't have time to think about it as more Dark arrived. He fought past the pain of the Dark magic continually thrown at him. His left arm was going numb, and it was all he could do to remain on his feet.

He whirled around with a bellow as a blast hit him in the back. Darius wanted nothing more than to shift and let loose a flash of dragon fire.

"We're here!" Con shouted in his head.

Darius tried to get a glimpse of the café through the Dark he was fighting, but he couldn't see inside. If only he could see a hint of Sophie he'd feel better.

He didn't know how long he stood there facing Dark Fae after Dark Fae. His right leg gave out, landing him hard on his knee. Darius rolled to dodge a volley of magic from the Dark.

"We gotcha," Kiril said as he helped Darius to his feet.

Within moments, Darius, Kiril, Rhys, and Con sent the last of the Dark to their deaths. When the last Fae fell, Darius leaned back against the building and closed his eyes for a second. Then he pushed away from the bricks and started toward the café.

"Whoa," Rhys said as he caught Darius before he fell. "Where are you going?"

Darius pointed to the café. "Sophie."

"I'll get her," Con said. Then he looked at Rhys and Kiril. "Keep him here."

Darius watched as Con walked across the street to the café. Once Rhys settled him against the building again, Darius slid down until he was sitting.

He kept waiting for Con to walk out with Sophie. Darius couldn't wait to see her face, though he didn't want her to see him like this.

The minutes ticked by slowly. Too slowly.

"Something's wrong," Darius said.

Rhys nodded as he looked at all the Dark littering the ground. "In more ways than one."

Darius climbed to his feet when Con walked out of the café alone. "Nay."

Kiril raked a hand through his hair and kicked at the pavement while Rhys whirled around to Con and let out a string of curses.

"Where is she?" Darius demanded when Con joined them.

Con shrugged, his black eyes full of sadness. "No one saw anything. I convinced the owner to show me the surveillance footage."

"And?" Rhys urged.

But Darius already knew. "Ulrik has her."

Con gave a single nod. "She didna go willingly. She made a run for it, but a Dark was there. He took her and Ulrik."

"I've got to find her before he kills her."

Kiril motioned to the Dark. "We've got to get this removed before someone sees."

"And Darius needs to heal," Rhys added.

Darius cut his eyes to Rhys. "I'm fine. I need to find Sophie."

"Why?" Con asked.

Darius jerked his head to the King of Kings. He knew what Con was asking. Darius wasn't yet ready to admit it to anyone, because he'd barely come to terms with it himself.

"Oh, shite," Kiril said, his shamrock green eyes wide.

Darius felt their gazes on him, but he didn't look away from Con. "Aye. Sophie is my mate."

"Then I suggest we find her," Con said, the corners of his lips tipping up slightly.

Darius closed his eyes. It might already be too late.

Ulrik could've already taken her life. Or worse—given her to a Dark. The dread bubbled inside him, coalescing with his rage.

The only way he was going to get Sophie back was to be the dragon warrior he once was. And regardless of what Con wanted, if the chance arose, Darius was going to take Ulrik's head. This was going to end once and for all.

No more would Kings have to worry about Ulrik finding their mates. No more would a King have to fight one of their own. No more would they have the Dark and Ulrik to contend with.

By the time the sun rose on a new day, Darius was going to make sure they had one less enemy to contend with.

"I know that look," Rhys said. "It's been a long while since I've seen it, but it's no' one you forget."

Con stepped in front of Darius. "We do this together."

Before Darius could answer, there was a push against Darius's head and he heard Ulrik's voice. Darius hesitated, but then opened the link.

"*I understand there was a lot of Dark in the city suddenly,*" Ulrik said, a smile in his voice.

"*They showed their stupidity again. They're all dead now.*"

"*That's a shame. I'm sure Taraeth isna going to be happy about that.*"

"*Taraeth can go bugger himself,*" Darius said. "*Where's Sophie?*"

"*With me.*"

Darius turned and punched the wall, the brick crumbling beneath such an onslaught. "*I warned you to leave her alone.*"

"*This is the part where you tell me you're going to kill me and that you'd do anything for her. Right?*"

"*Aye.*"

"*Then prove it,*" Ulrik said. "*Meet me.*"

"*Name the time and place.*"

"*I will. Bring Con.*"

And with those cryptic words, Ulrik severed the link.

"What happened?" Kiril asked.

Con's lips flattened. "Ulrik."

"Aye," Darius said with a nod. "He wants to meet me later."

Rhys rubbed his hands together. "Finally. The bastard will come to us."

Darius held Con's gaze. "He wants me to bring you."

Con crossed his arms over his chest and slid his gaze to Kiril and Rhys. "Ulrik may no' know either of you are in the city."

"We can no' count on that," Darius stated.

"Exactly. We'll need a plan that keeps Rhys and Kiril out of sight from everyone—including the Dark."

Darius twisted his lips. "That'll depend on where Ulrik wants to meet."

"Looks like we need to get our thinking caps on," Rhys said with a grin.

CHAPTER
THIRTY-SEVEN

The moment Sophie woke she had one thing on her mind—Darius. He'd warned her, repeatedly, that Ulrik would try to get to her while he helped the mortals. It had been a setup from the very beginning.

And she had played right into Ulrik's hands.

She felt like an utter fool, but she still wouldn't trade her life for those of the people Darius saved. Her life wasn't worth more than any of the others.

Sophie sat up from the bed and looked around. Everything was black and red. Even the walls were painted black. The room was huge with a ceiling that had to be twenty feet above her.

The bed linens were black with red accents. The chair was a black and red pattern. The rugs were black. Even the glass on the black table beside the bed was black.

The floating lights spaced along the walls and over the bed were confirmation she was somewhere she didn't want to be. Sophie scooted to the end of the bed. She looked to the door, waiting for it to burst open and someone to tell her she couldn't walk around.

But nothing happened.

She rose and walked around the room. There were some normal items, like a book, that made her think she might still be on earth. Then she opened the book and saw words in a language she'd never seen before.

Sophie hastily closed the book and wrapped her arms about herself. She really, really hoped she wasn't in the Fae realm, or even in Ireland where the Dark were.

She sat in the chair and tucked her legs to the side. How she wished Darius was there. He always knew what to do, which made sense since he'd been fighting the Fae and Ulrik for a long time.

Her eyes closed as she thought of Darius. He'd held her as if she were the most important thing in the world. He'd kissed her as if he had searched the very ends of the earth for her. And he'd made love to her as if he were worshiping her body, giving her unimaginable pleasure each time.

To think that she'd actually believed she'd never care about someone so deeply again that she lost herself. Yet here she was.

All she had to do was recall those first six months after Scott's betrayal. The pain, the emptiness. The desolation. Her world had been destroyed so vividly that she hadn't been able to put the pieces back together again.

On the outside everyone thought she had the perfect life. On the inside, she looked like a three-year-old had stitched her back together. There were pieces of her missing and pieces that would never fit together again. It made her a very . . . hollow . . . individual.

Strange how only a little time with Darius had changed all of that. Her heart would always carry the scars from what happened with Scott, but they were healed now. All because of Darius.

Sophie had survived on her own for a long time. She knew she didn't need a man, not even Darius.

But she wanted him.

That made all the difference in the end.

When Sophie opened her eyes, Ulrik was in the room with her. She sucked in a breath, hating that he'd taken her by surprise again. His hair was down and loose about his shoulders, the black length holding a hint of a wave.

"Praying?" he asked.

She looked him up and down. "Yes. For your soul."

He smiled, approval in his gold eyes. "That's no' something you need to worry about."

"It is. Darius is going to kill you."

Ulrik chuckled softly. "Ah, dear Sophie. You think you know what it is to know the Kings, but you've only touched the tip of the iceberg. Con has told all the Dragon Kings no' to touch me. It doesna matter how much Darius might want to kill me, he willna. Because we all know I'm going to challenge Con. And win."

"You're sure of yourself."

"I was sure of myself eons ago. I should've put friendship aside and fought him then."

His words caught her attention. "But you loved him like a brother."

"Where did that leave me?" he asked. He spread his hands wide. "Right here."

"Then challenge Con. Stop taking your petty revenge out on us."

Sophie knew it was the wrong thing to say the moment it was out of her mouth and the anger rolled off Ulrik.

He stalked to her, bracing his arms on the chair and leaning his face close to hers. "Petty? It was you fucking humans who began this. We should've wiped the stain of you from this realm the moment you arrived instead of promising protection. What has that gotten us? We hide our true nature and send away our dragons so as no' to offend your bloody sensibilities. You're a scourge on this planet!"

Sophie winced, sinking as far back in the chair as she could go. The few times she'd spoken with Ulrik he'd been as cool as ice. Now there was unmitigated wrath in his eyes, in his tone. In his very breath.

"I'm not the one who betrayed you."

He slammed his fist into the back of the chair near her head. "You're mortal. That makes you one of them."

Sophie decided to remain silent. Anything she said was going to set him off. As she looked into his eyes, she saw her death there.

"You can blame this on Darius. I would've left you alone had he no' sought you out. I watched the two of you shagging on the street in the shadows. I saw then what was coming. Passion like that leads to one thing—love."

Sophie blinked to keep the tears at bay. She didn't want to show any kind of weakness to Ulrik.

Ulrik straightened and ran a hand through his hair. "Enjoy your last few hours, doc."

As soon as the door closed behind him, Sophie buried her head in her hands and cried.

More and more whispers of the Reapers reached Balladyn. Yet every time he sought to find out more, there was nothing. Not even searching his archives proved anything useful. He wanted more, and not just because Rhi asked for the knowledge.

No, this was because Balladyn had a bad feeling that continued to grow the more he heard about the Reapers.

Nothing good would come of their arrival. He wasn't so much worried about himself, because if they wanted to come for him, nothing would stop them. Balladyn's anxiety was for Rhi. She was certain she had a watcher.

Balladyn had sent no one, and Taraeth didn't know where to find her. Besides, Balladyn knew every Dark Fae who had the kind of power it took to remain veiled. Not one of them could remain that way indefinitely.

Usaeil was stupid enough to send someone after her. She'd proven that already with having Inen follow Rhi. None of the Light had the kind of power to remain veiled either. Which left only one group—the Reapers.

It chilled Balladyn to the bone.

Were they out to kill Rhi? Recruit her? Sway her away from him?

The possibilities were endless, and he wasn't going to sit back and just let it happen. Rhi was his. He'd waited centuries for her. She belonged with him, and he was going to prove it.

Darius raked a hand through his hair, his frustration on high. They had a map of Edinburgh out on the table locating the places where Ulrik might want to meet.

All plans, however, were on hold as Con made a trip to Dreagan—without telling them what it was about. Kiril had called Ryder, but the resident computer nerd had no idea what would bring Con back during such a crisis.

Crisis. Shite. That's exactly what this was, and Darius could do nothing but wait to hear from Ulrik before he did anything.

He couldn't look at the map anymore. All he could do was think about Sophie, pray she wasn't hurt, and think of all the ways he was going to kill Ulrik.

"The Dark have no' made a move for it in weeks," Kiril said.

Rhys snorted. "They've no' given up on it."

"What?" Darius asked, their conversation intruding on his thoughts.

"The weapon," Kiril and Rhys said in unison.

Darius flattened his lips. "You're right. We've heard nothing about it lately. That's no' a good sign."

"No' at all," Rhys stated as he leaned his hands on the table and looked at the map. "With all the surveillance from our friends from MI5 going on around Dreagan, we can no' patrol as we normally did."

Kiril looked up from the laptop from his position on the sofa. "It doesna matter. Our magic is still there. The Dark can no' enter without us knowing it."

"But mortals can," Rhys pointed out as he looked at them.

Darius sank onto the other sofa and let out a string of curses. "The Dark want the weapon, no' Ulrik. It's in Ulrik's best interest if the Dark doona have it, because then the Dark could destroy him as well."

Kiril closed the laptop and set it beside him. "That's a good point. Ulrik wants us dead, but he wants to stay alive. He wouldna willingly give them the weapon."

"But he'd use it as a bargaining tool with the Dark," Darius stated.

"We doona even know what it is," Rhys said. He straightened and pointed to the map. "The Dark didna attack Dreagan again and again to simply give up so easily just because they managed to get a video of us, or because some of Ulrik's magic has returned."

Kiril rubbed his jaw. "What are you thinking?"

"That's just it, I doona know," Rhys said, weariness hardening his words.

Darius tapped his finger on the arm of the sofa. "Perhaps we're looking at this all wrong."

"Meaning?" Kiril asked.

Darius motioned to the map and the computer. "Every time Ulrik or the Dark have done something, we've reacted to counter it."

"As we're supposed to," Rhys said.

Darius nodded. "But what if it was all done in order to lead us to do exactly that?"

Kiril leaned forward and looked from Darius to Rhys. "While we've been chasing our tails trying to cover up things so we remain secret from the humans, Ulrik and the Dark have been leading us on a merry chase."

"I still say we should worry about the weapon," Rhys said. "I doona like discovering its existence now after all this time. I especially hate that the Dark knew of it before we did. And I doona like no' knowing what it is."

Darius agreed with everything Rhys said, as did all the Kings. "Sooner or later Con is going to have to tell us what the weapon is. Until then, we need to look at everything Ulrik and the Dark have done to see if there's a pattern we're missing."

"Or a sign of what they want," Kiril said.

Rhys threw him a look. "You know what they want. All of us dead."

"Who do you think will win between Ulrik and Con?" Kiril asked them.

Darius shrugged. He'd been thinking about that more and more, and he wasn't sure. If this had been before the banishment, Darius would've said Con only because Ulrik's heart hadn't been in it.

But now? Now Ulrik wanted vengeance, and he wanted Con dead.

"I doona know," Rhys admitted. "It could go either way. If Ulrik defeats Con, he'll come after us next."

Silence filled the room as they took in Rhys's words. Because if the Kings died, so did the women who were their mates.

CHAPTER
THIRTY-EIGHT

Con walked through the caves of his mountain without any need of light. He knew them like he knew every inch of Dreagan—by heart. But with his dragon eyesight—even in human form—he could see well enough in the dark.

Deep in the heart of the mountain, hundreds of feet below the cavern he used while in dragon form, was a narrow corridor. He had to shuffle sideways to get to the chamber.

He reached the entrance to the chamber and slowly walked inside. Con snapped his fingers and a shard of light hovered in the middle of the chamber shedding a yellowish glow over everything.

Con stared at the weapon the Dark so desperately wanted to get their hands on. He still hadn't learned how the Dark discovered the weapon, but he would.

There were only two Kings who knew of the weapon—himself and Kellan. Since Kellan had been sleeping in his mountain until recently, it wasn't him.

Con was almost 100 percent certain that Rhi didn't know of the weapon either. Which left no one else. Con went to great pains to keep the knowledge of the weapon from the Kings.

He and Kellan never spoke of it around them. It was too powerful to fall into the wrong hands. In truth, it should've been destroyed long ago. Con wasn't sure why he hadn't done the deed when he took over as King of Kings. He could do it now. It was why he was there.

Yet something stopped him.

He wasn't sure what. Maybe it was the need to learn who had betrayed them. Or perhaps it was because he'd guarded the weapon for so many thousands of years. He was responsible for it being kept as secret as their identity.

The Kings wanted to know what the weapon was, but if they knew, it would change everything. Because even though their very way of life was being threatened by the video and Ulrik's threats, it was nothing compared to what would happen if the Kings learned the truth.

Con knew he wasn't alone in the chamber. He wasn't surprised that Kellan was in his mountain. The weapon was too important not to be guarded, because not even dragon magic was enough to keep it safe.

"We can no' hide it forever," Kellan said from Con's left.

He didn't bother to look at his friend. "I'll keep it from them for as long as I can."

"That time is coming to an end. It's a weapon that can be used to destroy us, aye. But it's also said it could be used to help us."

"Nay," Con stated.

Kellan sighed loudly. "V is still missing. Ulrik is focused on Sophie who I'm guessing by your face is Darius's mate. The Dark are suspiciously quiet. We've mortals crawling all over Dreagan looking for any signs of dragons. We're no' sure if Rhi is on our side or no', and the

Light Fae are doing nothing. Aye, Con, we need to do something."

"No' this. Never this." He turned to Kellan. "As for the rest, we'll deal with it as we have everything else."

"Dragon magic can only conceal so much."

"It's all we need."

It was all they had ever needed.

Darius rubbed his eyes with his thumb and forefinger. The longer he went without hearing from Ulrik, the more uneasy he became. They'd located two places that favored privacy and seclusion. The weather would also help keep any mortals from venturing near.

He jerked when Ulrik said his name in his mind. Darius glanced at Rhys and Kiril and nodded, letting them know it was Ulrik.

"*I need to hear from Sophie.*"

Ulrik laughed. "*No' going to happen.*"

"*Then Con willna come.*"

"*Matters no' to me.*"

"*It doesna do your plan any good to lie. We know you want him there or you wouldna have requested it.*"

Ulrik was silent for a beat. "*This is about you, Darius.*"

"*Then why ask for Con?*"

"*I want him to see firsthand your pain when I kill Sophie.*"

Darius closed his eyes, attempting to remain as calm as possible. "*You do that, and you willna have to worry about challenging Con because I'm going to kill you.*"

"*We both know that willna happen. You'd never disobey Constantine.*"

In this, Darius definitely would. But he let Ulrik think what he would since it worked to his advantage. "*Show me Sophie's alive.*"

"*You'll come to the meet whether she is or isna. You'll*

find out then if she's still alive. We'll meet on the south end of Edinburgh. You know the place."

"*Aye.*"

"*In an hour.*" Ulrik closed the link.

Darius slammed his hand down, breaking the table in two.

"I gather that didna go well."

All three of them turned to find Con standing in the doorway. He stepped inside and let the hotel door shut behind him as he walked to them.

"Everything all right at Dreagan?" Kiril asked.

Con gave a nod. "As are Shara and Lily."

Darius pocketed his mobile and stared at Con. "Do you care to explain your sudden need to visit Dreagan?"

"Nay."

Rhys shrugged, his look saying that's what he'd expected out of Con when Darius looked his way. Kiril just sighed.

Con poured himself a glass of whisky. "Ulrik has been leading us on a merry chase for months now. This gives us what we need. We'll all go tonight. We'll save Sophie, and in the process, we'll capture Ulrik and end this debacle."

"Meaning you'll kill him once we're back at Dreagan," Rhys said.

Con downed the whisky. "I should've done it instead of banishing him. It's my mistake that must be corrected. He's ruined our way of life significantly. That ends tonight."

"Say this works," Darius said. "It willna end the Dark's need to come after us."

Kiril's lips twisted as he crossed his arms over his chest. "Actually, it might. The Dark have Ulrik as an ally. Without him, they know nothing. No longer will they catch us off guard."

"That's a big chance we're taking," Rhys said.

Con cut his black gaze to Rhys. "So you doona wish to be rid of Ulrik?"

"I didna say that," Rhys corrected him. "What I'm saying is that all of this might no' go away with Ulrik gone. The Dark are after the weapon. They willna stop until they have it."

"That's no' going to happen," Con stated in a voice as cold and lethal as death itself. "Like it or no', this is a good plan. Ulrik knows how we work. He'll be expecting you two, but if we work it right, this could work."

That made Darius smile. "Con's right. This is a verra good chance for us to end all of this right now."

"And if Sophie gets caught in the crossfire?" Kiril asked.

Darius looked at each of them. "That can no' happen."

Kiril sighed as he dropped his arms to his sides. "There will be Dark there. The place Ulrik chose is hidden well from mortals. It's perfect for us to shift if we must."

"We can no'," Con ordered. "Under no circumstances will any of you shift. We doona know who might be watching."

"Or what Dark might be recording," Rhys stated with a roll of his eyes.

"We have to do this," Darius said.

Con gave a nod. "I agree. To pass up this opportunity would be folly."

"Ulrik will suspect you'll try and trap him," Kiril said.

Con's smile was full of retribution and anger. "He willna be expecting what I have in store for him."

Sophie remembered that feeling of drowning when she'd discovered Scott's cheating, but this was so much worse. This felt like she was being sucked under a riptide.

Everything she wanted was slipping from her before

she'd ever had a chance to hold it. She hadn't even told Darius she loved him.

So many years she'd wasted being isolated and hiding her heart. Darius showed her all that she'd been missing. Her dreams were passing right before her eyes like dust in the wind.

And fate was laughing at her once more.

CHAPTER
THIRTY-NINE

Darius drove the Mercedes SUV, his hands tight on the steering wheel. The others were taking different routes, arriving separately in the concealment of the dark.

As he drove down the highway out of Edinburgh, all he could think about was Sophie. He'd come to the conclusion that Sophie was still alive—for the time being. Ulrik would want to kill her in front of him.

Darius couldn't think of that. He refused to allow his thoughts down that road. It was better if he concentrated on how he was going to get Sophie free.

And kill Ulrik.

Over and over he let the scene play out in his mind of taking Ulrik's head and ending this stupid war. Twenty minutes later as he exited the highway and turned right he pictured his reunion with Sophie.

Now that he'd admitted she was his mate to Con and the others, it was time he told her. He knew Sophie had feelings for him, but he was hesitant to tell her.

Her career meant everything to her. He didn't want her to have to choose, which is what would happen if he told her of his love.

As difficult as it would be, the best thing for Darius to do was let her go. Sophie could return to her work as a healer without having to suffer through their war, secrets, and MI5 investigating everyone associated with Dreagan.

Darius slowed and turned onto a dirt road. He drove for several miles before he came to the edge of a forest. Throwing the vehicle in park, he shut off the engine and got out.

He walked around the front of the Mercedes and looked around. The area was unnervingly quiet. Darius was on high alert, because he knew there would be Dark showing themselves soon. As if the animals knew evil was coming, they abandoned the area as well.

His boots crunched on the snow as he headed toward the trees even as flurries floated around him. The sun sank quickly, turning the already gray sky dark.

Not a branch rustled, not even a whistle of wind. The disconcerting stillness had him glancing around, waiting for an attack. But nothing came. Yet.

As Darius made his way through the trees, he thought of the past and how he'd gone mad with guilt and anger at losing his woman and child. Those destructive feelings ate at him until nothing was left. When he'd finally taken to his mountain, his soul had been a raw, festering wound.

When Con woke him for this war, Darius had left his mountain just as angry as when he'd gone in. Centuries of dragon sleep hadn't calmed him. Nothing had.

Until Sophie.

Darius told himself the wild, primitive hunger that he had was simply his need to relieve his body. In truth, it had been Sophie from the very beginning.

She's the one who soothed his battered soul. The one who comforted the dragon. The one who glowed each time he touched her.

He yearned for Sophie to a degree that should terrify

him, but it only made him smile. He'd never felt such longing for a woman before. He ached to be near her, craved to touch her.

Hungered for her kisses.

At one time he'd resented Kellan and the other Kings who'd defied fate and the world to have their women, who had put aside their pasts and found happiness. It looked like he was one of those as well—or had been briefly.

It was too bad he wouldn't have the future he so desired. It pained him to know he'd be leaving Sophie behind, but it was for the best.

Movement to his right caught Darius's attention as he left the forest and walked into the valley. A look showed there was a Dark on either side of him and one at his back. They kept their distance, but it proved that Ulrik had no intention of leaving this battle with anything other than victory.

Many times Ulrik had caught them off guard. Tonight just might swing in their favor. It better, because anything other than Sophie walking out of there alive was a loss.

There was no sign of Ulrik, but Darius knew he was out there. The seconds ticked by as the snow began falling faster and the temperatures dropped.

Darius scanned the expanse between them and the opposite tree line. Need tore through him to see Sophie, to hold her and know she wasn't hurt.

He wished now that they'd brought every Dragon King. Con, however, had other ideas. Darius was tired of playing this game with Ulrik. It should've never gone this way.

But hindsight was 20/20. Looking back, Darius knew they should've made other choices and decisions, but there was no turning back the clock. They'd set this course, and Ulrik was determined to finish it.

Darius caught sight of Ulrik walking from the trees ahead of him. Steps behind him were two Dark Fae. One had ahold of Sophie's arm, leading her. The other carried an unconscious Claire in his arms.

"What the fuck?" Darius murmured.

When had Darius gotten Claire? Then it didn't matter. There were two captives to free. It changed the plans slightly.

"*I see her,*" Con said into Darius's mind. "*Leave it to Ulrik to up the ante.*"

Ulrik grinned as he looked at Darius. All Darius could hope for now was that everything went smoothly, but then again they were dealing with Ulrik and the Dark. When did anything go smoothly with them?

When Ulrik began moving toward him, Darius did the same. They halted ten feet from each other. The Dark stayed just behind Ulrik with the women.

"We're here," Darius told Ulrik. "Hand over Sophie and Claire."

"I think I'll keep the lasses with me for a wee bit."

Darius clenched his teeth together. They'd expected Ulrik to do that very thing, but it didn't make it any easier for him. In fact, it only managed to stir his rising anger.

"That didna make you mad, did it?" Ulrik asked, his grin widening.

"Smile while you can. That willna last long."

"I think it'll last longer than you think."

Darius kept his gaze locked on Ulrik even though he wanted nothing more than to turn to Sophie. But he had to keep Ulrik's attention on him and not the women. "Because you've planned it all?"

"I have."

"You can no' know every detail. You doona know the humans well enough to predict their decisions."

Ulrik laughed sardonically. "I'm better at it than you, apparently."

"So a hundred years ago when you planned all this you knew you would take Sophie and Claire."

Ulrik's gold eyes went hard. "I'll no' waste my time attempting to explain things to you. You're nothing more than a brute, Darius. Why do you think Con always sent you out first in a battle? You doona think. Your emotions rule you."

"Con sent me out first because he knew I wouldna fail in my orders."

"Just like a good soldier," Ulrik mocked. "Always following orders."

Darius couldn't wait to show Ulrik that he was no longer just a soldier. Ulrik changed all that the moment he focused on Sophie.

Out of the corner of his eye, Darius saw Sophie shivering. Though her coat was thick, it wasn't enough in the cold temperatures. "Let's get on with this."

"Yes, let's." Ulrik took a step closer, determination and resolve making his gold eyes hard. "Where is he?"

CHAPTER
FORTY

Sophie couldn't stop shaking, but it had nothing to do with the cold and everything to do with the situation.

The air was frigid and the flakes fell harder while the moon glistened off the snow, making the area almost glow. It would've been beautiful if not for the dire circumstances.

The reality of dragons, Fae, and magic was staring her in the face. No more would she scoff at those who believed in such things. Now that she was experiencing it all first-hand, she wondered how some people instinctively knew it was real while others—like she used to be—were adamant that it wasn't.

No wonder the video showing the Dragon Kings shifting on Dreagan brought so much attention. Those who believed were looking for proof, while others wanted to verify it was all faked.

She couldn't take her eyes from Darius. He stood tall and magnificent in the moonlight. The tension was high, the situation daunting. Any moment now a battle would break out.

There was something different about Darius. He looked

more focused, more intense. Ulrik teasing him about following orders didn't strike the chord Ulrik wanted.

Or perhaps it did.

Even though she wasn't beside Darius, the fact she saw him did wonders to keep her on her feet.

Sophie wanted to touch him, to feel his strength and heat. But the Dark holding her kept her at his side. She blinked through the rapidly falling snow to the ten feet or so that separated her from Darius.

"We're here," Darius said. "Hand over Sophie and Claire."

Sophie listened to the exchange that followed with interest. It wasn't until Ulrik demanded to know where a man was that she knew this had all been nothing but a precursor to what was coming.

She looked between Darius and Ulrik, watching the two of them stare, unblinking, at each other. Sophie swiveled her head, glancing around to see if anyone was there. Then she spotted a man striding out of the tree line behind Darius.

The clouds parted and the full moon shone upon him as if to spotlight him to everyone. The man was tall and moved with the same predatory stride that Darius had. And even Ulrik, if Sophie was being truthful.

The stranger had wavy blond hair that was cut short on the sides and longer on top. He wore boots, a pair of jeans, and a light sweater despite the snow. He didn't halt until he stood next to Darius.

"Con," Ulrik said to the stranger. "So glad you could make it."

"I wouldna miss this," Con stated in a flat voice, as if he were bored out of his mind.

Con jutted his square chin toward Sophie and the man holding Claire. "Darius is here, and now so am I. Allow Sophie and Claire to leave. This is between us."

The tension thickened until she could've cut it with a knife as Ulrik and Con glared at each other for several long minutes.

"You know how I hate the mortals," Ulrik said. "What does it matter if two more die?"

Sophie's heart plummeted. There had been a part of her that had known this very thing might happen. She'd prayed and hoped that Darius would be able to free her, but now there was Claire as well—a true innocent in this mess.

"Hand the lasses over or I leave," Con stated.

Ulrik laughed then. "We both know that's no' going to happen."

"Allow Sophie and Claire to leave. This business is between us."

Ulrik smiled then, a callous, icy smile. "Between us? Is it, really?"

"You know it is," Con stated.

"I think no'." Ulrik reached over and touched Sophie's cheek.

She jerked her face away. "Don't touch me."

"I willna be the one to do that."

Claire moaned then, but it wasn't a sound filled with pain. It was one filled with pleasure.

Sophie glanced at Darius to see his lips thinning. The Dark holding Claire was smiling as he looked down at her. Sophie began to shake her head. "No! Claire is an innocent! Leave her alone!"

Ulrik's head turned to her and stared. Sophie could see the death he promised in his eyes, in the way he looked at the world and everyone in it. Almost as if he couldn't stand to be a part of any of it.

"Innocent?" He repeated the word as if it were poison. "None of you mortals are innocent. You sullied our world, destroyed our way of life. Every one of you deserved to be killed in the most vicious, heinous way possible. I was stopped once before I could finish the job. I'll no' be stopped again."

"We'll see about that," Con stated.

Ulrik snorted and turned his attention to the King of Kings. "It'll be rather difficult for you to do anything once you're dead."

Claire moaned again, louder. Sophie saw that the Dark who held her squatted to lay her in the snow and jerked open her coat. He produced a blade and cut Claire's sweater before doing the same to her bra.

Sophie could only watch in mute horror as he began to tease Claire's nipples, causing her to moan louder and longer. When the Dark Fae rubbed Claire's sex through her jeans, Sophie tried to rush them. But the Dark holding her held fast.

"Let her go, you monster!" she yelled at the Dark.

Ulrik laughed at her outburst. "Monster. What a curious word." He turned to her, his lips lifted in a sneer. "Would monsters make room on their realm for another species? Would a monster take them into their home and love them? Would a monster offer their lives for them? Nay, Sophie. I'm no' the monster. Your kind is."

She swallowed and glanced at Darius. He stared at her with a mixture of fury and fear that told her just how dire the situation was.

"Your kind," Ulrik continued, "takes whatever they want. You doona stop and consider what will happen to the earth or its inhabitants. It's all about your comfort. And your fear of what you doona understand. All your kind thinks of when you find something new is to hunt it and kill it. All your kind knows is to conquer whatever they think is theirs. You doona know how to love unconditionally. You doona know what it means to be giving and patient. So tell me, doctor, who is the real monster?"

"I'm sorry that happened to you."

He snorted, looking at her as if she were the devil incarnate. "Sorry? You're sorry? I doubt it. You'll say whatever is needed to attempt to get out of this situation." He leaned close, but his gaze went to Darius. "The fact is, lass, I'm going to kill you and make Darius watch. Then he'll know what it really means to lose a mate."

Claire was moaning constantly now, her body moving on the snow. Her jeans were bunched down at her ankles and the Dark had his finger inside her.

"I hear it was difficult for Kellan to watch Taraeth force Denae to climax in front of him," Ulrik said as he faced Con and Darius. "I'm curious as to your reaction, Darius."

"This is your last chance," Darius said. "Release them or you die."

Ulrik shot him a fake smile. "Be a good soldier and remember your duty."

Darius had never felt the need to kill as he did at the moment. It didn't matter what Con wanted, Darius was going to kill Ulrik slowly, enjoying every moment of his pain. "I remember my duty."

Ulrik's gaze slid to Con. "Nothing to say? Worried that you're going to lose? The thing is, *old friend,* you lost the moment you bound my magic and banished me from Dreagan."

"You made your decisions," Con said. "You knew the consequences of ignoring my calls."

"It was time you learned no' everyone will always do your bidding."

Con's black eyes were as cold as the north. "Someone tried that once. He was banished, unable to shift."

"Perhaps the rest of the Kings should know the true you. The Constantine who didna let anyone—or any-*thing*—stand in the way of being King of Kings."

"I challenged and won."

Ulrik simply laughed. It caused Darius to wonder just

what Ulrik wanted them to know and what Con didn't. Obviously there was something in Con's past that Ulrik thought might turn the others against Con.

If it was bad enough, it just might.

That in itself worried Darius. Con had his faults, but his main concern was Dreagan. Like the others, Darius didn't always agree with everything Con did, but no one else stepped up to do what Con did. Hard to judge a dragon when none of them wanted all the worries and stress of being King of Kings.

Darius looked at Sophie who was staring at Claire. Claire was practically naked, and any moment now the Dark would take her. Sophie would never forgive him if he allowed anything to happen to Claire.

"You know I'm no' going to allow that arse to take Claire," Darius said.

Ulrik glanced at the pair. "I believe you're already too late. You're welcome to try and stop them."

In the old days, Darius would've waited for Con's command, but this involved his mate. There was no waiting.

Just as Darius was about to make a grab for the Fae with Claire, Sophie slammed her fist into the balls of the Dark holding her. He bent over, a strangled cry emanating from him.

Sophie made a dash for Claire, knocking over the Dark touching her. Darius rushed the Fae when he snarled and turned to Sophie. Darius shoved him into the snow with a bellow and ripped out his heart.

He turned to Sophie. "Run!"

CHAPTER
FORTY-ONE

Sophie scrambled to her hands and knees and leaned over Claire, protecting her. She couldn't believe what she'd just done, but the opportunity had been there—and she took it.

"Run!" Darius shouted.

Sophie slapped Claire's face to get her to wake up. She gave her another smack on the other cheek while trying to pull up her jeans.

"Soph?" Claire asked, blinking up at her as if coming out of sedation.

"Get moving," she told Claire urgently. Sophie helped her sit up. "Now."

Claire was on her feet, yanking up her pants as they began running. Sophie hooked an arm around her friend to help keep her balance and looked around, waiting for Ulrik to come after them. Their feet sank in the thick snow, hindering their progress.

"What the hell happened? Where am I?" Claire asked as she finished fastening her jeans. "And why the hell is my sweater cut?"

Sophie looked over her shoulder at Darius. "Later."

"Yeah," Claire said sarcastically. "I'm getting that vibe."

They only got a few steps before two Dark Fae suddenly appeared in front of them. Sophie had no idea they could move that quickly.

She slid to a halt, but she couldn't keep Claire on her feet and they both fell into the snow. There was a commotion behind her, but Sophie was more concerned with the two Dark in front of her.

Claire began to moan, reaching for the men. Sophie went into protection mode. She shoved Claire's hands away and leaned over her so the Dark couldn't get to her.

But there were two of them against her, and their hands were everywhere. On her, on Claire.

Somehow Sophie was flipped off Claire, and one of the Dark was kissing Claire. Sophie scrambled through the snow to get to her friend. Her fingers were numb, but she ignored it. Sophie shoved the guy off Claire, but Claire followed him, throwing herself at him.

"Claire!" Sophie yelled.

Then she was grabbed from behind. Hands cupped her breasts as a mouth began kissing her neck.

That's when she heard a furious bellow behind her.

Everyone stilled, including Sophie. She heard someone shout Darius's name. Sophie tried to get the Fae off her so she could see Darius and find out what had happened.

The harder she tried to get away, the tighter the Dark held her. Sophie elbowed him, but it didn't even faze him. Claire, however, had already removed her jacket and cut sweater with the Fae kissing down her throat to her exposed breasts.

There was more shouting, and Sophie could hear Con and Ulrik. But she couldn't make out Darius's voice. The thought that he might be injured renewed her efforts to get free.

Sophie was tossed onto her back as if she wasn't fighting with all her might. She looked up into red eyes and lifted her knee toward his groan. The man deflected her blow easily, much to her annoyance.

"Darius!" Con yelled.

Sophie saw Darius loom over her and, with little effort, toss the Dark Fae away. Darius glanced at her, then stalked toward the Dark who had jumped to his feet.

Her lips parted when the Fae's hands drew apart and a large iridescent bubble appeared. When it was about the size of a bowling ball, he threw it at Darius. Darius effortlessly leaned to the side to avoid it.

Sophie followed the bubble as it landed in the snow a few feet from her. The snow melted instantly, and there was a sizzling sound as the bubble evaporated into the ground that turned black.

"Shit," she mumbled.

She swiveled her head to Darius to find him and the Fae facing off. Sophie caught a glimpse of Ulrik and Con who were standing toe to toe and talking, but she couldn't make out what they were saying.

Sophie twisted to find Claire and spotted two Dark Fae coming toward them. She tried to get to her feet using her numb hands. Stumbling, Sophie fell into Claire and the Dark. Instead of getting angry, he tried to take off her jacket.

She shoved his hands away and shook Claire to try and snap her out of it. The next thing Sophie knew, another set of hands grabbed her.

This time there were too many trying to disrobe her. As soon as the cold air hit her stomach, she knew real fear. This was going to happen. She was going to be raped.

Sophie kicked and screamed to no avail. She heard Darius shout her name. Through the bodies, she spotted him. His face was contorted with rage, then her vision was blocked.

The sound of a low, deep growl reverberated around them and shook the ground. Everyone paused. Sophie used the chance to scramble out of the pile of men holding her and saw a deep purple paw—or was it a claw?—covered in scales. It was beyond huge with talons that looked almost black in the night.

She followed the paw—claw—upward to a thick forearm. Her gaze kept moving upward to even more scales and a chest. Her head tilted backward when she reached the long neck and followed it to the head.

Of a dragon.

Sophie knew she was looking at Darius. She blinked as he spread his wings and his lavender gaze was focused on the Dark who tried to rape her.

He was enormous, his wings immense. No wonder he'd said he would destroy her flat if he had shifted when she'd asked. As she gazed at him, she recognized the dragon. Because it was the same one tattooed on him.

Out of the trees came two men running from opposite ends of the valley. One shifted right before her eyes into a dragon with burnt orange scales. Sophie turned her head to look at the other in time to see him change into a yellow dragon.

Then all hell broke loose.

Darius wanted to tell Sophie that it would be all right, but he couldn't. Not in dragon form. All he could do was protect her from the Dark Fae.

Kiril went after the Dark who were trying to have sex with Claire while Rhys kept another group of Fae from reaching the girls.

Darius's gut clenched when he saw the way she stared up at him with her eyes wide and lips parted. She'd wanted to see him. He wished he knew what she was thinking.

They should've known the Dark would take matters

into their own hands. Con had tried to stop him, but nothing was going to keep Darius from Sophie.

He motioned to Claire with his head. Sophie quickly nodded and scrambled to her feet. She touched his forearm before she rushed to her friend while the Dark were now focused on him.

The Dark had their teeth bared and were gathering their magic, ready to blast him with all they had. Darius was ready to kill more Fae, especially those who'd tried to force his woman.

With Claire's clothes gathered, Sophie got her to her feet. Half-dragging, half-running, Sophie finally reached the trees. It wasn't until Darius heard the Mercedes engine roar to life that he drew in a deep breath and let loose a blast of fire that killed the Dark closest to him.

Darius swiped at a Dark with his wings, knocking the Fae backward, right into Kiril's blast of fire. Dark Fae were pouring out everywhere, keeping Darius, Kiril, and Rhys occupied. And all the while Dark magic was slamming into Darius.

He wanted to take to the sky and make sure Sophie had gotten away, but there wasn't a chance. All he could do was hope that the girls were clear.

Darius caught a few glimpses of Ulrik and Con. Whatever words passed between them were over quickly as the two were now fighting in hand-to-hand combat.

A blast of Dark magic hit Darius on his left side. Almost simultaneously, he was hit on his right side with a double strike. He shifted back into human form, unable to stop the transition.

With his body wracked by pain, Darius pushed himself up on his hands and knees and stood. He wasn't as powerful in human form, but he could still take down a Dark.

Unable to take to the skies, it was only a matter of time before Kiril and Rhys were both back in human form.

Until then, the two of them were eradicating dozens of Dark Fae at a time with their dragon fire.

The slaughter of the Dark continued in brutal form until—finally—there were none but a handful left. Those soon scattered to the wind.

With a sigh, Darius looked to Rhys and Kiril. He hurt everywhere, but Sophie had gotten away. That alone made it all bearable.

Darius turned to find Ulrik and Con locked in battle, neither able to take the advantage over the other. Darius had always known Ulrik could've challenged Con, but to see Ulrik's power displayed so was a reminder of what was at stake.

"Shite," Kiril said as he walked up beside Darius.

Rhys's bare feet crunched in the snow as he stared at the duo. "I knew this day would come."

"This isna the battle," Darius said. "This is merely the beginning."

Kiril nodded slowly. "Darius is right. We'll know when they fight. They're testing each other's strengths."

"It's still a day I knew would come," Rhys replied in a soft tone.

Darius looked over his shoulder as he wondered about Sophie. He couldn't leave the city without one more visit to her.

"Shall we take Ulrik?" Kiril asked.

Rhys smiled and wiggled his eyebrows. "Try and stop me."

The three spread out and circled Ulrik and Con. Several times Darius tried to catch Con's eyes, but the King of Kings was too intent on his nemesis to notice them.

When they were in place, the three grabbed at Ulrik. As soon as they laid hands on him, he vanished.

"Son of a bitch!" Kiril bellowed in anger.

Rhys looked around. "No fucking way. This can no' be happening."

Darius stared at Con who stood with his chest heaving and eyes blazing. The heat of battle was still upon Con, which was why the three of them kept their distance until he finally turned away and let out a string of curses.

"That could've gone better," Darius stated.

Con stood with his hands on his hips as he looked at nothing. Several minutes passed before he faced them, once more the calm, collected man he always was. "No, it didna."

"I really hoped to end this tonight," Darius said. He would've, had the Dark not attacked Sophie.

Rhys put his hand on his shoulder and gave a nod. "We all did."

Seeing the Dark Fae on Sophie had sent Darius over the edge. No one touched his woman. He wasn't supposed to shift. He'd gone out of his way not to. Until those bastards touched her.

"I know," Rhys said.

Darius looked at him strangely. "What?"

Rhys raised a dark brow. "You do ken that you said that aloud, aye?"

Darius glanced at Kiril and Con, both of who seemed to be absorbed in something else. He then eyed Rhys. "I didna."

Rhys blew out a breath. "I'm glad you're no' fighting it the way I did. I tried, and it wasna worth it."

"I didna even know it was happening."

"You deserve some happiness, Darius. Take it without question."

Darius looked toward the city where Sophie was headed. "She's a doctor, Rhys. A damn good one. She has a career. If I take her as my mate, she'll have to give that up."

"Should that no' be her decision?"

"She asked me what would happen when all this with Ulrik was finished," he said as he looked at Rhys. "I told her I'd return to Dreagan. The look on her face said it all. She'll no' leave."

Rhys's lips twisted. "And we need you at Dreagan."

"Aye."

Con and Kiril walked toward them then, halting the conversation. Con's reticent fury was as frigid as the snow. Kiril exchanged a silent look with Rhys, an unspoken message passing between them.

Something Ulrik and Con had once shared.

Darius looked around at the scattered bodies of the Dark Fae. Looking back, it didn't feel right that Con and Ulrik had ended up like this. Two of the closest Dragon Kings now attacking each other.

He slid his gaze to Con, but Darius wasn't fooled by Con's calm exterior. The King of Kings radiated rage like the sun emitted heat.

"We doona have Ulrik, which means this war willna be ending," Kiril said. "No' to mention all the dead Fae."

Rhys shrugged. "The Dark are easily taken care of. Kiril and I will be in charge of that."

"Will we?" Kiril asked with a flat look.

"Aye."

Kiril raised a brow. "We cleaned up Edinburgh earlier."

"Quit your bitching, jerk."

Kiril punched him. "Dick."

Darius shook his head as he started toward the closest Dark. "I'm used to it. I'll do it."

"No," Con stated. "You have other business."

Darius halted and closed his eyes. Sophie. That was his business. Without turning to Con, he stated, "I might be awhile."

"I'm no' talking of Sophie."

Darius pivoted toward Con. "What then?"

"Wipe all traces of yourself from Edinburgh. Then head back to Dreagan. We're finished in Edinburgh for the time being."

Darius watched Con walk away. The three of them stood naked in the snow as the King of Kings walked amid the dead as if they weren't there.

"Go to Sophie," Rhys urged.

Darius didn't feel the snow on his bare feet. He didn't feel the cold as it swirled around him. But inside . . . inside he was hollowed and chilled to the marrow of his bones.

Because he knew he was going to have to say good-bye to his mate.

Sophie had been a means to slack his body's yearning. Her strength and intelligence only made her sexier. But it was his hunger for her that did him in.

Her beauty first captured his attention. Her body entangled him. Her mind and spirit ensnared him fully.

There was no doubt that she had called to him on a level he hadn't known existed before her.

Kiril walked up on Darius's left side. "Rhys is right. Go to her."

"I doona want to leave her," Darius admitted.

"You shifted in front of her," Rhys said with surprised look. "Even when Con forbade it. If that doesna prove she's your mate, then I doona know what will. Let her decide what she wants."

Kiril scratched his cheek. "You love her. Doona pass that up. You once thought you lost your mate. If you let Sophie go, you really will lose your chance at happiness."

"I'm no' sure that was such a good idea."

Rhys shoved against Darius's shoulder. "What the fuck is that supposed to mean?"

"Just that." Darius held out his arms. "Take a look

around. Ulrik and the Dark are knocking at our door. Con may win, but he may no'. Have each of you thought about what will happen to your mates if Ulrik defeats him?"

Kiril lowered his chin to his chest. "Of course."

"Nay, you have no'," Darius said. "If you had, you'd never have allowed them to get close to you."

"Unbelievable," Rhys said as he glanced at the stars. "After all you've experienced with Sophie you say this? You know who you sound like? Con."

"He's no' wrong," Darius stated angrily. "I doona want Sophie anywhere near this pile of shite we're stuck in."

Kiril crossed his arms over his chest. "I think that choice is out of your hands."

"That's where you're wrong. Her memories will be wiped, and she can go on with her life." As hard as it was going to be, it was the best for Sophie.

Darius loved her so much he was willing to let her go.

Rhys gave him a look of outrage. "Have you really lost your mind? Darius, whether her memories or wiped or no', she's in this. If you think Ulrik or the Fae will leave her alone, you doona realize the situation."

"I realize it perfectly. I'm going to exit her life."

"Good luck with that," Kiril said cynically.

Darius was going to do it. For Sophie. Because she deserved more. Because he wanted her to be happy.

Because he loved her.

The very thought of it was like a knife in his heart. Twisting and turning each time he imagined the Dark trying to take her. Their hands on her, their red eyes alight with excitement at touching her body.

Darius would love her from afar. He'd keep watch and ensure that she was always safe from the dangers in the shadows of their world.

It would be enough.

It would have to be enough.

CHAPTER
FORTY-TWO

Sophie drove like a madman. She kept looking in the rear-view mirror expecting to see the Dark Fae. With every mile that passed behind them, the more relaxed she became. She turned up the heat.

Claire groaned and grabbed her head. She sat up and blinked, looking down at herself in horror. "Why am I undressed? And why the bloody hell does my head hurt so?"

"Clothes are there." Sophie pointed to the floorboard. She didn't want to attempt to fill in the blanks for Claire.

"I was on my way to your place to check on you. A man stepped out in front of me, and that's all I remember until I woke up in the snow." Claire turned her head to her and stared. "You hit me. Twice."

Sophie shot her an apologetic look. "I had to wake you up."

"So tell me why I was asleep in the snow."

"It was Ulrik. You didn't talk to him again, did you?"

"Now look here," Claire said as she began to dress. "Keep that snobby British tone to yourself. He's a gorgeous man who showed interest. I'm a semi-attractive woman who is tired of being alone."

Sophie squeezed the steering wheel and prayed for patience. "Claire—"

"I didn't talk to him. I didn't see him," Claire interrupted her as she fastened her jeans and put on her jacket, wrapping it tightly around her.

"Good." Sophie was grateful for that. She knew how lonely Claire was and how charming Ulrik could be, so she'd had a moment of fear.

"I'd have thought you'd give me more credit than that."

She winced at Claire's sullen tone.

"It wasn't Ulrik who I saw before I blacked out."

"Did the man have red eyes?"

Claire was silent for a long moment. "You mean like those creeps that were on the street before Halloween?"

"Yes."

"No. I do remember he was incredibly gorgeous."

"I think he was working with Ulrik," Sophie explained.

Claire looked out the window and shrugged. "Makes sense. Did they drug me?"

"I'm guessing." Probably it was magic, but there was no need to tell Claire that.

"What else happened?"

"I got you away."

There was a beat of silence before Claire said, "You mean those other men didn't help?"

Sophie kept driving, her heart missing a beat. "Men?"

"I'm thinking one must have been Darius. I saw him talk to you."

"Darius was there."

"So he helped," Claire said.

Sophie nodded mutely. She'd thought Claire was out of it and hadn't seen anything. Was she wrong? Had Claire seen Darius shift? What about the other two dragons? And the Dark? Did Claire see Darius fighting the Dark?

"Did I . . . did I get raped?" Claire asked in a broken voice as she turned to her.

Sophie glanced at her. "No. We didn't let that happen."

"Good." Claire once more looked out the window.

Sophie flattened her lips. She prayed that Claire didn't ask anything else. At least not until Sophie talked to Darius and found out what she could tell Claire.

She thought of Darius in dragon form and wanted to smile. He'd been utterly gorgeous. She never imagined a dragon could be so beautiful. She was in love with a Dragon King. Sophie wanted to dance and shout it to the world.

Her smile faded as she realized she couldn't tell anyone who Darius was. It would all have to be secret.

"Sophie, you've gone pale."

She swallowed and swerved as she parked the Mercedes in front of her flat. After throwing it in park and turning off the engine, Sophie turned to Claire. "Hurry inside. Do you hear me?"

"Do you think they're still after us? What's going to keep them from getting into your flat?"

Claire had to be practical at that moment. Sophie squeezed the keys to the SUV in her hand. Darius had held them not that long ago. How pathetic that she thought she could feel the warmth of his hand on the metal.

"Sophie?"

"We must get inside."

"Whose car is this?" Claire asked.

Sophie looked out her window, checking the area around the Mercedes. "Darius's."

She opened the door and got out, slamming the SUV's door behind her as she hurried to her building. With a click from the key fob, Sophie locked the doors as Claire followed her inside.

Even as Sophie entered her flat, she knew she wasn't safe. Because sitting in a chair at her dining table was none other than Con.

Sophie noticed he'd changed clothes. There was no blood or torn sweater as before. He stared at her curiously while Claire gaped in astonishment. Sophie could understand why, since Con was a gorgeous specimen of a man.

"Hello, Dr. Martin," he said in a smooth voice as if she hadn't seen him surrounded by dragons taller than most of the buildings in Edinburgh.

Sophie closed the door behind her. "I don't suppose I should ask how you got here?"

"It's of no consequence," he replied.

Claire raised blond brows as she looked between the two of them. "Umm. What the *hell* is going on? This isn't Darius, Sophie. And tell me how you're meeting all these magnificent men."

Con stood and bestowed a smile to Claire. "You've had quite the ordeal. Perhaps you'd like to rest?"

"Rest?" Claire looked him up and down before shooting him a level look. "I think that's a *fabulous* idea."

Sophie had a hard time containing her grin when Claire removed her coat and tossed it at Con as she walked to the couch and sat down. She made sure to face them, her gaze locked on Con.

The long-suffering sigh Con expelled was enough to make Sophie smile, no longer trying to hide it. Then it faded as she realized why Con was there. An image of a massive purple dragon filled her mind.

His scales had been metallic. The color so vivid and deep that she had to touch him.

"Is Darius all right?"

"Yes." Con laid Claire's coat on the back of the chair. "He's fine."

Sophie sank into a chair, happy to know that he wasn't

hurt. "Good. That's very good." It was the jingle of the keys in her hand that prompted her to set them on the table and scoot them toward Con. "These are for Darius."

"We'll get the SUV soon enough," Con said without so much as looking at the keys. "How much does Claire know?"

"Claire is right here," Claire said acerbically from the couch. "Ask me yourself."

Con looked as if he were being summoned by a thousand screaming infants as he turned his head to Claire. "How much do you know?"

Without missing a beat Claire said, "I know quite a lot actually. How much do you know? Should I test you?"

"Claire," Sophie admonished, though it was hard not to smile.

Claire signed dramatically. "As I told Sophie, I don't remember anything after the man stepped in front of me on the sidewalk on my way here. I don't know what they did, because the next thing I remember is waking up half naked with Sophie. You want to fill in the gaps?"

"No," Con stated and turned back to Sophie. "And you?"

Sophie remained silent. Con knew she'd seen Darius and the others. She wasn't afraid, if that's what he'd come to learn. Instead of telling him all of that and causing Claire to ask more questions, Sophie returned Con's stare.

"Oh, for the love of Pete," Claire said as she slapped her hands on the couch and stood. She stormed past them, saying, "I'm going to take a nice long bath to help thaw out since no one will tell me what the flip is going on. It's okay. I don't need to know why my clothes were removed or why I feel as if I've been lying on a block of ice."

The bathroom door slammed shut behind her. A moment later the water turned on. Sophie understood how

Claire felt. She had been in nearly that same position not that long ago.

"Sophie," Con called.

She focused back on his face. "Claire won't stop until she has answers."

"I can give her some so she willna ask again."

"Will they be the truth?"

Con raised a single blond brow, which was answer enough.

Sophie cleared her throat. "Leave Claire to me. As for your other question, you know I saw Darius."

"As well as Kiril and Rhys."

She nodded. "I did. I'm not afraid, if that's what you're wondering. Darius told me all about the Dragon Kings and why Ulrik is doing what he's doing."

Con took the chair next to her and sat. "Since you were no' surprised to see the Dark, he must've told you of them as well."

"Someone is going to get hurt if this keeps up."

"You've no idea how true that is." Con looked away and placed his hands on his thighs. As if he'd come to a decision, Con met her gaze and stared at her a long moment. "Darius wasna supposed to shift. I ordered him no' to."

Sophie didn't need to have it spelled out for her. Con was telling her that Darius shifted to help her. He'd disobeyed Con. For her.

"Do you love him?" Con asked.

"I do," she answered without hesitation.

Con inhaled deeply. "I assumed as much by the way you looked at him earlier. Since you know all about us, you know how important it is that no one know our secret."

She recalled the video Darius showed her. "It's not so secret anymore."

"You're speaking of the video. Did you believe it when you saw it?"

"Had I seen it before Darius told me who he was, no."

Con grinned. "Most doona."

"And the ones who do?"

His smile dropped. "That's a problem we're dealing with that doesna involve you. I doona need to tell you that Claire can no' know any of this."

"I know," she said, glancing at the bathroom door. "I understand."

Sophie wondered why Con didn't ask her if she was coming to Dreagan. Perhaps he thought she was. The problem with that was that Sophie wasn't sure what to do. She wanted Darius, but she wasn't ready to give up her career.

Then she recalled how with just a look Darius could have her aching for his touch. And his voice. His voice was a seduction all its own.

"I think we're finished," Con said as he rose and walked around the table.

Sophie followed him with her eyes as he stopped at her door. He looked back at her and said, "Think carefully, Sophie."

The door shut behind him as she wondered how the hell he could've known what she was considering.

CHAPTER
FORTY-THREE

Darius paused on the street and raised his face to the sky, blinking through the snow. He longed to shift and let his wings catch an air current that would take him high above the clouds. He wanted to lose himself in the freedom of it, to help diminish the ache in his chest.

But he couldn't shift. Just like he couldn't have Sophie.

He took a deep breath and walked into Sophie's building. He reached her door and knocked. It was thrown open almost immediately. She flew into his arms as soon as she saw him. He closed his eyes, loving the feel of her against him.

"I was so worried," she said against his neck.

Darius pulled away and tugged her inside the flat before he shut the door. "No Dark followed you?"

"I didn't see any."

He touched her face. "I'm so sorry that happened."

"None of this was your fault. I should've listened to you when you said you shouldn't leave me at the café."

"That's no' on you. I should've waited until Con and the others arrived."

The bathroom door opened and Claire walked out with

a towel wrapped around her. She rolled her eyes as she walked to Sophie's bedroom. "I think I might throw up if I have to keep listening to you two."

Darius frowned down at Sophie who shrugged.

"I forgot," she whispered.

A few minutes later music blared from the bedroom. Sophie smiled and led him to the sofa. She curled up in a corner and tugged him down beside her.

"Claire is still trying to figure out what happened. By the way, Con was here a few minutes ago."

"Was he?" Bastard. Darius was going to find out what Con wanted with her.

She laced her fingers with his. "I think he wanted to make sure I didn't say anything to Claire about all of you."

"It's always more than that with Con."

Sophie glanced away, telling him that Con had grilled her on her feelings. Darius wished they'd managed to capture Ulrik. Then he might feel better about Sophie's safety once he left. All it did, however, was spur Darius to find Ulrik that much quicker.

"I know I saw the video, but seeing you in person was breathtaking. I had no idea how big you were," she said, awe in her voice.

He grinned at her words. He'd been worried that she'd be scared of him, but he should've known Sophie was made of sterner stuff.

"I wasn't expecting your scales to be warm."

He loved the sound of her voice as she whispered his name. Her moans of pleasure were so damn sexy. Darius got hard just thinking of her body and the way she felt in his arms.

"I want to see you as a dragon again," she said.

Darius lifted her hand to his lips and kissed the back of her hand. "We're watched too closely now. None of us should've shifted tonight, but I saw the Dark touching you, and I shifted before I realized it."

"Thank you for saving me and Claire."

Darius couldn't look into her beautiful olive eyes. It hurt too much.

"You're leaving."

He closed his eyes at her words. After a moment he looked at her and nodded.

"So Ulrik is finished with me?" she asked, the smile gone as she leaned away from him.

"Con assures me that Ulrik willna bother you again."

"But you can't guarantee that."

"Nay."

She pulled her hand from his. "So you'll leave with Ulrik's word that he won't bother me?"

"You have a life and a career, Sophie."

"I thought we had something special." Her gaze was full of hurt and a large dose of anger.

This was the part Darius had been dreading. "We do."

"Then why throw it away?"

"Because what you do is special. No' everyone has your skill," he argued.

She blew out a harsh breath. "That's nothing but bull-shit. You're afraid. I thought I'd be the one making excuses, not you."

"I'm immortal!" he bellowed and jumped to his feet. He raked a hand through his hair. "I live on Dreagan, Sophie. Do you want to give up your life and friends to go with me? Do you want to give up your goals as a doctor? Do you really want to face the Dark and Ulrik every day? Because that's what it'll mean if we stay together."

She simply stared at him, her arms crossed over her chest. Darius touched a lock of her red hair before he walked from the flat.

Every inch of him ached. Not from the battle with the

Dark. He didn't feel those wounds. No, he hurt from walking away from the woman he loved.

Even as his heart demanded he return to her, his mind knew he was making the best decision. Sophie wasn't ready to give up her career. He'd seen it on her face. Why put either of them through more time together only to make the break that much worse?

It was better this way.

If it wasn't for the war, Darius would walk into his mountain and sleep once more. That time would come soon enough. Until then, he would have to get through each day as best he could.

He reached the sidewalk and strode past the SUV, his thoughts turning to Ulrik. There'd been no sign of Ulrik since he'd disappeared when they tried to take him. All Darius could hope for was that Ulrik turned his attention away from Sophie. Without Darius and the other Kings in Edinburgh, that chance was much better.

The lie he told Sophie was for her benefit, but they would keep watch over her. It wouldn't be Darius though. He didn't trust himself to remain in the city.

By the time he returned to Dreagan, he was a mess. He couldn't talk to anyone and went directly to his mountain—though he didn't go inside. He climbed to the top and stared in the direction of Edinburgh, wondering what Sophie was doing.

Darius remained there for several hours ignoring the snow that piled around him. Then he turned to retrace his steps down the mountain. With Dreagan watched by MI5, everything had to be done as a mortal would. It was infuriating.

Halfway down the mountain Darius saw Rhys sitting on a rock. Rhys stared at his hand that was held palm up catching snow. Darius paused for a heartbeat before he continued to Rhys.

"Can you see her from the top?" Rhys asked.

Darius hooked his thumb in the belt loop of his jeans. "You know I can no'."

"But you feel closer to her."

Darius looked at the ground. Words stuck in his throat as he thought of Sophie. How had something that began so simple ended so complicated?

"You'll never get her out of your blood," Rhys said as he looked at Darius. "You'll still taste her on your lips years from now. That hunger you have, that'll only intensify."

Darius clenched his jaw. He didn't need Rhys to tell him anything. He felt it already.

Rhys slowly closed his fingers around the small mound of snow in his palm. "That ache will begin to crush you from the inside out."

"Is that how you felt with Lily?"

"Aye, but I didna wait so long to take her. As soon as I made love to her, I knew there was no turning back." Rhys opened his fingers and tilted his hand so that the snow fell to the ground.

Darius eyed him, wondering what he was getting at.

Rhys stood, his aqua ringed dark blue eyes pinning him. "If you want to know what it'll be like, you need to talk to Rhi."

"Stop," Darius said and held up a hand. "I doona need to hear this."

"I think you do."

Darius shook his head and let his hands fall to his sides. "I lost something once, long ago. I know the sting of it."

"You think you do," Rhys argued. "You're just getting a taste. Wait, my friend. The pain hasna begun yet."

Rhys turned and walked away without another word. For several minutes, Darius remained where he was.

He knew exactly how bleak his future looked. Odd that he had closed everyone off for a tragedy thousands of years ago. That time in his life had been what he thought was the worst that could happen.

How very wrong he had been.

Sophie stared out the window with a cup of coffee in her hand. She hadn't been able to sleep no matter how badly her eyes hurt. Because every time she closed them she saw a purple dragon.

She saw Darius.

"I could refill that cup a third time, but it'd be a waste if you aren't going to drink it," Claire said from behind her.

Sophie looked at her friend through the reflection of the window. Claire had slept like a baby the entire night. At least Claire would remember nothing and be able to go on. Sophie didn't have that privilege.

"I know," Sophie said. "I thought I wanted it, but I don't."

"When was the last time you ate?"

Sophie thought back and shrugged. "Sometime yesterday, I think."

"You need to eat."

"I can't." The mere thought of food made her want to be sick.

Claire came to stand beside her. "You could call Darius."

If only Claire knew how many times Sophie had begun to call him. "No."

"Hmm," Claire said as she looked down at the street. "The Mercedes is still here. Neither Con nor Darius took it."

Sophie shrugged. She didn't care about the SUV.

"I wonder who'll come for it."

Sophie was trying hard not to snap at Claire and tell her friend she didn't give a bloody damn about it. Darius had ended things, and she couldn't wrap her head around it. The tears were coming, but Sophie was still in shock.

Claire turned her face to her and smiled. "What do you think about Dreagan whisky?"

She looked at Claire with a frown. "Whisky? I don't like whisky."

"Yeah, I've tried a few, but never really liked the taste either. I hear Dreagan is the best there is. You know it's made here in Scotland."

Sophie shrugged. Of course she knew that. Darius had told her it was his home. "Yeah."

"I think their logo is really cool."

"That's nice." Sophie's last nerve was wearing raw. She wanted to be alone, but she didn't have the heart to tell Claire that. She also didn't want to tell Claire anything about Darius, because to repeat any of it right now might break her.

"Oh," Claire said as she came to stand beside her, licking the spoon she had taken from stirring her coffee. "I called a friend at the police station. That Mercedes you don't care about is registered to Dreagan Industries."

There was something about all of this that Sophie should be concerned about, but all she could think about was going to Dreagan. She could return the SUV.

If she went, then that meant she was leaving her career behind, leaving her friends behind.

"Go," Claire urged.

Sophie looked at her. "What?"

"Go to Darius. You've found what I've looked for my entire life."

She looked helplessly around her flat. "Claire, it means giving up my life."

"Is he the kind of man that makes you long to be with him?"

"Yes."

"Is he the kind of man who makes you feel complete, who makes you feel as if you're better when you're together?"

Sophie nodded, tears gathering in her eyes.

"Is he the kind of man that is worth letting go?"

"No," Sophie said as the tears started.

Claire smiled sadly and wrapped an arm around her. "Then don't be stupid, Soph. Go tell him what he means to you."

Sophie handed her coffee cup to Claire and ran to her room. She changed in record time, grabbing the keys on the table as she rushed out, Claire's laughter following her.

"Good luck," Claire said right before Sophie slammed the door behind her.

Once in the Mercedes on the road to Dreagan, Sophie had time to think about what she was going to say to Darius. If he was even there.

Oh, God. What if he wasn't there?

He'll be there.

Sophie went around a car going slowly. She'd tell them that she was there to return the SUV. Then casually ask to see Darius.

She groaned at such a stupid move. If only he'd be there when she drove up. But what were the chances that he would be standing there at that time?

Sophie wasn't sure how to do this. She hadn't gone after a man in . . . ages. After she let Darius think her career was more important than him, it was going to take some serious groveling.

But what did she say?

She was sorry? She felt sick every time she imagined a day without him. He was worth giving up her career for, because theirs was the kind of love she hadn't really believed existed. She felt it every time they touched, every time he looked at her.

The miles passed quickly. The closer she came to Dreagan, the tighter the knots in her stomach became. And then her mind halted. How the hell had Claire known about the dragons? She'd said she didn't see anything, but obviously she had.

Sophie would keep that secret for the time being. Claire had been through enough. And perhaps if Sophie never spoke of it, neither would Claire.

When Sophie finally turned down the long, winding drive to the distillery, she was so nervous she was nauseous. Her hands were shaking when she parked the SUV. The parking lot was devoid of any cars, and she realized the distillery was closed to the public. But there had to be someone around.

Sophie grabbed her purse and exited the car. Her knees threatened to buckle when she stood. Closing the vehicle door, she looked around at the beauty of Dreagan. The buildings she could see were all whitewashed with red roofs dusted with snow. There was a row of tall hedges at the back of a gift shop that obviously sectioned off something from the public.

Was that where Darius was?

Sophie looked down at the keys in her hand. She had one shot to talk to him. She couldn't screw this up.

She took a deep breath and lifted her head, taking a step. Only to come to a halt at the sight of a tall man with wheat-colored hair and the most unusual shamrock green eyes.

She recognized him as one of the men from the night before. Another dragon. He simply stared at her, waiting for her to speak.

Sophie swallowed and held out the keys. "I came to return this."

"Nay, you didna, lass. You came for Darius."

"I did come for Darius," she admitted.

One side of his mouth lifted in a smile. "That's good." He then turned on his heel. "Follow me."

CHAPTER
FORTY-FOUR

Darius was walking through the mountain connected to Dreagan Manor when his mobile vibrated in his pocket. He pulled it out and saw a text from Kiril telling him to meet in the library.

He only wanted to be alone, but Darius knew he had to see what Kiril wanted first. Darius continued through the tunnels to the doorway into the manor.

Despite the time of day, and the fact that most of the Kings and their mates remained in the manor, it was quiet. Darius heard voices, and the closer he walked to the library, the clearer they became.

He was at the door to the library, reaching for the knob when he heard Sophie's voice. Darius froze, his mind reeling. She wasn't supposed to be there. Guy was on his way to Edinburgh to wipe her memories even now.

Darius slowly opened the door and pushed it wide. He looked inside to find Sophie's back to him as she stood talking to Kiril. Kiril's gaze looked over her shoulders and met his.

"Is he here?" Sophie asked.

Kiril tilted his head slightly. "Aye."

"I'd like to see him. He made a decision about our future without giving me a chance."

"Are you sure about that, lass?" Kiril asked.

Sophie bowed her head for a moment. "I need to tell Darius this, not you."

Darius walked silently into the room. "You shouldna have come."

Sophie whirled around, her long red hair spinning with her. God, she was so beautiful it hurt to look at her. His hands fisted at his sides to keep from touching her. It was pure hell to have her in the same room with him.

"Why?" she repeated, a stricken look on her face. She licked her lips. "I was so hurt last night that I let you walk out. I can't live without you. My career doesn't matter if I don't have someone to share my life with. You made me see that."

"You say that now, but what about five years from now?" Darius didn't look at Kiril as he quietly walked from the library. "You'll regret it then."

"You can't know that. Only I know what's in my heart, and it's full of you, Darius. I know your body. I know your taste, the feel of your hands on me. I know that I like having you near, and that despite everything, I fell in love with you."

Darius couldn't look away from her olive gaze. Her words were everything he wanted to hear and more. "This world isna for you. You have a chance to walk away."

"There's no walking away from you." She took another step closer. "I thought I liked my life controlled. Then I met you. I loved how out of control things were. I thought I never wanted to trust again, and then I trusted you."

"People need you at the hospital," he tried to argue.

"I can open a practice in the village I drove through. I'll be near Dreagan, near you."

He shook his head. "I doona want you turning to me

five, ten, twenty years from now hating me because you gave up your career path."

"I love you." Sophie walked to him and put her hands on his chest. "I love you, Darius. I love that you tried so hard to keep me from knowing what you are. I love that you're a dragon. I love that you disobeyed Con to protect me. I love how you look at me. I love how you touch me. I love so very much about you."

He took her hands and brought both to his lips, placing a kiss on the back of each. "I've longed to hear you say such words."

Sophie's heart pounded in her chest. She was putting everything on the line, something she'd sworn she would never do again. But for Darius she would risk it all. "But?"

"I think you'll be better off away from me."

"Do you love me?"

"Doona ask that," he said as he stood and walked to a window.

"I believe in you. I believe in us. I love you, Darius. I love you as a man. I love you as a dragon."

She wanted him to know just how much she felt for him, but her words didn't seem adequate enough. Tears threatened, because she felt as if she were losing him.

"I love you," she said again. "I swore I'd never fall for anyone again, but you broke through my walls without me even knowing."

She stood staring at his back as tears ran down her face. Sophie had given it everything she had, but it wasn't enough. This time it was her fault. She was to blame for losing out on the best thing in her life.

Now she really would be alone, because there wasn't a soul out there who could compare to Darius.

She nodded as the truth of it sank in. She wouldn't waste any more of his time. "You're a good man. Don't let Ulrik get the better of you. And . . . I hope you find happiness one day."

Sophie turned on her heel. She reached for her purse on the sofa with eyes blurred by tears. With her head held high, she walked from the library. She had no idea how she was getting to the nearest town, but she would walk if she had to.

She had only taken three steps when she was pushed against the wall and Darius's lips were on hers. The kiss was frantic as they both wound their arms around the other and held tight.

When he finally ended the kiss, his breathing was harsh and ragged as he looked down at her. "I love you, Sophie Martin. I love you with everything I am."

The tears came faster, but they were tears of joy now. "I love you, too."

They embraced, simply content to hold each other. Sophie had no idea how long they stayed that way before Darius leaned back.

"I only want your happiness," he said.

"I'm happy with you." She smiled up at him. "I'm better when I'm with you."

"Aye, lass. You make me whole." He kissed her again, slowly.

When he ended the kiss, Sophie touched his face. "I love my job at the hospital, but what I really thrive on is helping those who need me the most. The ones like Lily who couldn't get to the hospital for whatever reason. I can do that here. I can do what I love and be with the man I love at the same time."

"Sophie," he said with a frown and a dash of hope in his gaze. "Are you sure?"

She threw back her head and laughed. "Yes."

He smoothed back her hair from her face, his smiling crinkling the corners of his eyes. "Once you do this, there's no going back."

"I don't want to live without you."

"Even in this war?"

"Even in this war. I'm a shell of a person until I'm with you. You brought me to life again. I want that every day. Through the good times and the bad. Through sickness and health and everything in between."

Darius gazed deeply into her eyes. "I want you as my mate. I want to spend eternity with you."

"But?" she asked with a raised brow.

"Humans were no' meant to be immortal. There's a chance you could go insane."

She shrugged and ran her hands over his shoulders. "There's a chance I'll die in a wreck tomorrow or get cancer in a decade. I've lived safely for too long. I want to take chances and love—all with you."

"And the children? You know that can no' happen."

"I was never the maternal type," she said with a smile. "I'm not greedy, Darius. All I want is you."

"You have me. All of me." He pressed his arousal into her sex. "All the time."

She laughed and kissed him. "I like the sound of that."

"Will you be my mate, Sophie? Will you spend eternity or however long I live with me?"

"Yes."

He lifted her in his arms and strode to the stairs to take them two at a time. Sophie was laughing and enjoying his smile. She glanced back over his shoulder to see Kiril, Rhys, and two women looking up at them with a smile.

Had she really gotten a happy ending? Sophie could scarcely believe it. She hadn't thought them possible, but she knew with Darius anything was possible.

With him she opened up her heart and soul once more, knowing he would protect it as fiercely has he had protected her.

Who could ask for anything more?

EPILOGUE

Four days later . . .

"Well, it's close to Dreagan," Darius said as he watched Sophie closely.

She walked around the office space with a smile on her face, her fingers trailing along the walls and vacant desks. "It's perfect."

"I can no' believe the hospital let you go so easily."

Sophie shrugged, her smile growing wider. "This is going to be all mine."

"What did the hospital say, Soph?"

She walked into the next room. "They doubled my salary."

Darius crossed his arms over his chest and widened his feet. "And?"

"And what?" she asked as she leaned out of the room. "I don't know how Ryder found this place, but I need to get him a dozen boxes of donuts for this. It fits all of my needs."

"I'm glad. Now tell me the rest of what happened at the hospital."

Her smile died as she walked out of the room to lean against the wall. "They tried to tell me what an asset I was. I told them until they found a replacement I'd be happy to help with surgeries if they needed someone."

"What else?"

"Claire wants to come work for me."

Darius was shaking his head before she finished. "You know she can no'."

"I'm going to need a nurse, and the fact is, she's good."

"Need I remind you of what occurred with her and Ulrik?"

Sophie walked to him, a seductive smile playing about her lips. "I remember."

Darius tried to look away, but he couldn't. He grabbed hold of her and pulled her against him and kissed her. "We can no' remain long. Shara and Lily are waiting to go dress shopping with you."

"They can wait. We need to christen every room."

Darius laughed as he lifted her in his arms and walked to the back room that was going to be Sophie's office. They'd start there first and work their way to the front. He didn't care if she arrived naked for their mating ceremony. She was going to be his, and that's all that mattered.

Perth, Scotland

Ulrik tossed back his fifth whisky. He was in no mood to deal with anyone, least of all his uncle. Yet Mikkel walked into The Silver Dragon as if he owned it.

"Did you have fun?" Mikkel asked.

Ulrik didn't bother to answer him. He stared out the window and poured more whisky into his glass.

"You keep failing with the Kings." His uncle laughed. "If you'd told me your plans, I could've helped."

Ulrik wasn't failing. In fact, he'd learned a great deal

from both Con and Darius, whether either of them realized that or not. The fact they'd nearly taken him was what had him in such a foul mood.

And the longer Mikkel remained, the harder it was for Ulrik to pretend he was bending to his uncle's rule. Ulrik wanted Con to suffer, but he couldn't stand much more of Mikkel's interference.

It had to end. And soon.

"Perhaps now you'll stop being so stubborn," Mikkel said.

"If you've come to lecture, you can leave."

Mikkel laughed. "Oh, I'm no' here to lecture, nephew. I'm here to tell you there's a new plan. I've made sure Ryder is going to have a visit soon. With all the attention on Dreagan, this should make things interesting."

Ulrik turned to his uncle. He needed a diversion.

Rhi snuggled against Balladyn's chest. They'd made love so many times she'd lost count. The Kings weren't going to be happy with her, but she honestly didn't care.

For once she was happy. It was time for that, time for her to be selfish.

She felt her watcher's gaze on her. Rhi opened her eyes and looked across the hut to where she knew he stood. He hadn't left. What did he think of what she had done? And why did she even care?

"Rhi," Balladyn whispered as he rolled her onto her back and pinned her arms above her head as he kissed her.

Yes! This is exactly what she needed. To be desired and loved, to feel pleasure and ecstasy.

She arched her back as his mouth found her nipple. When she looked at him, she could only stare in shock at silver eyes looking back at her.

* * *

Ryder sat at the monitors as he opened another box of jelly-filled donuts. It was a good thing he was immortal, or he would have to seriously consider cutting back.

He did his routine of checking on sightings of Dark Fae as well as taking a look at Ireland where most of the Fae lived. But no matter what he did, it didn't take him long to type in an address and wait for the camera to allow him in.

Ryder set aside the donut and stared at the quaint stone house on the outskirts of Glasgow. How many times a day did he watch it? There were so few instances when he'd been rewarded with a glimpse of her.

Kinsey.

He longed for her. Their affair was something he kept from the others. When he'd had to leave Glasgow a few years ago and return to Dreagan when Hal fell in love with Cassie, Ryder knew his feelings for her went much deeper than just a fling.

While the other Kings were falling in love, he couldn't stop thinking of her. Then Con sent him back to Glasgow to fight the Dark.

Ryder had hoped he would see Kinsey, and he had. Just not as he would've liked it.

He closed his eyes as he heard her scream in his head. It was the worst night of his life. Made even worse knowing he would never see her again.

V walked into the small village in Belgium and smiled as he spied a woman sitting alone on a bench. V walked to her and sat.

Her frown disappeared when she saw him. Her smile was tentative, but grew as she returned it.

"Hello," V said.

"Hello."

He glanced around at the village. "It's a nice place."

"Not really," she said in a thick Dutch accent.

His smile widened as he held out his hand. "Then let me make it more interesting."

As soon as she put her hand in his, he pulled her into his lap and kissed her. Her moan of pleasure spurred his desires. He stood, lifting her with him as he walked to a clump of trees. There he set her down and pressed her against the bark as he yanked open her shirt to reveal her breasts.

She was just as ravenous because she quickly unbuttoned his jeans and slid her hands inside to cup his arousal. In minutes he was inside her.

V began to wonder why he had slept in his mountain for so long. It was time to spread his wings—in more ways than one.

Read on for an excerpt from
the next book by
DONNA GRANT

SMOKE
AND
FIRE

Coming soon from St. Martin's Paperbacks

After a moment, she flipped on the lights and began to take off her clothes. Everything was piled in the chair. Mostly because she wasn't obsessed with folding every piece of clothing. But also because she didn't have the time or inclination.

Kinsey removed her bra and grabbed the olive green tank top and put it on. Then she washed her face and brushed her teeth before climbing into bed.

Except, unlike the last two nights, she didn't fall right to sleep. She was wide awake, staring at the ceiling.

And thinking about Ryder.

Foremost in her mind was their kiss. Her lips still tingled from it. His taste . . . chills raced along her skin. She could still taste him.

The power, the desire.

The hunger.

If he hadn't pulled back, she wouldn't have been able to. For three years she'd yearned to have his lips on hers again. When it happened, she'd been too shocked to move at first.

But her body remembered what to do. Her arms went around his neck and she eagerly opened for him.

Her body pulsed with need. A need that only Ryder had ever been able to call up—or quench. She squeezed her legs together and rolled onto her side, but it didn't do any good. Her sex ached to feel Ryder slide within her, filling her as only he could.

Kinsey had no idea how long she laid there thinking of Ryder and replaying all the times they'd made love in her mind when the door opened.

She remained on her side. The light from the hallway lit the room in an expanding triangle as the door opened. A large form filled the crack before the door was quickly— and quietly—shut.

Kinsey didn't move a muscle. Who was in her room and why? She was getting ready to scream Ryder's name when the form stepped away from the door and the shadows there. The glow from the moon shed little light, but it was enough for her to see wide shoulders and a profile she recognized all too well.

Ryder.

With her fear gone and replaced with curiosity, Kinsey slowly released the breath she'd been holding. Ryder was in her room.

Ryder was in her room!

What the hell? She was furious.

Wasn't she?

Unfortunately, fury wasn't anywhere close to what she was feeling. That was reserved for exhilaration. And anticipation.

Her heart rate increased, and it became difficult to breathe. All because Ryder was in the room. She wished now she was on her back so she could watch him. He'd moved out of view, walking behind her to the opposite side of the bed.

When the bed shifted with his weight, Kinsey could barely contain herself.

What about your pledge to ignore him? Weren't you done with him?

She was just a woman, a woman with desires. She'd have to be dead not to want him. And she was anything but dead.

He'll break your heart again.

It was already broken. What did it matter if she gave in and took some pleasure? After the past three years, didn't she deserve that much?

At this, her subconscious was quiet.

There was a sigh from Ryder as he lay back upon the bed. For several minutes, he didn't move. Then he turned toward her, stroking her hair.

Just like her dreams!

Had they been dreams? Was this the only time he'd come into her room? She'd been dead on her feet the past two nights, so a nuclear blast could've gone off and she wouldn't have known about it.

Her heart beat double when his hand came to rest on her waist. Then, slowly, he scooted close until their bodies were molded together, her back to his front.

The covers stopped her from knowing if he had his pants on, but there was no denying he was bare-chested. She used to run her hands all over his chest and the dragon tattoo every chance she got.

And she wanted to do it now.

"I'm so glad you're here," he whispered.

Kinsey squeezed her eyes closed. Those words hit her squarely in the chest. She wanted to believe him, to take those words and hold them against her heart forever.

But Ryder used to say sweet things like that all the time before he left her.

"Doona ever leave, Kins."

If he kept this up, she was going to cry. To have the man she was in love with leave unexpectedly, and three years pass with no contact only to have him say everything she'd dreamt he would say was brutal.

And glorious.

This time she knew what was going to happen. This time she understood her place in his world perfectly.

This time, she'd be the one to leave.

She played a dangerous game. She was the lamb and Ryder the lion. He'd shredded her heart and her life effortlessly before. He could do it again.

Warm lips met her shoulder where he placed a light kiss. "Doona be afraid of me. I'll always protect you."

Kinsey moved back against him, allowing her shoulder to rub against his bare chest. Heat radiated from him, cocooning her in everything Ryder.

Another kiss was placed on her ear before he tenderly nuzzled her neck. She felt his cock thicken and grow against her back. Her nipples hardened and moisture gathered between her legs.

She knew Ryder well enough to know he'd never take advantage of her when she'd made it clear she didn't want him. If she was going to have her night in his arms, she was going to have to make the move.

Kinsey covered his hand draped over her waist with hers. Then she turned her head to look at him over her shoulder.

He froze, waiting to hear what she would say or do. Kinsey took his hand and placed it on her breast. They gazed at each other for long seconds.

Then he squeezed her aching nipple through her tank top.

Ryder stared into striking violet eyes, unable to believe that Kinsey wasn't just awake, but wanting him to touch her.

He ran his thumb over the hard nub of her nipple. Her lips parted and her eyes rolled shut. His cock jumped with yearning. He wanted inside her right that minute, but he pulled himself under control.

Three years had passed since he last held Kinsey. He wasn't going to rush anything. They had the entire night without interruptions. Hours of nothing but them, the night, and desire.

Ryder rolled the nipple between his fingers, hating the shirt in his way. She rocked back her hips, rubbing against his arousal and causing him to moan.

"I missed that sound," Kinsey whispered

He moved so he could roll her onto her back. Her lids opened, meeting his gaze. Desire was there, thick and evident. No longer was she trying to hide it or pretending that she didn't want him.

"What else did you miss?" he asked

She touched his hand and then his face. "This and this." Then she placed her hand on his chest, right over the dragon head. "This." She reached down and cupped his rod through his pants. "And this."